CHILDHOOD WITH

...Memories of a provincial S

CW00499949

CHILDHOOD WITH A-MA-LING

...Memories of a provincial Spanish girl in the 1950s

Victoria F. Leffingwell

Translated by the author and R.L. Leffingwell

ISBN: 9798736465958
Imprint: Independently published

Translated by the author and R.L. Leffingwell

Cover design: Inma P.-Zubizarreta, 2021
Cover photo: Victoria F. Leffingwell
Author photo: Victoria F. Leffingwell

And when you look back
You can see the path that
you will never pass again

A. Machado and JM Serrat

For Feipang
telling jokes in heaven and cajoling the angels

CONTENTS

PROLOGUE

Today I dreamed of A-ma-ling.

Sometimes, when we talk with friends or family, one remembers and tells who was our first love, the person we first kissed, what we thought when we first saw the sea, what we were doing when a famous person was killed, how was our first flight by plane, what book has marked us, what kind of food is our favorite, just to give a few examples.

But we almost never stop to tell who our first friend was. Well, some people do. Like Elena Ferrante, with her wonderful friend. But that is literature, not ordinary life...

My first friend was better than wonderful: she was my playmate for several years, and together we discovered many things, some of them that would serve us "for a lifetime." We learned the different kinds of people that we had around us, how to act in the various circumstances that presented themselves, and how to escape from small conflicts.

Turgalium, despite its pompous appellation of "Very Noble and Very Loyal City" (granted by a king hundreds of years before, when Spain was still not more than a handful of dispersed kingdoms), was, in the first half of the fifties, little more than a rural town: communications with other cities and towns were scarce; there were, it is true, line buses that took people to different places, but they took hours, if not days, when traveling to more remote places.

Few people had cars, actually they were hardly needed. The milk did not come in a carton or in bottles like now: you went with a churn or a large pot directly to the dairy farm, so it had to be boiled and made to foam up three times to avoid illnesses or contaminations. Carts and wagons circulated through the cobbled streets. The Plaza was the neuralgic point where on Sundays people strolled, round and round, dressed in their best clothes and with the curious peculiarity that every time they passed friends or acquaintances they said goodbye, time and again, for as long as the walk lasted — many goodbyes in the same morning.

There was no television, no electronic "devices," the houses had no heating. To heat the rooms, charcoal braziers were used, or fireplaces in the most buoyant households. There were no vitro-ceramics stoves; food was cooked over a sort of charcoal fueled pipe, or on, or in, the so-called "economic" stoves, large iron and brass contraptions stoked with wood; and, many years later, cooking was done with butane. In short: we did not have many things that now we find essential, but the city did have many churches, convents and palaces, silent witnesses to the times when Turgalium had reached its zenith thanks to the gold brought by the *conquistadores*; on its promontory it had an imposing Arab Castle and a quite run-down medieval city, where many families had settled into the huge centuries-old houses. That part of the city, separated from the rest by some remaining wall and large doorways, was known as La Villa, and those who resided there were "the villains," or *villeins* as translated here, wonderful people, but very poor, who hunted lizards and snakes and fished frogs and tench, which they sold house to house every day to eke out their meager economy. The people who lived below did not go to La Villa, or as the protagonists of this book would say: "it was forbidden," although its inhabitants were clean and hard-working people, they never hurt anyone, and their only wish was to be able one day to live "below."

Spending my childhood in that small city was the most wonderful thing that could have happened to me. This is not an historical novel, nor is it a political one. It is just one that tries to show with small brushstrokes, and under the vision of little girls, what Spain was like in the early and mid-1950s, for middle-class families, although with upper-middle-class pretensions, and where the children were oblivious to anything beyond playing, dodging punishment, and spending their days in the best possible way.

And isn't that, deep down, what we all want?

Let's go back to childhood, if only for a little while.

I have structured it in eight sections, somewhat ordered in introducing new information, but independent, so that you can read it without having to follow any order.

Enjoy as much as I have while writing these pages. It is for all of you, dear readers!

A note:

All the characters in this novel are real; the anecdotes and adventures that have been narrated here, not all or not completely. They are the fruit of the author's imagination, sometimes a little crazy, and that of the child Ma-ring, which serve to fill in and recreate the ambiance of those distant times.

The two protagonists are two girls who begin their story of friendship when they are not yet five years old, so it is important to read the stories imagining them from the perspective of a child's mind. If the author's imagination has achieved this, it is now up to yours, dear readers.

And apologies: First, to Titing - as in all stories there must be a "bad guy," in this one it has fallen to the lot of poor Titing, A-ma-ling's brother. And second, for anything unpleasant or offensive in the words of Ma-ring — please bear in mind that this tiny girl's mind really understood things as she describes.

SECTION ONE: FAMILY

When we lived in the Plaza, I still didn't have any friends because I was very young. If I left the house, I would do it with my mother, the servants, or once, with my brother Man-o-Ling, and that "excursion" I almost prefer not to remember; it was not long before it ended in drama, because I got lost.

But when I was not yet five years old, we moved to a huge house, on the Paseo de Ruiz de Mendoza, an evocative name that sounded like its bearer was someone brave and conquering, although I don't know if he really was, and where you could get lost easily in that house of many, many rooms, in an area that seemed to me to be very far from where we lived before, and that's where I got my first friend.

Our houses were opposite, in fact our numbers followed, six and seven, but it did not seem so, since between the two there was a large kind of garden, or small park, and only in some winter months, when the trees were bare of leaves, and from the upper floors of both, could we see that, in the distance, there was another house.

My first friend was called A-ma-ling.

Our mothers were friends, of those called "lifelong" friends, which meant that they had been friends for at least one hundred and thirty years, and living so close it was logical and normal that our paths crossed.

She was the same age, I think she was a few months older, but I was the one who was always bossy in our relationship, because I had lived in two houses, and she only in one.

Physically the only thing we had in common was that we were both small.

And not very tall.

In everything else, opposite.

My friend had very fine, shiny blonde hair and huge blue eyes; mine, on the other hand, were dark, almost black, and very vivid. Her nose was straight, mine upturned, that's why in my house they used to call me snub nose, or *chatunga*.

In general her little face was very sweet, like a good girl. Mine? Well, if I want to tell the truth, that of a very naughty baby, that is, it is better not to say; we were totally different, and it is possible that that is why we were such good friends and we were so happy and congenial from the beginning, because I encouraged her and took her to unknown worlds, and she partially stopped my most wild and naughty ideas.

We always had great conversations, we spent a lot of time together (in fact, except when we had to eat or sleep, we were with each other all the time), and our relationship was better than good, we could say almost perfect, except for some occasional anger for some trifle, which we resolved instantly.

And when twice a year we would go to Las Viñas, a winery and olive plantation that my family owned a few kilometers from our city to spend a long season, or she would go to camp for a few days in the summer, we both cried and we were very sad with the separation and the fear of not ever see each other again.

Not surprisingly, given our age at the beginning of the friendship and during later young years, many of our "themes" focused on the respective families, something almost inexhaustible and that took us hours.

OUR MOMS

My mamá, who was called Mamá Chong, was gorgeous and very tall. Imagine, wasn't she tall, she reached to the top of the big safe!

Her hair was short, a little curly because they put it that way at the hairdresser, and it seems to me that first it was black, but then she changed the color many times, although they never made her blonde.

Besides, my mother was very fat, when she gave you a hug she surrounded you with soft meat, not like the mothers of other girls who were very thin and their bones stuck in you, buff! What a drag.

She always wore many gold and gemstone rings on her hands, and all the time her nails were painted, her eyes or face were not, but her nails were.

She didn't care how other parts were, but she wanted her hair and nails always to be perfect.

Mamá Chong loved all of us kids very much. Well, it seems to me that she loved some of them a little bit more, like Feipang, although if we asked her, she said no, that she loved us all the same.

And besides, she was very good, not like those other mothers who were nagging all day; no, ours left us alone.

The only thing more difficult with her was that we must never make her upset, because she had a disease called "Discompensation of the Heart," and if she had a disliking, she could die and turn into a corpse right away, so we were always forbidden to do that, because then we would have been orphans, which are those who do not have a mamá or papá.

But with the other things, no problem.

At first there were only three of us: my sister Ne-ning, my brother Man-o-ling and I, who was the youngest, and I think the worst of the three. Then the storks brought us my little brothers, Feipang and An-dong-ni, and I stayed in the middle.

Being in the middle of all the kids, I don't think it was the best, because the older ones could do many things, because they were older, and the little ones too, because they were small, but since it couldn't be changed, I had to put up with it, although sometimes it was good to be the one in the middle, because I would hang out with the big ones or the little ones as it suited me.

And besides, I really liked having all those brothers and sister. The house was always full of people!

And our mamá took great care of us all.

We were very lucky, because when they did the moms raffle, we got the best of all mothers.

My friend's mamá, whose name was IsabelM, was not as pretty as mine, nor was she so fat, although she didn't stick you either, and she couldn't wear heels either because she limped a bit; but she was pretty good too. Many, many years ago, when she was young, she had pricked herself with a needle, with bad luck that it broke, and a chunk remained inside her body.

So a typical conversation between us was:

—Do you know that my mamá has a half needle inside her body? A-ma-ling would say to me.

And I:

—But of course! You've told me more than a thousand times!

—But what you don't know, is that if the half needle reaches her heart and pricks it, she will be instantly dead, she said triumphantly.

My mamá, on the other hand, only had that "heart discompensation" thing, something she told us all the time, and that I didn't know exactly what it was, but I figured it must be that the heart was very fat in some parts, and it fell the wrong way, and that although it was a very long name and that impressed us a lot, it could not be compared to having a half needle freely going around through the body, as happened to her mother.

From the great revelation of what would happen if it reached the heart, we spent many hours imagining the trajectory.

—Where do you think the half needle will go today? I asked. And she:

—It seems to me that it is in one of her knees because it hurts a lot.

—What will happen if the half needle hits one eye today? I insisted.

—Today I don't think so, it must be very low and moving slowly, A-ma-ling replied.

—And what would happen if the half needle reaches the heart while she is asleep, and she doesn't realize that it has pricked her? counterattacked I.

—Well, nothing, as soon as she wakes up, she will realize that she is dead, and she will have to run to get mourning suits for us, A-ma-ling told me.

Because when someone in the family died, like a father, or a brother, or a grandfather, or someone who was one of those who are something, even if they are only cousins, you had to wear black, and that way everyone knew that he was a relative of yours even if you didn't cry, or even if you weren't very sorry, because it was a brother or a cousin who had been nagging you a lot, and you didn't care if he was a corpse.

The issue of the half needle took us hours and also, IsabelM, without realizing it, encouraged us, because sometimes we heard her say:

—I think the weather is going to change. The half needle is giving me a lot of pain.

With that we attributed to the half needle almost magical powers, which also announced when it was going to rain, or when we would be very cold, and much better than the man in a picture they had in their living room; that man was made of paper, he was very old, and had a hood, a long coat and when it was hot he would uncover and take off his hood by himself, but as soon as it was going to rain the next day he would wrap himself up, put the hood on down to his eyes, and that way he stayed very warm.

My friend and I looked at him every day to find out, but what IsabelM told us was much better and she never failed.

As you can easily understand, on that subject of diseases, A-ma-ling always beat me: What was a simple "discompensation heart" compared to a pricking needle?

Nothing.

But there was another subject in which I always triumphed, ha.

A-ma-ling told me:

—You know? Today they weighed my mother and told her that she weighs eighty-five kilos.

Well, there I was laughing because I knew I was going to win.

—Eighty-five kilos? I said. —What nonsense, my mother weighed herself yesterday and she was ninety-eight kilos! So just face it and don't brag.

And of course, she had to recognize the superiority of the ninety-eight kilos over the eighty-five rubbish, and she pondered and pondered how to make her mother gain those kilos of difference.

One day we were with our mothers, when they were talking about diets (to lose weight, naturally). IsabelM said: —Oh! Mamá Chong, I don't know what I'm going to do, I don't eat almost anything and I'm just getting fatter and fatter. Why don't you tell me what you eat for the discompensation of the heart? Maybe that would help me.

A-ma-ling smiled, she was very happy, she winked at me a little because we still didn't know how to do it well, and she said very softly so that no one would hear her:

—You see, smart aleck? Now you are going to have to face it. I'm sure my mamá will get past yours!

And she was so happy.

OUR DADS

A-ma-ling's father, whose name was Don AngelB, was a drawing teacher at the technical institute, and I also think something from the police, inspector, or chief or I don't know what, but he was the one who commanded all the guards the most.

My father, Papá Bo-ling, was Chief of Telegraphs, and also a professor of mathematics, so the two of them, for our private accounts, were more or less tied.

My papá was also gorgeous, like Mamá Chong. He had glasses over his eyes, so he could see everything double. I too would have liked to have one of those, especially when we ate cakes, but it was only he who had them.

And a mustache that tickled a lot and made me laugh when he kissed me.

Around his face every day grew many hairs and that was his beard, but in the morning someone called Man-ó-lo Barbéro would come with a very big knife and he would take it off in a moment. It seems to me that my papá was a little scared to do it by himself just because he didn't want to be left without a piece of his face and be ugly, although I would have loved him the same way even with just a little piece.

Her papá knew how to draw very well.

Mine, much better, because my grandfather had been a painter to the King and Papá Bo-ling had concentrated a lot on how he did it, and he watched him every day when he left school and had learned.

And when he was little, he had even gone to the King's Palace once, and there were all the princes and princesses really alive, not like the ones in our stories, and my papá told me that they coughed, and that they went to bed, and ate, and they did all the same things as us, only they were princes and had to be called Highness, instead of their normal names.

Since they both knew how to do it, that's why they taught us to paint.

Papá Bo-ling taught us how to draw horses and cows and cats and lots of critters, even a spider that had a very fat head and many legs, I think twenty or more, and also little houses with a blue door and four windows with flowerpots full of flowers, and fields with green grass and stones, and even castles.

What my papá taught us was much more precious and interesting than hers, because they were things that had many different shapes and colors, and we could do it even if we didn't have the critter, or the house, or the field next to it, look, they were things that were out there, while what Don AngelB taught us were things of stripes and dots and circles and things like that, which was called draftsmanship, and do not think that it served us too much, and I don't know what it has to do with draft on ships, but he said it was very important and later on we were going to be very happy to have learned it. Well, I don't remember if we were happy, I don't think so.

But we did like one thing: after making the figures with pencils and rulers, he let us use India ink, which was a very black special ink, which could only be used for those drawings. At first, we got a bit stained, especially our fingers, but as soon as we learned a little more, almost not. And that was very important, because the ink from India was not like the ink from Spain: if it stuck to your fingers, it wouldn't come off until many days had passed, even if you rubbed your fingers with the sandstone powder for cleaning kettles.

That's why we liked what my dad taught us a lot more, and although we both thought the same, I didn't tell her, so as not to bug her.

Because it was better to leave the arguments and fights for important things, don't you think so?

Her papá, unlike ours, could swear when he was home.

It was one thing that Papá Bo-ling was not allowed, and only when he was very, very angry he would say: "Dang!" and then we knew that the thing was serious indeed.

Mamá Chong could not bear the words that were called profanity, and of course, they could not be said in her presence, and although I did not know exactly how many there were, I think it had to be thirty or more, it seems to me that Man-o-ling had them written down on a piece of paper, but he had it hidden in his room and he never showed it to me.

But poor Papá Bo-ling, though he knew them all by heart, could never use them. That's the way it was. So that's that!

I'll tell you a dialogue on the subject between A-ma-ling and me:

—This afternoon, my father said 'Heck' when we were at the table.

—Really? and what happened then?

—Well then he said: "Damn it, the soup is cold!"

—And your mother, didn't she get angry?

—No, she told the maid to warm it up.

—Well, Mamá Chong says you can't say those words. They are only used by "stewp, stewp" people.

—And who are those from the "Stewps"?

—Well, I'm not very sure, but I think they are people who only eat stew made with snakes and nettles.

—Uff! Disgusting!

From there, as you can understand, most stew was eliminated from our diet, and if they put it in a meal we would refuse to eat it, even if they were angry with us and said we were capricious, but it was a very important thing, if without realizing it, we ate stewps instead of stew and we became one of those who spoke bad.

BROTHERS AND SISTERS

My friend had a sister and two brothers.

I had a sister and three brothers!

Well, those who followed me were very small and almost did not count, but they were brothers after all...

And her sister was younger than mine! So, that also added to the small children, although the true truth is that I know if they added all the years of the four that they were, and the five of us the count stayed more or less equal, but it was not a matter of going around with sums and silly stuff like that: what counted was the number, and that's that!

So I say, I had one more brother, almost a baby, yes, everything has to be said, and unlike all of us who had dark hair, he was blond like all A-ma-ling's brothers, a beautiful angel, and that also added points to the count, that is, a brother to add, look at it however you want to look at it.

MAN-O-LING AND ANGELMARING

My brother Man-o-ling was close friends with A-ma-ling's older brother, whose name was AngelMaring.

And I don't know why he was called that, because he was neither an Angel nor a girl to be called Maring.

But really that was his name.

Maybe it's that when he was born he looked like an angel, like my brother An-dong-ni and then they forgot to change it. I don't know, and I never asked my friend.

They both knew a lot of things, and since they were very good to us, they taught us quite a few of them.

The two of them were the ones who taught us to talk with the Pee, which was a secret language, and it seems to me that only the two of them knew, and very few other boys.

It was a pretty difficult way to speak at first, but once you got the hang of it, it was almost as simple as Turgaliuman.

What you had to do was put the p with the vowel that came before, behind each syllable, for example if you wanted to say

"Cómo estás?" in the language of pee it sounded like this: *"Copomopo Espestaspas,"* and like that with all the words that you used.

And you had to say it really fast!

It was a top secret language, and after we learned it, A-ma-ling and I used it all the time, first to practice and not forget it, and also and most importantly, for when we wanted others not to know what we were saying.

If we wanted to call someone dumb or ugly, the secret language was terrific; we just put on a normal face and said what we wanted, without the person in front of us finding out. Swearing no, because of that disgusting stewp stew.

My father, Papá Bo-ling, bought us three fat volumes called "Our Children's Book"; I don't know why it said "book," when the truth is that there were three books, but that's what they were called.

And Man-o-ling, who was a very good brother, and the most handsome in Turgalium, and who read much better and faster than us, read to us many times.

So we both learned all the mythology, and the signs of the zodiac, and the oceans and seas, the countries that are in the world, the people who lived in Egypt before, and what they did as soon as a cousin died, or a father, or anyone: they wrapped them with many rags so that they would always stay still, and became mummies, and to make them smell good they put many bottles of perfume and cologne on them, and then they put them in the pyramids, but very deep inside so they won't escape.

In those books was written everything you needed to know when you were twenty or older, and although we two were only six when Man-o-ling began to read it to us, we learned a lot about all painters, not the ones who paint houses and walls, who we knew by sight in Turgalium, but about those who paint pictures like my grandfather; about the writers, the musicians, and a lot of other things that our other friends didn't know, the ones that didn't have those books.

Although knowing all that sometimes also led us to some problems...

A-ma-ling told me:

—I want to be Zeus!

And I said:

—Are you silly or what? You cannot be Zeus because you are a girl, and Zeus is a god, that is, a boy. You have to ask to be a goddess, and I am quite good to let you choose, because we are at my house.

—Well, I want to be Zeus, and I asked it first, so you just face it, and that's that.

Because sometimes she was a little pig-headed, or a lot. It must be because she was the youngest of her family, and as my grandmother said, she was very spoiled, which meant that she always had to be what she had chosen, and she insisted on being Zeus, although I had explained to her a thousand times that she could not be, so we didn't reach any agreement, we got angry, we told each other that we were never going to get together anymore, and that we wouldn't be friends and each one of us was going their own way...

Until the next day, when we had forgotten the whole fight.

But for me, Zeus being a girl sounded terrible and it couldn't be.

Man-o-ling and AngelMaring had a beautiful collection of decals.

And the "reeps" were traded, which was said like that when you had more than one of the same.

Those decals came in Nestlé chocolate bars, and since that was our usual snack, chocolate on bread, it was pretty easy to get decals.

I liked a chocolate called "Dolca" much more, which was not so sweet or pasty, but rather more bitter, but there were no decals with it, so we hardly ever had that kind. It didn't matter so much to me either, because our brothers let us look at all the pages of their albums, and they didn't even notice if our hands were very clean because, as I said before, they weren't the kind of brothers who bugged, not like Titing, the other brother of my friend, who was a complete demon, and who always annoyed us, and on top of that he laughed.

What a difference!

And our older brothers taught us to ride a bicycle, and even when we cried a little, if we fell and scraped our knees, they would not say anything to us, nor would they tattle on us so that everyone would laugh. On the contrary, they put a little spit on their handkerchiefs, and they cleaned the blood and the dirt, and they put us back on the bike so that we would not get scared, because Man-o-ling told us that if after falling you don't got on right away again you could never ride again, because then you just thought you were going to fall again, and you were so afraid that you would fall for sure, and it was true because that happened to a girl who was in the park, she fell, and since she had no brother to explain to her about riding her bicycle right away, she never ever rode again. Buff, what a bore.

TITING

Titing taught us almost nothing, and the few things we learned from him I think they must not have been very good, because IsabelM was always saying:

—Don't teach bad things to the girls!

But I do remember that he taught us to say "Doggone it," which was something he said all the time, and that only really old people could say, like over ten years or so.

We would leave her house or mine and A-ma-ling would ask me:

—Are we going to the big or to the little park, doggone it?

And I would answer:

—Better to the one big one, doggone it.

—But the big one is very hot now, doggone it.

—Okay, well, we shall go to the small one, doggone it.

We soon realized that the doggone it thing was too tiring and we stopped using it: it couldn't compare with talking in Pee!

And all the other things we learned from Titing did not last long either, so it did not serve for life, as gods and goddesses, and other things from the book of our children, and that really was good.

Titing had a close friend named Luisito. And that one was a good boy! He was not his neighbor but ours because he lived on our street, not the one that was in front of the park, but the one of JoeyStreet, but they were friends despite that.

IsabelM told us:

—His parents are really "rich"! What a pity that there are so many deaths in that family!

We knew they were normal; come on, made of flesh and bone, not like the desserts our mamás always said were so rich, like a *tocinillo* made of syrup and egg yolk, so then Titing explained that being "rich" also meant that they had a lot of money, fifty thousand pesetas or more, but Luisito didn't notice it because maybe he didn't know that they were so rich, or perhaps he thought that they only had about four thousand pesetas. The truth is that we never asked.

His family was always in mourning, their whole life, forever and ever, because when they were almost going to finish to mourn one, another died and hah! begin again, what a dragging drag.

Titing, as I told you, was of almost no use to us, because the things he had, a slingshot, a pirate's patch and so on, we were not interested in at all.

I mean, he was a brother for the count we kept, but actually we should have said that A-ma-ling had two in total compared to my four. What a trifle of a brother...

My brother Man-o-ling told us that Titing was called "*Bocarrana*," Frogmouth, but we should never tell him, because he would get very angry.

It seems to me that he told us that they had given him that name because his mouth was very big, like that of frogs, and that only nonsense came out of it, but we called him that when he was very naughty, which was almost every day, and yes, he got all furious and wanted to hit us, thank goodness Lupeng defended us, and while she tried to calm him down, we ran away.

But of course, it is that with brothers and sisters you never know what is going to happen to you, and if you have bad luck, you have a lousy one that almost does not count, and if you have it good one then you can breathe easy...

AN-DONG-NI

The year my brother An-dong-ni was born, Isa-bel-i-ta the seamstress made me a beautiful pale yellow coat. It was a woolen coat, very warm, and I wore it on the day of his christening.

My brother was very small, and I have already told you that he almost did not count as a brother, but he was beautiful, all pink and we loved to look at him, touch his face, and put a finger so that he could hold it with his little hands.

He was like a doll, but it was one made of flesh and bone.

As I lived in the same house, they let me hold him sometimes, but I couldn't tell A-ma-ling so that she wouldn't get envious, and when she was in our house we just touched his face, and kissed him and were very careful not to break it, because the little brothers, especially when they are of a class called "babies," are very delicate, like some glasses that Mamá Chong had and where she put the "toasted cream," which was a sweet delicious light brown desert and then, on top, it had a white meringue pompadour, which we had on my dad's birthday, and we could never touch those glasses because they could break, and we only looked at them when we entered the large dining room.

The truth is that my new brother was so soft that we would have liked to hug him and kiss him all the time; but as we couldn't, we couldn't.

An-dong-ni had been brought to us by a stork of the kind that lived above the Brothers' church. There were always two or three there and they were our neighbors too, like JoeyStreet and other neighbors, although they did not look like us, because they had feathers instead of skin, and it seems to me that they did not have teeth or fingers, and they did not speak, they only moved their heads to say yes or no, but they knew how to fly and could go to many cities and see many things, and they were the ones in charge of going to Paris to pick up the children they made in a factory when a family asked them, and although they were different from the others, they were also neighbors.

One day when Feipang was very annoying because he wanted to have a little brother to play with, and he was with the same teasing all the time, and he cried and threw himself on the ground and all that he always did, Mamá Chong told us, Man-o-ling and me, to play with him, but Man-o-ling had to go out with a friend and I was busy with something else, (the real truth was that neither of us wanted to play with him, because although the two of us were much older, he was a bit of a cheater, and he always won whatever we were playing), and poor Mamá Chong no longer knew what to do with that annoying child.

Suddenly she remembered our neighbors, she went up to the large terrace and spoke with one of them so that, please, bring us a small child, that we needed it urgently, and that it had to be a boy, please stork make no mistake and bring us a girl, because if it was a girl we would have to throw it away, because it would not serve us.

The fattest stork shook his head up and down, which meant yes, not to worry and that he would bring us a child.

When all of us were eating at the table of the big people, well everyone but Feipang, because he ate at a little table and a chair that they put for him in the hall, because he threw things on the floor, and that was a filthy pig thing he did, Mamá Chong told us:

—I think they are going to bring us another child to play with Feipang very soon, so don't make too much noise so he doesn't get scared when he arrives.

We were all very happy, and as soon as we finished eating I ran to my friend's house to tell her.

That night we went to bed so calm and the next morning, when I woke up, my sister Ne-ning came running to my bed and said:

—Run, get up right away; they have brought us the child!

So I went quickly to Mamá Chong's bed and there it was: It was real! A beautiful little boy, with blond curls on his head, and he wasn't even crying because he was so happy to be in our house.

And Feipang I'm not telling you!

Now he had a brother to play with all the time and boss him around.

The thing is that An-dong-ni didn't know how to speak, walk, or do almost anything, because in the rush, Mamá Chong forgot to tell the stork to bring us one who knew how to do it, and the one he brought us was a bit silly, and he only knew how to say *gugu*, and on top of that he was hardly understood, but hey, at least now we had one.

But Feipang was a little greedy and believed that the new child was only for him, and as soon as one of us got near An-dong-ni, he would get very angry and say,

—It's mine! Don't touch it, it's mine! If you touch him you will find out!

But we didn't pay much attention to him, because we all knew it was for the whole family.

When A-ma-ling came to my house that afternoon and I showed her my little brother, she was very happy too, although we had some problems.

Because she wanted to have another.

And that was what Man-o-ling called being "monkey see, monkey do" which meant that she had to do what other people did, and what she wanted then was a little brother like ours.

She went home and told IsabelM what the stork had brought us, and that, please, please, talk to the fattest stork, who was the one in charge of bringing the children, to ask him for one like ours, as if one so precious could be repeated. Hah!

But IsabelM was not friendly with our neighbors the storks, and could not suddenly go and ask for a child, so no matter how much she asked and asked again, A-ma-ling was left without a little brother.

And she cried and whimpered and all that, as Lupeng told me later.

Because sometimes she was very boring...

And this is how I said it: —Look, hold on and give thanks that I let you touch our child, if you weren't my friend, don't think I would let you.

She gave me thanks, but she made me promise that she would put the booties on him by herself every day, and to make her stop nagging, I said yes, but I put my fingers crossed behind my back, which meant no, haha.

For An-dong-ni's christening, Feipang and I wore our new clothes. My coat was very beautiful, as I have already told you, and inside I was wearing a dress made of a very soft cloth called "*de villela*," pale blue and yellow, and then patent leather shoes and socks. I was gorgeous, even all the old adulterers told me that, and they weren't going to cheat on me, right?

We went to church to get him baptized and made a Christian of him, and they took away something called "Being unfaithful," because Mamá Chong used to say that if babies died being unfaithful, they would go straight to limbo, which was a very strange place because it was not heaven, where God and the Virgin of Victory were, and many angels were flying around there, nor hell, where Pedro Botero lived, and he was the one who had a very long tail and a fork that measured many meters, with which he was sticking those who had fallen there all the time, and it wasn't even purgatory, which was on the middle floor, between heaven and hell.

That Limbo was a real drag, because most of those who were there were babies and they did nothing but cry, and pee and poop on themselves, and those who were older did not even know how to dress, they put all their clothes on backwards and they were really ugly, so we didn't want An-dong-ni to have to be in such a bad place, if by chance he turned into a corpse.

When they had taken away being unfaithful, we all went to the Virgin's castle so that she would meet him and he could be friends with the Child there, but since he was made of stone and our child did not know how to speak, I think they did not become very good friends, but I don't know; besides, Feipang wouldn't have liked the two of them to hang around there either, with how greedy he had become.

And then we went home to have Chocolate with sponge cake and pastries! Everything was delicious, and since we knew the names of everyone who was invited there, A-ma-ling and I had a super yummy time, and they let us take the baby in turns for a long time.

TrickyJoey's mother, Paula, I think she also got a bit envious when she met our little boy, because she wanted to have one for her, but she was already very old, because she was about fifty or forty-six or more, the kind who are called old women, and since Mamá Chong used to say to her: "Paula, small children are a lot of work and you don't want to have a bad night," so she convinced one of her sons to order one from the stork, and that son must have made the order when he was a little asleep, because they brought him Two! - two girls who were called twins, because they were just equally the same.

Paula was super glad her son got those babies, although those girls weren't even half as beautiful as our baby, but now she had something to play with, and she decided to have a big party the day they took away their being unfaithful.

They invited my papá and Mamá Chong, because they were friends, but Papá Bo-ling couldn't go because he was working that day, and Mamá Chong couldn't go either because she had to do something called "breastfeed," and that was because An-dong-ni did not know how to eat alone, because he had no teeth, and also he could not take the spoon, because he had very small hands, so for that she had to put him first on one side and then on the other for him to suck, I think what came out was soup or puree and custard, soft things and also milk, and so on all the time, for breakfast, for lunch, for tea time and for dinner, and she had to be at home always, because if she left, the baby would cry and be very sad. So about the party:

Ne-ning had to write a very long letter to her boyfriend Cheng-Chu.

Man-o-ling had to play a game of table football with his friends.

Since there was no one else left, because Feipang was very rude and threw things on the floor when he ate, and besides, I was much older than him, they decided that it would be me to go on behalf of the family.

It was my first party alone and I was happy, although I was a little scared, that's the truth.

On the day of the christening party they fixed me up with my dress and coat, my cute patent leather shoes, and when they were combing my hair, A-ma-ling arrived.

She had not been invited, nor any of her family I think.

My friend leaned close to my ear and said:

—Before you go I have to tell you something, but in secret, top secret.

As soon as they finished preparing me, we went into the parlor, there was never anyone there, and she told me:

—Since I'm not going to be there, and I won't be able to eat anything, don't forget to bring me things from the party, but nobody must find out what you have taken, come on, promise me that you are not going to tell anyone.

I gave her "Holy Word" that I would keep the secret and so she remained calm, and as there was still a while before they took me away, we both stayed in the parlor, which was a room that we loved because it had a table and six chairs with a very high back, like princesses and also two armchairs, it seems to me like for the king and queen; they were made of wood and yellow cloth with very beautiful black branches, and there was also Mamá Chong's piano, and on the walls there were some rags called tapestries, which we liked a lot, and when no one saw us we went in there and we pretended we were the princesses of the kingdom: we could command all the other girls, and they always had to obey us, even if we sent them to do very strange things, such as walking backwards or eating a raw toad.

But the time came, and she went home, and Fau-sti-na the nanny took me to the Plaza, and there she left me holding Paula's hand.

After they got rid of all of the unfaithfulness for the twins in church, we went to their bar to celebrate.

They had prepared a table at least sixty or seventy meters long, all covered in white and with many dishes. There was everything there: sweet-rolls stuffed with ham, French fries, squid, croquettes, pasties, dishes with cheese and with *chorizo* and with salami and with tenderloin, Russian salad... and millions of desserts: tarts, pies, cakes, sweet *ensaimadas*, bacon, egg yolks... All kinds of foods.

Although there were many things, I could not eat anything: I was so worried thinking what I was going to take to my friend, and how I could take it without anyone noticing that although everyone around was with their mouths full, and the truth is I was a little hungry, I was not able to eat.

Finally I decided that I would bring her some eclairs that looked very delicious: filled with yellow cream and on the outside they were covered with chocolate. At a time when no one was looking, when I knew none of them were seeing me, I put two in each pocket. Uff, what a break! I could finally dedicate myself to eating a lot!

From then on, as I had my order done, I was able to do whatever I wanted, play with other girls, and on top of that they let me hold the twins a little bit, so I had a lot of fun.

When the nanny came for me, I did not want to leave, but could not start to whine like a little baby girl, so I put up with it and I went with her.

It was night and in the sky there were many stars and a very fat moon; I wanted to stop all the time to look at them, but Fausti-na told me to stop the nonsense, that we had to get home at once, that it was very late and I already had to be in bed, instead of on the streets.

Although she was very unfriendly, I asked her:

—Can we stop by A-ma-ling's house for a moment? I have to tell her something very urgent!

Well, nothing, she would not allow me to stop, although I asked her three times, and said please before asking.

As I saw that she was not going to take me, I stopped talking to her, and I did not want to be with her ever again. Well, what an unpleasant witch and an idiot! Surely if it had been my mother who was going with me, she would not have minded stopping for a moment at IsabelM's house, or my brother Man-o-ling either, but that dope did not take me.

When we got home I had to tell everyone everything, well, not everything, I couldn't say about the eclairs because it was secret, but I told everything else, and how well I had behaved, and everything I had done and eaten, and the people who were there, everything everything.

And since it was very late, at least nine at night, I got into bed to sleep.

The next day I woke up because my nanny was screaming like crazy, with some screams that reached to the upper park and lower park and Doña Margarita's.

—Miss Mamá Chong: Have you seen this? The whole girl's coat is dirty and full of chocolate stains! Oh, what a shame, how beautiful it was! She will never be able to put it on....

And many more things that I do not tell you.... She was very angry.

With so much shouting, Mamá Chong went to the "donkey" in the hall to look at the coat and see what happened.

That donkey was not a real donkey, it was a place where we would put our coats, jackets, umbrellas and those things when we came back from the street, and I don't know why we called it the donkey, but we really always called it that .

When Mamá Chong saw the coat, she got quite sad and called me, and since I was already behind the door hearing what was happening, I went right away.

My mamá asked me what had happened, but I couldn't tell her anything about the Holy Word, but since she was getting a little angry, I had no choice but to tell her, look.

It turns out that the eclairs had been squashed in the pockets, and everything was smeared with cream and chocolate, and the coat made a mess, because it was yellow, surely if it had been brown it would hardly have been noticed, but in this one it got noticed, and a lot.

I thought that Mamá Chong was going to get very, very angry and that she would never want to be my mother again, but she took me in her arms, gave me a kiss and said:

—Look, *chatunga*, that's not fair to do, because you cannot take other people's things, that is stealing, and stealing is a sin. Also, if you had asked Paula for some cake for your friend, she would have given it to you, and she would have wrapped it up and the coat would be clean, but since you didn't know that, we're going to try to clean it and you're not going to do it again, right?

You can't imagine how happy I was!

My mamá still loved me, and she didn't even tell me that I was bad or naughty like others did, so I gave her a huge kiss and went to breakfast!

(Well, I was a little mad at A-ma-ling because she had made me spend one of my "holy words" for nothing...)

FEIPANG

The brother who followed me, but was four years younger, was a bit of a cheater, that's the truth....

Almost since he was born.

Although Mamá Chong thought he was the best, haha, but she didn't know many things he did.

One day, when he was almost two years old and still did not speak much, he began to wrinkle his neck, let's say, to put it inside. When I saw him doing that the first time I thought that maybe he wanted to be a turtle, because we had seen a few that were where the statue of Doña Margarita was, in the garden park below, and Feipang many times wanted to do what the animals did.

But as he kept doing it, I saw that he had that mania.

Mamá Chong took him to see Don Teodoro, who was our doctor and always came to my house when I had tonsillitis, or my ears hurt, or one of my brothers had a stomach ache, or whatever.

And A-ma-ling and I went with them to find out about everything, look, we liked to know what was happening and we were not like other girl children, ha.

Don Teodoro looked at him and touched him all over the neck, he put a spoon in his mouth, but the other way around so that his tongue would be lowered and the little bells would appear, which were two balls that we have before reaching the swallowing tube and said:

—Mamá Chong, what Feipang has are tonsillitis and lymph nodes.

We heard that too.

He said he had to eat many many ice creams and little pieces of ice, look how lucky, especially in the summer.

But it seems to me that Don Teodoro was wrong, maybe he was also very old and could not see very well, because Feipang kept hiding his neck more and more and said that it hurt a lot.

So my papá and Mamá Chong took him to Madrid, which was where all the best doctors in the world were, those who knew all things about people and animals, and one of them told them that they were not tonsillitis or lymph nodes, what happened was that someone had dropped him from above, and that somehow it broke little bones in the neck, and then they had stuck back together really rotten and for that reason the neck was shorter, and that's that.

And he also told them that putting another bone there was very difficult, because they had to cut off his head first and there would be a lot of blood, put that new bone in, and then sew the head back together, and that was very dangerous because sometimes, by mistake, they put on the head of another and it looked very bad, look, and on top of that, maybe you didn't even know that one or he was really ugly, or I don't know.

And since they didn't have that new bone either, Mamá Chong and Papá Bo-ling, although they were very sad and crying a lot, they said what a shame, what sadness and all that, but well, what can we do? They left him like that.

But then another problem came:

Since Feipang was very clever and had heard the whole conversation from behind the door, he decided that he was going to always do whatever he wanted, and that everyone was going to find out what's what.

Then he became very spoiled, although he was not the smallest in the house, as was the case with A-ma-ling, because after him was my brother An-dong-ni, but that didn't count for much either, that's the truth.

So Feipang every time he wanted something he would say:

—Either buy it for me, or I'll throw myself on the ground and take off my shoes!

And he made a very scary voice to scare us.

And also, if he wanted something from one of us, he would tell us:

—Either you give it to me, or I throw myself on the ground and take off my shoes!

And if you were at home it did not matter so much, because the floor was clean, but if he did it on the street it made you very disgusted, and since it did not matter to him to throw himself in a puddle or wherever he was, he always ended up dirty and sticky and everything and we did not like that at all.

Mamá Chong used to say to all us kids:

—Children, if Feipang wants something, please give it to him, you know that if he doesn't get it he becomes very angry.

And we almost always did, but sometimes we didn't.

One day A-ma-ling and I were going to play in the big garden park, and he insisted on coming with us, and forced us to take him, although he didn't know how to play a lot of our games, but he was very pig-headed and in order not to put up with him we said okay.

We went downstairs, got to the park and while we were playing something called the week, which was a wonderful game, he saw a kitten that was there, near the *churrería*.

He started talking to him and I think they became quite friends.

Suddenly, he left the cat where it was, came to our side and in a very powerful voice said to us:

—Hey, you two, either buy me that cat or I throw myself on the ground and take off my shoes!

(Which was what he always said and he had us all bored with that).

So we had to stop playing and listen to him.

I tried to convince him that we couldn't buy the kitten, because we didn't have money, we didn't know who it was from, or anything, and A-ma-ling also said many things to him, but he was very stubborn, took off his shoes and got on the ground screaming and saying that we were very bad and that we were going to find out.

And thank goodness that the owner of the cat came, because we no longer knew what to do with that boring child!

We went up to that man, who was quite old, and I said to him:

—Good morning. Could you leave us your cat for a few days? My brother Feipang has become a very good friend of it and wants to take it home with him, and if we don't give it to him, he will be very mad.

—Well, I'm very sorry, he told me, —I can't give it to you because I live alone and my cat keeps me a lot of company, but if your brother wants, he can come with us and I'll let him play with him.

I told Feipang right away and he said well, that he would go with them, and to tell Mamá Chong that he would be back soon and not to worry.

As neither A-ma-ling nor I knew that man and we did not know if he was a gypsy, or the bogeyman (although he did not carry any sack), or who, and so that my brother would not get lost and then we would have more problems, what we did was stop playing and get a little behind and follow them without them noticing, to see where they were going.

My brother began to tell the old man things, and he and the cat only laughed and laughed, I don't know if he was telling them jokes or a lie because we couldn't hear what he was saying, but they were breaking up, and that's because we were more separated from them and for some moments we had to hide in a doorway so they wouldn't see that we were following them.

The three of them arrived, my brother, that man and the cat at the old man's house, and thank goodness that he lived in a lower floor, the kind that are next to the street, not like ours which were very high up and with stairs, because otherwise we wouldn't have been able to spy, but since there was a window,

A-ma-ling and I stood next to it to hear everything they were saying, all of it.

When we were so entertained watching and hearing what they were saying, TrickyJoey came over and said:

—But what are you doing here? Don't you know that this is Bogey Cut-lard's house?

We did not know, but they had told us things about that bogey, that he was very bad, and that if you did not go to bed on time, or eat everything that was on the plate, or things like that, he would come to see you, he split you on all sides and took out the lards, which are things that are under the skin, before the blood and the bones and everything we have inside, and if you don't have those lards then everything goes outside and you turn into a corpse, and you die, and that's that.

So then we got really worried, because look, how were we going to get to my house with Feipang without lards? And on top of that about his neck! Surely Mamá Chong was going to get really awful, and the discompensated heart thing would be getting horrible, because that was a fine upset, and neither of us knew what to do.

When we were thinking and thinking, the door of the house opened and Feipang appeared, with the cat on one arm and a huge bag on the other side, so happy and without any cut or crack anywhere, I mean, he was whole.

We ran to his side to ask him if he was okay or if he had a cut or something and he said:

—Come on, let's go home, I've done a good business!

The three of us and the cat shot out of there, and as soon as we got away a bit and we were already in the big upper park, my brother said to us:

—What a nice guy! He has given me his cat and on top of that he has given me this bag full of lard, so I'm going to give it to Mamá Chong right now, so that she can take it to the nuns in the Villa, and they will make us some sweet-rolls of the kind that I like so much. Take me home, you silly!

Neither A-ma-ling nor I said anything, we just kept walking and that's that.

NE-NING

My sister was eight years older than me and she was gorgeous, more than an actress in the movies, but she was not an actress, she was a flesh and bones sister and we lived together in the same house.

Ne-ning didn't pay much attention to us. Almost no attention at all, and she scolded us a lot because she said that we bugged her a lot and were always spying on her.

But sometimes she would make us sticky croutons, which was like fried bread and it was delicious, or she would sit and watch us while we wrote in our notebooks, so that we would not get out of the lines.

And other times she let us look at her while she painted her eyes, and that was a very complicated operation, because she had to keep her mouth open while doing it, so she couldn't speak, or argue or anything, and it was a great luck for us, although she said that sometimes we were a little trying and that is why she had to scold us.

The first time she let us look, we both sat on the edge of the bathtub and she told us that we had to be quiet, as if we were in church, not to make any noise, because if she heard us she could make a slip.

First she dipped a very fine brush in a small bottle filled with black liquid, which looked like the bottle of India ink but was special for the eyes, and very carefully she ran it over the eyelid, it had to be next to the eyelashes. It couldn't be anywhere else.

The first eye was very easy, but painting the second was very difficult, because it had to be exactly like the first, and once we took the little paint bottle and the brush without her knowing, to do an experiment, and we saw that it was really difficult, and that you had to keep your mouth open all the time, and that although the first eye would have been very precious, when you reached the other it would be very ugly, and that was a big drag, because then no one could see you, not even close friends, nor your boyfriend, and you had to stay hidden in your room until it was erased, but my sister had both eyes the same, exactly, and she told us it was because her mouth was open, that it was a secret, and that we must tell no one, not even Lupeng, and we gave her a Holy Word and a Word of Honor, both of us, to keep her calm.

Then, with a metal gizmo, she curled her lashes and painted them with a very small brush with a paste called mascara.

She was gorgeous!

But another day when we took the gizmo, almost, almost that thing ended in tragedy.

I tried to curl A-ma-ling's eyelashes, but since she was not still, because she said that it was tickling her, and also since they were blonde and did not show much, it almost left her without an eye, and that would have been a problem because, look, how were we going to explain it to Mamá Chong and, above all, to Ne-ning? If we appeared with one eye in the hand, we would have had to confess that we took that thing to curl our eyelashes, and they would have been very angry, and also, then they would have seen that the whole bathroom was full of blood, and we would no longer have never ever been able to look at how her eyes were painted.

But we were lucky, the eye stayed in place and nothing happened, so we put the curling gadget back in the bathroom cabinet, and that's that.

Ne-ning had many high-heeled shoes.

That meant that they were shoes that when you put them on, you suddenly grew a lot, without having to take either calcium-20 or cod liver oil, which was a very disgusting thing that they gave us on Thursday mornings, before breakfast.

Every week, the night before Thursday, which was still Wednesday, Mamá Chong would say to the nannies:

—Don't forget to give the children the cod oil!

Phew, and they never forgot.

It was so that we would grow up, it seems to me, and so that our bones would not become soft, like those of poor Doña Marting.

Because Mamá Chong wanted them to be very hard, and since she had never tasted it, she didn't know what a drag it was.

And we had no way of sneaking away.

Until one day when I noticed what Feipang was doing; he was the cleverest of all of us, and I started doing it too: he opened his mouth without saying anything, not even ugh how disgusting, they gave him the spoonful of oil, then he closed his mouth and was silent.

As soon as the nanny was gone he ran out and spit it out!

And then he ate breakfast so peacefully!

From that moment the nightmare ended, because I did the same as my brother, and my bones did not get soft. Ha!

The *calcio-20* itself was good, and we would not have minded taking two tablespoons, but always we only had one.

Well, as I was telling you, my sister had many high-heeled shoes, which were also called "needle heels," but the heel is not like a sewing needle, come on, but like the fat ones for knitting.

Walking in heels was very difficult, very difficult, and very dangerous, because you could break your leg or, if you were unlucky, break your head and have all your brains pop out, and have to live all the time with your brains in your hand, or in a bag, and with how sticky and slimy the brains are, don't think it had to be very comfortable, really.

But since we liked danger, as soon as we could we went to my room to put on her shoes.

My bedroom was called "The Girls' Room." It was a beautiful room, all the furniture was made of shiny pine wood, and although Ne-ning was much taller than me, because she was older, the two beds were the same, it seems to me that Mamá Chong made my bed like this so that it would serve when I grew up, because if she did have to change it all the time maybe she wouldn't find another one like Ne-ning's; we had a bedside table in the middle of those beds so that they were separated, and near mine there was a closet that had three parts, one was for my sister, another for me, and in the middle, there was one that was for other things, like belts and hats and gloves and socks and panties and T-shirts and all that, and we also had a huge mirror with a dresser and a stool, where A-ma-ling and I could get up and look at ourselves making a lot of different faces.

Hanging over the table, we had a picture of the Virgen del Pilar, which was of something called alabaster, with the Virgin and a little boy on top of a column. I couldn't reach there, not even climbing on top of the bed or the stool, but Ne-ning did, and every time she went to the street she would kiss the picture and smear it a little with the color that she had put on her lips, but I didn't say anything to her to show her that I was very good, well-behaved and polite.

For us to be alone in my room don't think was easy, because Ne-ning spent hours and hours, thousands of hours every day, scrunched up in the center of the closet, not where the dresses were, she put herself where the drawers were, above there was a flat part, and she'd do nothing more than write and write letters to a boyfriend of hers, who was called Cheng-Chu. All three parts had a key, but my sister always kept the middle one hidden and it was never sticking in the lock. Maybe it was she thought that we were going to take those letters to read them and laugh, what a silly....

As soon as we had the slightest opportunity, and we saw that she was not there, we entered right away, to try on heels and practice!

If my sister caught us red-handed she would start screaming:

—Mamá, the girls are taking my heels again! Scold them!

And Mamá Chong would scold us a little, but very little, to make her shut up, even though we knew she wasn't really scolding us.

The thing was Ne-ning was so many years older than me that her world was another world.

LUPENG

Lupeng, A-ma-ling's sister, she was really good to us!

As she was younger than Ne-ning, she didn't have needle heels, but "low-heeled" shoes, and those were much easier to wear, and she left them to us for a few moments, although those were also a little dangerous, because our feet were smaller than hers, and if you were careless, they would bend and a bone came out of your ankle, and that would hurt a lot and you had to wear a bandage for many days, and then everyone found out that you had put on heels and said things.

She also let us paint our lips with her lipstick. We were really ugly, but we exploded laughing when we looked in the mirror!

And she would tell us stories about Alaska!

In Alaska the Eskimos lived in their ice houses called igloos, and there it was always very cold, much more than in January in Turgalium, also all the time, even in the summer, but we liked those stories very much, and we would have liked to live there.

But since our houses were made of ordinary walls, not ice, one day I said to my friend:

—Hey, A-ma-ling, why don't we ask TrickyJoey to give forty blocks of ice to us, and we'll make an igloo for ourselves?

—And where are we going to get money to pay him for so many blocks? she answered.

—Well, I don't know, we can ask Grandpa Edua-rding, my grandmother, all our brothers, and if they lend us a little, then we'll let them come in for a while, but not to live there.

Because TrickyJoey always had a lot of ice stored; I don't know where he got it from, maybe he would go to Alaska every night to buy it, but I don't know for sure, and every morning someone who was at the bar would take the ice around the houses to cool the iceboxes, which were like cabinets with a very heavy door, with a part where the large chunk of ice was put, and at the bottom of the ice, it had a tray so that the melting water could fall there. And then it had many shelves, like in the clothing closets, but no clothes were put on, we put the food there so that it would be very fresh and not spoil, nor would the flies that were around eat it.

A-ma-ling's icebox was yellow and very tall, but ours, although shorter, was more beautiful: green and white like marble, but it was not marble, and it had a door, with a pure silver border that took a lot of work to open it, so I never opened it, but Feipang, even though he was smaller than me, was always opening and closing it, and if you asked him why he did it, he would always answer:

—I want to take a little bit of ice, that makes my mouth very cool!

But what he wanted it for was not to eat it, that was a lie, he wanted it for throwing at people who passed by on the street. He would stand on a balcony, and as soon as he saw that someone was underneath, Pumbaa!, throw the ice on him; he would hide immediately so they would not discover him, and then he would spend an hour laughing out loud.

The truth is that we never asked TrickyJoey to lend us ice for the igloo, but sure, sure, if we had told him, he would have given us a lot of ice blocks and on top of it not charge money for it, because he was our friend, but because we didn't, we put up with it and we continued living in our normal houses, look, we didn't have any others....

At A-ma-ling's house they had a very fat and very large tome, which her sister Lupeng read to us many times.

It was so big that we couldn't even hold it between the two of us, and when A-ma-ling had a cold, or a cough, or a fever, which was often in the winter, and she had to stay in bed all day not only at night, Lupeng and I also flopped onto the bed, one on each side, and she read it to us and we listened to every single tale of that volume, and we did not care not to be on the street because we were very warm there, and although A-ma-ling and Lupeng and I knew that there must be a lot of microbes, which were like very tiny bugs, around the bed, we spent many hours listening to stories.

They were stories from China, with stories of Chinese men and women and their traditions, of how they were dressed; of the things they ate and did, like they planted rice, which was what they ate every day, just like my brother An-dong-ni, who when he caught that mania he always had to eat rice, and if they didn't give him that, he started to cry and say:

—I want my rice! Give me my rice! I want my rice now!

Like this all the time, until they prepared it for him to shut up and be still.

In addition, in that book they said what they did to the poor little Chinese girls: all Chinese men, what they liked was that women had teeny tiny feet, so what they did was that they bandaged them, and it seems that they put on some pure iron shoes so they wouldn't grow and they were always really like dwarf feet, and although that kind of shoes and bandages were hurting a lot and the girls cried a lot, they could not take off those shoes, not even to sleep, and a girl who took off bandages and shoes, as soon as the chief of all the Chinese found out he ran to the house, drew a very sharp sword and cut off both of her feet, gosh, so that she would learn to be obedient; with that story we cried a lot, but thank God we weren't Chinese and our feet could get big if they wanted.

There were also stories in the book of how they married and stayed with their husband's relatives, instead of going to their own home by themselves. A-ma-ling thought it was because the Chinese woman did not know how to make the bed or prepare the rice, but Lupeng told us that no, that it was a tradition, that is when something is always done and that's that, and they had that way of living, even if they knew how to make the bed.

When the Chinese stork brought them a child, they had to wrap them with rags, like mummies, even if they were alive; I think it was so they wouldn't put their fingers in their eyes; or they put them in a sack and they would stay still while they made the rice.

There were many more stories, five hundred or a thousand, and we loved them. We would cry or laugh depending on what the story was about, and in the end, almost always all the problems were fixed, more or less as happened to those who were not Chinese.

But A-ma-ling and I sometimes got fed up with so much Chinese and preferred what "Our Children's Book" told us, much more variety.

In addition to the fat books that our older sisters or brothers read to us, we also had our own books.

Ne-ning and Lupeng read some novels of somebody called Corintellado and that were about boyfriends and girlfriends, about kisses that boyfriends and girlfriends gave each other on the mouth, Puff, that's disgusting, with all the slobber, because once we got hold of one of my sister's without her knowing it, we began to read it, and what a bore.

And thank goodness she didn't find out, because if she had done for sure she would have told Mamá Chong to scold us, on top of which we didn't like it at all.

Ours were so much better.

In ours we had fairies and gnomes and witches, and we also had princesses and queens.

And fairies could fly with transparent wings that they had, and we really liked that.

One day we said to Lupeng:

—Can you make us some fairy wings?

—I can try— she told us, —but since I've never done any, I don't know if they will be okay.

—Come on, even if they're not very transparent, make us a few, we replied.

She made us four and they were very precious and beautiful, with threads that looked like gold and silver, and many little holes for air to pass through.

So I said to A-ma-ling:

—Let's try them, see if they work.

We climbed on a fat stone in her garden, we held hands, we counted to three and, come on, let's fly!

But we didn't fly.

We hit the ground with a thump, and we got blood on our whole faces!

And on top of that we couldn't even cry, so that no one would scold us.

That day we decided that we were never going to be fairies, that it was better to remain regular children, and we switched to other less dangerous books.

She had one called "Antoñita the Fantastic" and I had another about "The Adventures of Celia."

The one about Antoñita we liked a lot, but Celia's a lot more, because the poor thing, even though she only had one brother, Cuchifritin, that one was really bad, and he didn't stop for a minute doing bad things, much worse even than my friend's bad brother, which is saying something, and since she only had one it was more noticeable, because at least we got some of the good ones, so every time we read those adventures of Celia with her brother, we had to cry a lot, a liter of tears at least, for the pain it gave us, and we would have liked her to live in our city, and even on our street; as my house had many rooms to spare, she could have stayed there, because it seems to me that Mamá Chong would not have cared at all, because there were already many people, and it did not matter one more girl, and thus she would have become our friend and almost my sister, and she would have had a good time with us, but we didn't know where she lived.

As the post office was on the ground floor of my house and all the postmen lived there, and I knew them because I lived upstairs, we thought it would be a very good idea to ask them.

We went into the Post Office and as soon as I saw a postman I asked him:

—Mr. Car-pi-tong, (that was his name) do you know where Celia lives?

—No, right off hand I can't think of it, but wait a moment, I will look for her address in my notebook, he told us.

And the thing is that he had a very fat notebook containing all the addresses of all the people, even those who lived on Little Street or Shops Street, or in streets that were very far away, of which we did not even know the name.

But as much as he searched and looked in his notebook, he couldn't find where poor Celia lived, so we couldn't invite her to live and play with us.

But we kept reading all her adventures and wept a little; that's the truth.

Our two sisters were tied for one thing: they both taught us how to cook.

Well, cooking, what is actually cooking, was not much, because those two things they taught us were not ordinary food, which is eaten every day, such as soup or Russian steaks, but they were much better and above all, they tasted much better than ordinary food.

Our kitchen was very large, but much uglier than hers.

Because A-ma-ling's had a door that when you opened it a terrace would appear, not as big as our terrace above, which was five or six kilometers large, but hers was a terrace above the garden, and there was lots of plants and flowers, chairs to sit on and a table and many other things.

In our kitchen there was the entrance door from the hall, three square windows very small, from which you couldn't see anything because they were high up, and another door where the white cupboard furniture was pushed up against it.

The door was shared with the maids' room, but since the cupboard was tight against it, they couldn't open it, and they couldn't go into the kitchen at night to eat all the food while we were sleeping, which was what they wanted to do, but Mamá Chong was very smart and that's why she put the cupboard there; so tough, take that!

In my house and hers, inside the kitchens we had something to cook called "Economic-stove" but I don't remember why it was called that.

Out at Las Viñas winery we also had another Economic Stove, but in the one there we had to put wood. My brother Man-o-ling cut out equal chunks every morning. And they had to be exact, of the same equal measure, because otherwise Ne-ning would get very angry and say they were useless. We didn't put wood in the one in Turgalium, because we didn't use it, but it served us to put things on top.

Next to the economic stove was the ovenstove, which was where food was made.

Charcoal was put in a hole that was like a tunnel, it was blown with a bellows for a long time, until the charcoal that was black turned red and was very hot. It burned a lot if you touched it.

And above that hole it had two holes, which had many circles of iron, one circle inside another, where the pots and pans were put to make the soup and macaroni and fry the breaded steaks and potato omelettes and all other things that we had to eat, because if they were not put there they were raw and that was very disgusting, look, because if the steaks were not fried they were full of blood, and the eggs also seemed like snot, uff, what a disgust...

Ne-ning taught us to make coconut yolks, balls of coconut called *yemas de coco*!

One day when she wasn't writing those letters to her boyfriend Cheng-Chu, and because of that she must have been very bored, she told us:

—I think you're being pretty good this afternoon, so I'm going to teach you how to do something.

She took us to the kitchen, put some rags tied onto us so we wouldn't get stained, and said to us:

—Come on, now to work, we're going to make coconut yolks!

We both loved coconut balls, but we did not know that they could be made, because we had always seen them on a plate, each one inside its paper, or in a cardboard box when they were to give to other people, so you can imagine how happy we were.

A-ma-ling looked at me with wide eyes and said softly:

—As soon as we learn, I'm going to make sixty-five coconut balls for myself.

—And besides, I put in, —we can start a coconut balls factory and sell them at the Thursday market.

—And (I continued) take them to the tile factory and have Uncle Edu-ard-ong sell them for us and then give us the money.

—And when we sell them we will have at least thirty-eight pesetas, was her last contribution to the dialogue.

But making coconut yolks don't think it was so easy:

First you had to make something called "syrup," which I don't know why they called it syrup, because it was water with sugar, but it really was called that.

Since we couldn't reach up enough to stir the syrup pot, which was the best of all, Ne-ning let us blow a lot with the bellows; taking turns, although she was my sister, but so that A-ma-ling would not get envious.

Then you had to put that syrup on top of the grated coconut, we mixed everything for a long time, it got very sticky and everything stayed between your fingers.

And then they were made into little balls. We liked that very much, because we did it on the marble table, which we loved and my friend was always saying:

—As soon as I'm forty or fifty years old and have a lot of money, I'm going to buy my mom a marble table just like you have!

Because we both knew it was a beautiful table....

And when all the balls were done, they were rolled around a plate that had sugar, but regular sugar, not syrup.

And they were placed in paper molds, like those for muffins but smaller: and so the coconut yolks were ready.

The first day we made them they were very ugly: some were like chickpeas and others like small balls, they didn't even go into the molds, but if you closed your eyes and didn't look at them, the flavor was of coconut balls, so we covered our eyes with one hand, in addition to having them closed so that by mistake we would not look, and think we were eating macaroni, or anything else, and with our free hand we took handfuls of coconut balls, until we gobbled them all up!

Another day, when we almost knew how to make the coconut balls, and they came out very round and the same, Ne-ning told us:

—Because you have been very good students, now I'm going to show you another way of making them! You know I am very good when you behave!

Well! get a load of that... when she was the one who was always scolding us...

But A-ma-ling and I looked at each other and shut up, just in case.

The second way was much easier, we did not need that sticky syrup or anything, just the grated coconut, egg whites and sugar, and then make the balls, which at that time were almost perfect, and then put more sugar on the outside and, Ta-dah! to their little paper beds to rest. Delicious.

Lupeng taught us how to make Candy Lollipops!

But if I don't want to tell a lie, so that afterwards you always go around saying that I'm a liar, the truth is that she made them, we looked at how she did them, because the lollipop was very dangerous, and you could burn and die while you were doing them.

Lupeng put a lot of sugar in a pan, as if she were going to fry it, although everyone knows that sugar does not fry like a cutlet, and when it was turning dark brown she put honey in it, and come on, stir and stir the sugar, which no longer seemed even sugar with honey, until many little bubbles started to come out, which meant that it was already well fried.

So she put that in some paper cones, and then she put some wooden sticks in them.

We had to wait a long time until they got cold, but when we peeled the paper, you can't imagine the lollipops we had made: Fat and delicious! We had never eaten any like them, and we had almost made them ourselves!

And since they both knew how to sew well, they taught us!

My sister Ne-ning knew how to sew everything, but what's called everything, not like poor Mamá Chong, who always had many magazines that taught you to sew, but I don't know if she just forgot to read them or what, because she never read them. She only looked at the pictures, we call them "santos," who were not the kind of saints who are in churches or hermitages. The saints in my mother's magazines were photographs, yes, just photos of tablecloths and sheets, and other things like those that are used in houses, and that she looked at and looked at again and said:

—What a wonderful bed set! It is really beautiful! I'll see if I will make it.

—What gorgeous tablecloths! Let's see if I cheer up and start a similar one.

So with everything she saw.

But she never did any of the saints stuff... I'm sure she would forget the next day.

What she did know how to do was something called darning, and then it must not have been a bad word because she never said a bad word, and that was when a sock had a hole in it, she would put a glass egg inside it, pass a thread on one side, then on the other, back to the first side, and so on, all the while, hours and hours, until the hole disappeared and the threads covered it, and it was no longer noticeable that there had been a hole there before. Like magic.

That glass egg of my mamá was really pretty!

IsabelM also had a darning egg, but it was made of wood, very ugly.

So we loved to sit at the round table and watch Mamá Chong, passing and re-passing the threads through the sock, and our dream was to one day have an egg all to ourselves, but not made of wood or something else. It had to be glass and the same color: green and yellow and white.

Ne-ning didn't have any eggs, not even wooden ones, but it didn't matter because she didn't have to do that darning thing. Also she did not know how to do it. But she did know how to sew everything: pants, skirts, jackets... Everything that was first a rag, when she sewed it became something else.

To learn all that, she went to a place where they taught her about sewing.

It was called the "Academy of Dressmaking," which meant really that every kind of clothes could be cut out and sewn there, but in truth they had given it that name of dressmaking and it was called that.

It was like a school, but they didn't teach reading or writing, neither did they teach addition and division. You already had to know that before going there, because the teacher didn't know anything about the EM with the A, nor did she have a notebook with lines like ours, she only knew how to turn rags into things to wear and nothing more.

My sister told us in the afternoons:

—I'm going to Cha-ring's house, to my Dressmaking class.

We really wanted to go to that Cha-ring house, and see what the tailoring was, because the truth is that it sounded great.

One day, after asking her a thousand times, she let us go with her.

It was very far away, near the Plaza where we used to live, on a street called Sillerías, Seat Makers Street, and A-ma-ling was very excited thinking that the street was full of chairs and she kept saying to me:

—As soon as we get to the Sillerías street, I'm going to sit in seventeen different chairs. First in a gold one, then a silver one, then a short one, then...

And so on all the time. I was dizzy, but I held on, because she was my friend. Later someone said it was where, a long time ago, they made seats to put on horses, but usually I think it's chairs.

When we finally got there, we saw that it was a normal street, with houses on both sides and sidewalks and people on the balconies, and some shops at the bottom of the houses; no chairs, not even the most common ones, I didn't care, because I didn't have hopes about the gold and silver chairs, but A-ma-ling was very sad and believed that everyone had cheated and deceived her. And as I said:

—Who told you about the golden chairs, Titing? Well, you already know that you can't trust him, that he tells a lot of lies! Come on, stop whining, or they are going to think you are a little girl like my brother An-dong-ni.

She must have seen that I was serious, because she fell silent.

We went into Cha-ring's house and there were really wonderful things there: needles, pins, scissors, cloths of all colors, papers, rulers... everything, and she was so good that she let us fiddle with everything, everything, but she told us that we had to be very careful with scissors and needles, Ha! as if we didn't know that needles broke and entered the body to make you a corpse! Well, maybe other girls didn't know, and that's why she explained it to us.

Between Cha-ring and Ne-ning they taught us to thread a needle, which was a very difficult operation, because you had to pass a thread through a very small hole, and it took a long time, but it was necessary for sewing.

And since we almost knew how to put thread on the needle, one afternoon my sister Ne-ning taught us to sew buttons.

Until that day, we believed that the buttons were glued to the cloth with glue, but no, it was done with thread, and it was very important to know how to do it, the most important thing about sewing.

And as Ne-ning used to say:

—This is the first thing you have to learn, because if a button falls off your blouse or dress, and you don't know how to put it back on, you're going to look like La Per-nal-a.

And that really scared us, because La Per-nal-a was a lady who was normal before, but who had become a witch because she did not know how to sew her buttons, and she always went along the streets dragging her feet and wrapped in many rags, one on top of another. She must not have had a house, or a bathroom, because she was very dirty and uncombed, and she didn't have teeth because they had fallen out from not washing them. See? That is why when my father forced all of us to brush our teeth after eating, and we did not like to do it, if he had told us that we would end up like Doña Per-nal-a we would not have minded running out to wash them, but I don't think my father knew Mrs. Per-nal-a, because he was locked up working, and she was always on the streets, and he only told us that we had to clean them. So we quickly learned how to sew buttons just in case. And it was quite difficult, but we did it.

And Lupeng taught us to sew hems, which was what was at the end of the skirt. There was no need for glue either, because the cloth was folded, it was folded again and then the needle was poked through with thread and that's that. When we learned I said to my friend:

—A-ma-ling, this is going to help us a lot! Now when we have something secret that we don't want anyone to take away from us, we put it in the hem, we sew it again, and that's that! And as we will wear it, there will be no danger that any of our brothers know!

But she wasn't so convinced that my idea was that good. Because she said:

—If it's a small thing, we can put it, but what if it's big, eh? The lump will be seen and everyone will know.

And there I had to agree with her.

But the important thing is that we learned to sew, thanks to our sisters.

GRANDPARENTS

Other girls had two grandparents and two grandmothers, but not me and neither did my friend, and that was a big drag, but that's what we had.

I had only one grandmother, Mamá Chong's mamá.

Although her name was Ma-Li-ya, we just called her grandmother and that's that. Because that name was only used by her sister, her close friends and her cousins and like that, we couldn't, and look, she wouldn't have cared because she didn't care about those things, but even my friend called her grandmother (and she wasn't even her relative or anything, because A-ma-ling had another blood type) so as not to be confused.

My grandmother had green eyes and blonde hair; the truth is that she was no longer so blonde, because some things called "silver threads" had gotten into her hair, but there were parts that yes, they were still quite blonde and I loved it. Since Nening and I had very dark hair and mine was almost black, we were a little envious of her, although we didn't say anything to her.

And I don't even want to tell you how envious we were about her green eyes!

But since we couldn't change ours to that color, what we did was look at hers.

When I said:

—Grandma, you have the most beautiful eyes in the whole world!

She always answered:

—Don't believe it, they're cat eyes.

But it wasn't true, they were grandmother's eyes.

The thing is that she liked cats very much, and maybe she thought that if she had cat eyes she would become one of them.

First she lived in a very large, very large house, near the Plaza. Mamá Chong was telling her all the time that she couldn't live there alone, that anything could happen to her, that she wasn't calm in case she got sick at night, that if this and that if that, but my grandmother told her:

—Don't be boring and don't pester me, Mamá Chong, I've told you a thousand times that I like to be at my own home and do whatever I want and don't nag me anymore.

Because the truth is that she was very happy there: she got up very early, fed her cats, ate anything for breakfast because she did not care about meals, and went to many convents to see her goddaughters.

Those weren't her real daughters, the only real one was Mamá Chong. They were normal women who had become nuns and to do that they had to have something called "herdowry" (which was not some kind of herd, no, it was like money to buy a nun's dress, buy sweets for others who were locked up there and things like that), because my grandmother and other friends of hers gave it to them, if their parents were very poor or if they got very boring teasing all the time that they wanted to be nuns.

In exchange for the money they had to pray every day for my grandmother and for us, but she liked to go check that they were doing it. It seems to me that she did not trust much in case they were liars and they said yes and what they were doing was painting their nails or eating coconut balls.

One day at my grandmother's home she said to A-ma-ling and myself:

—Children, tomorrow tell the nannies to put some nice dresses on you because I'm going to take you both to a wedding, but I want the three of us to go alone, so hush-hush! At home you say that you are going to visit me, and you will see how well we are going to spend the day.

(That hush-hush was a secret code that meant that we couldn't tell anyone, not even Mamá Chong or our sisters, and I warned my friend to be very careful, not to let anyone know without realizing it.)

As we had not been to any wedding before, we were very happy, and we ran home to choose the costumes to wear.

We did not have many, that's the truth, only the one for Sundays, the daily ones and then the uniform, not like the Lol-i-tang neighbor, and we couldn't borrow any off that one because as she was super-adulterer, she must be twenty years old or more, all her suits would be very big, and very horrible and we would have left-over cloth everywhere, also she was not our close friend, only a neighbor, so I told my nanny to iron the one for Sundays very well and my friend did the same at her home.

The next day A-ma-ling came in very pretty. She even had a barrette in her hair! And I was also very nice, in a very beautiful dress that I had only worn twice and that had belonged to Ne-ning before, but got too small.

Because since my sister was much older than me, when she grew up and could no longer wear a dress because it squeezed her a lot, what they sometimes did was shrink it, I don't remember very well how they did it, but suddenly it got my size. One day when I told Titing about it, he told me that it was very easy: they would put the dress in a tightly closed box, then the magic words were said, the box was opened and the dress was small, but since he was such a liar, I don't know if they did it that way or not.

When we were already fixed and waiting to go with my grandmother, Feipang came and asked us: —Where are you two going so dolled up?

That was a word that Man-o-ling had taught him and he wanted to use it all the time so he wouldn't forget it.

We told him that out there, to go take a walk, but he didn't believe it and wanted us to tell him the truth.

What pressure!

Luckily the baby came crawling, because he still didn't know how to walk very well, and while he was distracted with him we ran down the stairs.

My grandmother was already waiting for us downstairs and the three of us went to the wedding.

We didn't know which church she was going to take us to. We went past a lot of them and didn't stop at any.

Very strange.

Finally, after walking two hundred kilometers or more, we arrived at the convent of San Pedro, which wasn't very pretty, not like others in Turgalium.

Because in our city there were seven or twenty-three convents, I don't remember exactly, but there were a lot of them, and they were all full of nuns dressed like nuns, even at night they had nuns' nightgowns that were a bit ugly, that's the truth, but the poor things had no others and they had no choice but to put up with it.

We entered the church. There were quite a lot of people but we didn't see any groom waiting for the bride to arrive.

Because Ne-ning had told us one day how weddings were done and we knew it by heart, well, we even did a wedding with one of my dolls and a rag doll that Lupeng made for us and it turned out great.

We're looking and waiting and no boyfriend came.

A-ma-ling said softly to me:

—Maybe he doesn't want to get married and has gone to Madroñera or Melilla.

Because Melilla was very far away, much further than Madroñera, and look, Madroñera was far away, because when we went to Las Viñas we had to go through there and I knew it.

The boyfriend of Man-o-ling's nanny had been sent to that Melilla when he started doing something called "drafted," and he told us that it had taken a long time to arrive, that we never should go because it was a very bad place, a drag.

Well, nothing, the boyfriend still did not come.

We were already getting very worried, when nuns began to arrive in the center, between the rows of benches.

Nuns and more nuns. Eighty or one hundred seventeen at least.

And then a bride.

In a wedding dress, but we thought she had the face of a nun too.

In her hands she carried a very precious crown of pure gold.

She kept walking and walking until she reached the altar, where the priest was waiting.

And the groom had not arrived!

Poor thing, what a shame, because the groom had to arrive before the bride, that was like that and it couldn't be changed, look, what can the poor thing do if he didn't show up, eh? Because to have a wedding it was necessary to have the two, a groom and a bride. What a problem.

I asked my grandmother when the groom was going to arrive and she told me:

—Now you be quiet, the ceremony will begin in a moment.

While she was answering me, the bride goes and throws herself on the floor. Can you believe it?

Like my brother Feipang when he wanted something. She must have been extremely angry with the one from Melilla because he hadn't arrived.

The other nuns next to her took the crown and wanted to put it on her head, but she was still on the ground.

At last two nuns, who seemed to me to be quite rough, raised her up, forced the crown on her head, and an altar boy came with a small tray and a ring.

The priest said:

—Today you are going to marry Jesus Christ, MariPuri (which was what she was really called, her real name, because my grandmother had told us about it while we were walking to the convent). From this moment on, you will be called Sister Azucena Del Valle, and that's that. Don't even think about answering when they call you MariPuri, because I'll give you a fine. Come on, the ring.

They put the ring on her and then another nun came, who must have been very bad and very disgusting, because she took scissors from a bag and began to cut poor MariPuri's hair.

And look, her head was full of beautiful ringlets!

Well, nothing, the bad nun took them all off, and on top of that she didn't have to know how to cut her hair, I don't think she was a real hairdresser, but had told a huge lie to the other nuns to get the scissors, because it left her ugly and with horrible hair.

Then two more came from behind and began to take off her wedding dress.

And MariPuri wasn't even crying!

We both got very angry, on top of that Melilla's boyfriend not even even showing up, they cut off her ringlets, they took off her white dress, well we wanted to go where she was and kick those nuns so bad in the shins, but Grandmamá said that we had to be still and in silence, that now was the best moment, so we kept quiet and kept looking.

When they took away the wedding dress, do you know what those did? - you can't even imagine it. The two of us were open-mouthed: they put a nun's outfit on her! In other words, they take away her beautiful suit and ta-dah!, dress her like all the others, poor thing, what a great shame.

And we started crying a lot of tears!

My grandmother was very happy to see us crying and said that we were very "sensitive," which must be a very good thing because everyone around us shook their heads yes. We would have to ask Man-o-ling as soon as we got home, and to explain it well.

Then many prayers came, many songs of the nuns and after many hours we were finally able to leave the church.

They took us to a room that was secret, only the nuns could enter there every day, but since that was a special day because of the wedding, they let us who were normal, come on, made of flesh and bone.

As soon as we arrived, MariPuri, or Azucena or whatever they call her now, came up to my grandmother and said:

- Godmother, today is the happiest day of my life! I have finally been able to marry Jesus Christ! Thank you very much for making my dream come true!

A-ma-ling and I really heard all this, really.

And look, they had made her ugly, but she was so happy.

She gave us kisses and said that as she was the goddaughter of my grandmother she would pray every day for us, so we never had anything bad in our lives and so much more that I do not remember. Then A-ma-ling said:

—¿Why haven't you sent a telegram to the guy in Melilla telling him what time the wedding was? We could have helped you write it if you didn't know how to write it, and he would have jumped on a bus very fast and would have arrived on time.

They all looked at us very strangely and my grandmother said:

—These babies are tremendous!

So I told my friend to shut up and we went to where the cakes were.

GODMOTHERS AND GODFATHERS

In addition to the parents and relatives, we also had some who were our godmothers and others the godfathers, who got put there just in case Mamá Chong or my papá would suddenly be a corpse and we would become orphans, so that they would take us to the school or Don Teodoro if we had sore throats, and also for them to come into the kitchen to see how the food was going, or see if we needed new shoes, or if our coats had become small.

All of us had to have those, but Feipang and I had a bit of bad luck with ours, the others didn't. I will tell you.

Ne-ning's godmother had no name. That was her name, the godmother, and she was also Mamá Chong's godmother. They had used the same one because when my sister was born they were so busy, between changing her diapers, preparing meals for her and all those things you have to do when a baby comes, that they didn't have time to look for another one, but my sister didn't care much, because godmother, although she was very old, was quite good.

That godmother lived in the street of the chairs or seats, yes, Sillerías, where A-ma-ling got so disgusted near the Plaza, and at that time Mamá Chong, Papá Bo-ling and Ne-ning lived in the first house we had before we changed to the big one, and because they were so close by she could go many times to see her, to kiss her and to put on cologne and a bow in her hair so that she would be very beautiful, and sometimes even to give her a bottle.

When we changed, even though we lived very far away, they kept seeing her many times, so that no one would believe that they were no longer friends, and since Ne-ning already knew how to make some donuts, she prepared many of the ones she liked for her snack time.

The godmother lived in a horrible house, all full of furniture and paintings and all those things that are put in the rooms, there was nowhere without furniture, and you could hardly look anywhere without seeing something. How tiring! I didn't like going there at all, even though she was very good and gave me many kisses and also chocolates, not like her disgusting maid who as soon as she saw me enter the house she gave me a pinch of the bad ones, the kind of twisting ones, and even if I had done nothing, or almost nothing, she comes to pinch. She had that mania, it seems to me that she had learned it when she was little and lived in the Huertinas and it never went away, and even though I kicked her a few times to make her leave me alone, she wouldn't stop. But she only did it with me. Nothing with my sister, very clingy, just telling her all the time that she loved her very much, that she was beautiful, that this and that and many stories.

So one day I approached the godmother and said:

—Hey godmother, I love you a little, but it seems to me that I'm not going to come to your house again, because that one pinches me and they hurt a lot.

The godmother told me not to worry, that she was going to scold her that afternoon and that if she did it again I must tell her right away, that maid would find out what's what, so I was pretty calm.

In that house with so many pieces of furniture there was one that I did like a lot: It seemed like a sofa, but it was something else called "You-and-I," where two people couldn't sit in a row, because the seats were in different places, and when two people sat down, one looked to one side and the other to the opposite side, but if they got sideways, they would see each other.

When I asked her why it was that way, she told me that it was a special sofa for when two people were not yet close friends; at first, as they did not know each other, they had nothing to talk about and could be very comfortable looking at each one to their side, but later, when they already knew the names and that, they could lean over and look at each other a little and start talking. If they became close friends, they moved to another place and that's that.

Ne-Ning went many times to eat with her, especially on Sundays, but we other kids only went "for a visit," which meant that we were there for a while, while Mamá Chong had lunch with her and then we left.

And as in that house, although they had so many chairs and furniture and cabinets, they didn't even have notebooks to paint, or colored pencils, or dolls, or anything to play with, it was a lot of boredom. Better not go, although sometimes I did not escape.

My sister's godfather was gone.

He was not the godmother's husband, because she was very old and they don't have husbands, or even parents.

When Ne-ning was born, Uncle José Manuel (who was Mamá's Chong's brother), ran to the house and told them that he was asking to be the godfather, that she was a very cute girl who hardly cried and they mustn't be looking for anyone because he had asked them first.

But two or three years later, some very bad guys came with guns full of bullets, they killed him and my sister was left alone with her godmother.

And look, my papá had warned him, he said very clearly:

—It is better that you are not a godfather, if something happens to me, then you have to act as a father and you will get very tired, you like to get up late in the morning and with a baby at seven o'clock you already have to be on your feet.

But he said that he didn't care, that maybe something would happen to him before, that he wanted to take the girl in a stroller that he had bought, and that could only be done by papás, mamás and godparents and end of discussion.

As he got so capricious they let him, and look, poor Ne-ning was quickly left without a godfather, buff, and thank goodness they didn't put another bullet into the godmother...

Man-o-ling had some godparents who were great.

His godmother was called Ga-bing and she was French, that is, she was not born in Turgalium and not even in Spain, because she was from a different country called France and those French lived there, although they were made of flesh and bone like us, but his godfather, that was called Man-o-Long, he was Spanish. And a dentist.

Dentists are a bit like doctors, but they do not know anything about the guts, or fever or wounds and that, they only know how to take out teeth when they are poor, and other times they cover the holes and that I think is called making "filling," because if you were unlucky enough for a mosquito to drill you in a tooth or in a molar, then you had a hole left, and it hurt a lot and you had to go straight to the dentist's house and tell him you had a hole. Then he would cover the hole with I don't know what, a little cement or a small brick and it never hurt you anymore.

And the thing is that Mamá Chong was very good, but she was talking all the time and the mosquitoes took advantage of it to get into her mouth and bite her teeth and molars. And they were very hard, not like when they bit me, that they did it in soft places, like a leg or in the neck, but what those bugs wanted was to bother and bother and that's that, and they did not care whether they bit in a hard place or a soft one.

Where Man-o-Long was almost always, which was called "The consultation," I did not like going in very much, in case he told me to sit in that scary armchair that he had there and where you had to be with your mouth open all the time. Or for a while, even if you weren't painting your eyes, but one day when A-ma-ling was hurting a lot inside her mouth, Mamá Chong and I went with her so that she wouldn't be too scared and wouldn't cry a lot.

He sat her down in that terrible chair, told her to open her mouth, and a moment later said:

—You can close it now. It is nothing serious, only that you will have a tooth and I have to make a tiny cut.

She began to shake a lot but we held her hand while Man-o-long cut her and in a moment it was all over.

And Ga-bing came with a tray full of fresh chocolates!

Yes, because she, my brother's godmother, was the only person in the world who knew how to make them and didn't have to go to a store to buy them or to the pastry shop, and since she was very close to my mother, she always did a lot for all of us, although she gave Man-o-ling a separate packet of candy chocolates with strawberry and plum fillings that were delicious.

I really liked going to Ga-bing's house, and not only because of the chocolates but because she was very good, she told me many things about France, her little brothers and her friends there, about the trips they made, about her school and the nuns she got, how they had played, well, many great stories and Jua-ni-ting, who was her daughter, taught me how to make a scarf with wool of many colors!

So even though Ga-bing wasn't really my godmother, it was as if she was and whenever I could I went to her house.

An-dong-ni also had some very super-nifty godparents, that is, very good.

Those were not from France, but Mar-u-xing, the godmother, had a sister who lived in Canada, which was even further away than Paris, because you had to cross an ocean.

An-Dong, the godfather, was always laughing and told us many stories, and since he worked with Papá Bo-ling we saw him almost every day. They were godparents who loved him very much, and not only him but all of us.

Mar-u-xing, every time I went to her house she would tell me:

—I can't understand why they say you're bad, with how funny and nice you are!

She was one of the good adulterers, I tell you, and whenever she saw me with my friend on the street or on the upper park she gave us many kisses and hugs.

But look what happened to me: my grandmother asked to be my godmother and Mamá Chong said that was all right, she was letting her. Then she ran off with me, put me in a pretty large bag, went to see those nuns from the convent of San Pedro who were friends of hers and said:

—I need you to make me the most beautiful christening skirt in the world, because I have to take this girl to San Martín to have her take off the unfaithful thing, and since it is January and it is quite cold, inside you put a very good lining so that she is warm.

So the nuns began to sew very quickly and in five minutes they gave her a very beautiful dress, they put it on me and took me quickly to church.

When she arrived, Don Ra-fa-el (who was the priest at the time) said:

—Where is the godfather? You have to bring one, if not, there is no baptism.

So my grandmother went out to the atrium, saw a gypsy there and told him to come in with her for a moment, please, that she would beg him please, and afterwards she'd buy him a bottle of wine.

The gypsy was very happy, he went in with her, grabbed one end of the dress and that's that, they made me a Christian right away.

(My mom told me that long after that day, because before then I didn't understand anything because I was a baby.)

But since they didn't know him at all, they didn't know his name and he didn't even live in Turgalium but had come to a fair, he didn't count, and I was left without a godfather. Besides, my grandmother was a grandmother too, which is much more than being a godmother, that is, I couldn't say like my brothers or sister: "I'm going to see my godmother," no, I had to say: "I'm going to see grandmother." On top of that, she wasn't just my grandmother, she was also everyone else's, so really bad. A godmother who almost didn't count, but hey... Mamá Chong, I think she was a bit silly that day, she should have told my grandmother to wait a while while they were looking for a regular godfather, even if he wasn't a dentist, but Ne-ning and Man-o-ling were a bit annoying wanting to pick me up and put my booties on, and maybe she didn't realize it, and then they couldn't take me to baptize again, it was very forbidden, it could only be done once; if you went another time, the priest would warn the guards, they would catch you and put the whole family in jail, and you were now one of those called "lowlifes" and it couldn't be.

But when I got my friend and told A-ma-ling all that, she told me not to worry, that she didn't have a godmother either, not even one who was also a grandmother, because hers had been her father's aunt, a very old and very fat lady that died of the so much that she ate. All the croquettes and soups and like that turned into lard, the lards squeezed her so much that she couldn't breathe and one day when she was trying to eat a chicken drumstick she became a corpse and they had to take her to the cemetery for being so dead, so she was left without a godmother. A tragedy.

And Feipang was another who also did not have a normal godmother or godfather.

As he was born on Ne-ning's birthday my sister said:

—Hey, Mamá Chong, this year I don't want you to buy me anything for my birthday, what I would like is to become Feipang's godmother.

Papá Bo-ling told her that it was a lot of responsibility, what he meant it was a lot of work and all that, that Feipang was quite fat and very heavy, that when they went to church she would be very tired and a lot of things, but she made like she was listening to him, but paid no attention.

As we still lived in the Plaza, the church of San Martín was very close, almost opposite.

When Mamá Chong went to Pep-i-tang's hairdresser salon to have her hair color changed because she no longer wanted to be a redhead, my sister grabbed Feipang very quickly, wrapped him in a blue shawl, went to see Paula who was living under us and told her to accompany them for a moment, that she had to take the baby to make him a Christian right away, in case he died suddenly that day, which was very urgent.

Ne-ning knew that she had to bring a godfather, but Paula told her not to worry, that around the fountain there were always many villeins, that she would ask someone and then invite him to some glasses of wine, that they liked that a lot.

So they caught hold of one of them, and look, he must have been pretty good because the poor guy grabbed Feipang so that my sister wouldn't have to go upstairs with that boy who weighed so much, and as soon as they got upstairs they baptized him.

At noon, when we were all eating, she told us what she had done, and although my mamá had a bit of one of those upsets that she could not have because her heart turned upside down and it was very dangerous, she held on and said okay, but that she should have waited a bit, because she wanted Feipang to have an ordinary godfather, and she wanted for him to have a godfather who was a brother of my papá whose name was the same, but since it was already done there was no solution.

So Feipang was even worse off than me because his godfather was a villein and his godmother was his sister. Can you believe it? At least my godmother was a grandmother, because look, a sister... And as I told you before, in that of the godmothers and godparents we both had very bad luck, but in other things not.

SECTION TWO

RELATIVES - NEIGHBORS

A-ma-ling's house, just like ours, was in a building that had one floor right next to the street, and was called The Ground Floor, and then two floors on top of it.

But everyone who lived in hers were relatives. In ours, no.

For Mamá Chong did not have brothers or sisters, just her mamá who besides was our grandmother, uncles, aunts, cousins, nephews and nieces, and her godmother; and Papá Boling's were living in Madrid, so all our cousins and our aunts and uncles were there, and they couldn't come to live in Turgalium, look what a drag...

On the ground floor were the Mail and Telegraph offices.

The First Floor was where the Chief of Mail lived with his whole family.

On the Second our parents lived along with us, we were the Hermanos Birmanos (which is, like, Burmese Brothers or Sino-Siblings). And also my grandmother when she moved to our house, and maids and a few others who cleaned and made meals and all like that. On top we had a big terrace and from up there you could see all the old part, the castle, the churches, the palaces, and all the houses, which were very old and also a lot of new ones, and things like that.

But nobody who lived or worked in the other two floors was from our family. Friends or neighbors, yes, but no cousins or aunts or uncles, although they all loved us a lot, but I would have liked it better if all our cousins were living with us; what happened was that if they couldn't they couldn't, and that's that.

A-ma-ling's house was between the City Hall and the house of Doña Ma-rting, a very ancient lady who must have been like sixty years old, or at least fifty-three.

Doña Ma-rting lived alone and without any cousin or uncle, not even a brother, even a little one. In her house were only her and her maids, so when she was out on her look-out balcony, which seemed like all the time, and she saw us, she often said:

—Girls, do you want to come up for a while and keep me company?

And the two of us went running up the stairs, and thank goodness they were less than in our houses.

She must have wanted to be really great friends with us, even though we were only little girls, because when we were in her parlor, while we told her things she stuffed us with all kinds of stupendous treats: sugared almonds, sections of mandarins, candied hunks of squashes... It was all delicious, and when we cleaned off one plate they filled us another.

She was a pretty ugly lady, dressed all in black, and did not walk very well. She always had a cane nearby to help her, and she'd say to us: Ay! These bones of mine are killing me!

We didn't see her bones with swords or rifles or pistols or like that to kill her, but we didn't say anything. Maybe those bones were quiet while she had a visit, even little girls, but we didn't say anything because we were behaving ourselves.

She laughed a lot at the things we told her and then her bones must have hurt less, and stayed quiet without wanting to bug her, because we saw her much happier than when we got there, and this even if half the time our stories were fibs that we made up as we went along, but she rewarded us over the top, even lots of times she'd give us a bill for one peseta or even five for us to buy ourselves ice cream if it was summer, or lemon sponge cake if it was not a hot season.

We spent the pesetas on whatever we wanted to, but we didn't tell her. It was better for her to stay content, the poor old lady.

The part behind my friend's house had a huge garden that stretched all the way to the beginning of the Slope of San Andrés, and we had all kinds of adventures there, because we could play with the flowers, make little houses with stones, take our dolls there and give them a bath in a bucket... everything.

But it didn't have a terrace like ours, ha!

It didn't have an entrance hall either, with a glass floor and ceiling!

And besides, the downstairs door of my house had two lions! Well, they were not real lions, like the ones in the jungle, they were lion's heads, smaller than the ones in Africa and in the circus, but they also were very scary.

On the bottom floor of her house, to the right of the entrance door (that didn't have even one Lion), were the offices of her grampa, Don Edua-rding, who was already very old and he must had been at least sixty two years old, and the offices of her two uncles, the ones who were not National Teachers, not even of the normal kind.

Grampa Edua-rding was always dressed very elegantly, with a suit, a tie, a grey overcoat that went down to the ground when it was cold, and a beautiful hat, and wherever he saw us on the street or on the stairs he smiled at us and gave us a kiss, and sometimes, even when it wasn't our birthday or anything, after asking us if we'd been good, he also gave us some pesetas so we could buy things and sweets. We always said yes, we have been very good, just in case, and since there were not people around, they couldn't tell him that we were a couple of fibbers.

A-ma-ling's family had a tile factory.

Yes, the kind you put on the floors of the houses; they also made wall tiles, the kind you put on kitchen walls and bathroom walls, and they were very shiny and we liked them a lot, but the factory was in a different building. But the tiles samples, and where they had all the papers and the list of the people who bought the tiles, were on the ground floor of the house at Ruiz de Mendoza, in some very ugly rooms that they called "Thoffices," and there only very grownups went in, we only stuck our heads in the doorway, and we didn't like that much either because there were just papers and people sitting at desks moving those papers around. Well, what a bore to be there instead of going for a walk, buff.

And, on the other side of the entrance door there was a big place, which my friend's family was letting a guy use, who had a bar with tables and chairs and a long counter where they set little glasses of coffee with milk, or ones with wine or with many other things.

That place was called "New Spain bar," but we all knew that the bar belonged to "TrickyJoey" and since he was our friend we went in there like he was in our family, because he was a neighbor and loved us a lot and almost always we left with something: olives, French fries made by Paula - the mamá of Joey, who was her son, and she was the owner of another bar in the Plaza, right below where we used to live, and for that she was my friend too - peanuts and some kind of sarsaparilla... it seems like everybody was agreed to give us things and we really liked that. So for that whenever we went in there we felt very happy, because if the grownups wanted to treat us well we were not going to take away their pleasures.

The first time we saw the sign on the bar A-ma-ling asked me:

—So the Spain we live in is the old one?

Since this wasn't very clear to me either I had to make something up and tell her a lie:

—Of course, silly! You still don't know that Spain is centuries old and is very worn out now? They have to make a brand new one and they started with the bars.

Then they'll knock down all the houses and the churches, the schools, the roads and the shops and everything, everything, and besides, they'll put new names on the streets.

And she:

—But how are we going to know how to get to places then, if the streets have different names? And what if we get lost?

So, A-ma-ling was my friend but as for imagination, what is called imagination, she didn't have a drop and she didn't know how to find creative solutions to problems.

—Look A-ma-ling, I said to her then —they'll have to write down the new names on a little paper for us and that's that. Besides, if we don't know how to get to school, better for us, we will have the day off.

When she saw that we could skip school because we didn't know how to get there, she was very pleased and forgot all about new and old Spain, and better for me, because I was running out of lies to tell...

On the first floor of her house, which was called the principal, her grampa and aunt Cánd-e-li-tang lived, and in summer another one of her aunts came, who other times lived in Madrid, aunt Pep-i-tang, with her sons, A-ma-ling's cousins, who were real drags and we had a real mania about them because they were always whimpering and asking for stuff and we stayed as far away from them as possible.

About this aunt Pep-i-tang, A-ma-ling and her sister Lupeng were always saying "my aunt lives on Wood Street!"

Since at that time neither she nor I knew Madrid, the stuff about Wood Street sounded stupendous. We both kept trying to figure out what that street must be like:

—I think that all the houses and the roofs there are wooden, I said.

—And the floor of the street must also be wooden, she answered.

And I:

—And in the middle of the street it seems to me there is a wooden river...

—Hey! There can't be a wooden river. Wooden rivers don't exist, she said then.

—Who said? You don't know it, but should realize there are all kinds of rivers: of wood, of glass, of iron, of aluminum foil... is it possible you don't remember the Nativity scene? Don't we put an aluminum foil river there, huh?

And face to face with this she had no choice but to be quiet and admit that, well, maybe Wood Street really had a wooden river, and with that we closed the topic for the time being.

Her flat was on the second floor.

Our was too.

We had to go up fifty two stairs to get up there.

And she did too more or less, but I don't remember the exact number, and since we always went up running we didn't care whether they were many or few.

Our big brothers went up there two by two and came down three by three, but we only went down two by two for the last two and someone was always waiting below in case we fell.

One day we tried the three by three thing and Fel-i-crung, who was one of my neighbor sisters, helped us and we didn't fall down or anything but we didn't want to do it anymore by ourselves because we didn't like it so much even though it seemed like fun.

But her flat was not like ours because the whole thing wasn't for her, her parents and her brothers and sister, but in one part her uncle Em-i-long lived, who was a National Teacher, right, for the whole nation, that means that he could be a teacher in our city or in places very far away like Madroñera or Talavera, a very big town because a queen always lived there, and that's why it was called that, Talavera of the Queen.

That queen must be very old now because she has been living there for ever, and my friend asked me:

—How old do you thing the queen of Talavera is?

And I, who had no idea of how old that good lady was, told her a very high number to impress her:

—Well at least one thousand three hundred eight! She is ancient!

—And how much longer do you think she is going to live?

—Well, forever! Don't you see that if she dies the town would have to be called something else and that would be a mess for the mailman?

The result was that we left the poor queen alive, and the town with its name.

Along with uncle E-mi-long lived his wife and his daughter, who was cousin Eng-ag-ing, a very good and very obedient girl, who was a bit littler than us but just as tall.

Sure, it was very easy for her to be good! She didn't have brothers to bug her or bother her, and she didn't have to share with them either, not toys, not presents, not anything at all; that way anybody could be good, naturally!

Low conversation so nobody could hear us:

—My mamá and my aunt Cánd-el-i-tang say that we sure could learn something from her, A-ma-ling said.

—We'll no, she is a dummy and is always holding her mamá's hand. We can go around without anyone holding our hands, I answered.

—Maybe if we loaned her some brothers she'd get normal. Why don't you lend her your brother An-dong-ni who is very little and doesn't even know where he lives?

—But how could we get him out of my house and put him in hers without anyone finding out?

So with this project we had a few hours of entertainment: how we would do it at night when everyone was asleep; how we would wrap him in a blanket and we would cover his head so that if by chance anyone saw us crossing the park and squealed, they wouldn't see who it was; how we would have to put something in his mouth so he wouldn't cry or scream; how we would take along his clothes and his booties... and a lot more of the necessary preparations when you take a child to live in another house.

In the end we were never able to carry out the semi-kidnap plan.

We forgot about it.

We always had so many projects and things in our heads that it was very hard to remember all of them.

And cousin Eng-ang-ni had to continue being a good girl.

My friend's flat, although it was also big, was smaller than ours, and besides, with that cousin and her parents living there, it seemed smaller yet, but I loved it and always wanted to be there, but she liked ours a lot better, most of all the glass floor and ceiling in the hall, and the dining room, which was enormous, with the walls painted purple, with chairs that were covered in velvet of the same color, and where there were two sideboards which we never managed to open because the doors were a bit stuck, and also a pure silver picture called the "Sacred Heart of Jesus," but it didn't have a heart, or at least we didn't see it, and which was in a room which we hardly ever used, only on papá Bo-ling's saint's day and Mamá Chong's saint's day and sometimes on Christmas.

That room had a lot of balconies, but we couldn't go out on them because they were very high above the street and you could fall on to the highway which was underneath and was called the Madrid-Lisbon highway, because if you kept walking for many hours you'd get to Lisbon, which wasn't even in Spain, I mean it was really far, and cars drove on it, and when Mamá Chong saw us going to that room she always said:

—Girls, don't even think of going out onto the balconies, you could fall!

And we were obedient and we did not do it, but sometimes, and this is a secret, while one of us stood guard the other peeped through the iron bars.

They never caught us because we were well synchronized.

The other balconies, the ones in the living room, in the parlor and the bedrooms must have been less dangerous because they never said anything to us.

Maybe it was because that part was called Incarnation Street and the other not.

I do not remember.

Every time she entered the hall, A-ma-ling threw herself on the floor, looking for some little holes between the glass bricks where we would be able to spy at what they were doing on the first floor.

But she never found any.

And look, she searched and searched!

I told her:

—Don't keep searching and searching, I live here all the time and I never found any!

But she insisted just in case I had forgotten to look at one of the squares.

There were many bedrooms in our house: the girls' room, the boys' room, my grandmother's room, the maids' rooms, my parents' room and a lot more.

Besides, my parents' room was really two bedrooms, but one side did not have a wall or a door, just an arch; in the summer they moved the bed, the armoire, the night tables, Mamá Chong's easy chair and the rest of the furniture to the "outer" bedroom, which had two balconies facing the park garden and was more refreshing, and in the winter the reverse move, to the "inner" bedroom which was next to the hall and was a lot warmer, and the day of the move was a big mess, because there was a lot of furniture all over the place and you almost couldn't get past them, but it was a mania of Mamá Chong and we had to let her be because that's why she was our mamá and it was the way she liked to have it.

In A-ma-ling's house there were only two big bedrooms and one more for the maids.

Her father and her two brothers slept in one of them.

In the other her mamá, her sister and she.

I also would have liked for Mamá Chong, Ne-ning and I to be in the same room and for Papá Bo-ling and Man-o-ling to stay with my two little brothers, and that they would have to put up with their crying or their blasting poopers, but no, in our house it was different, and look, I told Mamá Chong how they did it in A-ma-ling's house, and although she was very nice about everything, in this thing she never wanted to pay attention to me.

The middle floor of our house was where Don Eli-ang lived with his wife and their three daughters, who were at least twenty years old, so they were all adulterers, so that's why they could use high heels and some skirts that were called "tube," but they were not tubes like for toothpaste, they were cloth like other skirts, I don't know why they were called that; and the middle sister (who was called Africa although she was from Spain and also was a teacher) told my friend and me that it was very difficult to walk when she wore it: one day she let us put on one of hers and it was true, it was very difficult, so we liked much better being little girls than adulterers and did not have to put on those tubes.

The three sisters were our friends and they loved us a lot, but we couldn't go to their house all the time, only sometimes, especially when their papá was not there. They didn't let us.

Don Eli-ang was very thin and coughed all the time: in the morning, in the afternoon and at night, he was always coughing, even when he was asleep, one of his daughters told us, so he was very tired and did not know what to do to keep from coughing so much, because that was a total drag. Imagine, if we coughed a little bit when we had a cold and did not like it, how fed up that poor guy must have been!

They did not let us get very close to that man, it must have been that Mamá Chong and IsabelM did not want that awful cough to stick to us, and because of that if we saw him on the stairs we pressed against the wall, and we ran up or down very fast in case one of those cough bugs jumped at us and never wanted to leave, because then we'd always be coughing like that poor guy. I think that's why Mamá Chong didn't want us to spend much time in his house even if he wasn't there in case those bugs were hiding in the parlor or in the living room or under some cushion.

But since all three of them were so super nice to us, we loved to be there.

When we were in that flat one of us would look around a bit to see if we could see one of those evil bugs, while the other one talked with the sisters or the mamá, who was so very good and gave us delicious cookies, but we never saw even one, that's the truth.

One day Doña Amp-ang asked us:

—Don't your rag dolls have any children?

When we said no, she said she would make us some, and the next day when we went there she gave each of us three. They were so cute! And they looked just like Mamá-dolls, except smaller, so we got very happy, and the oldest sister, who was named Pur-e-sang, one day made them a lot of little baby outfits so they were very beautiful and very warm. They were all so nice that probably their father was also very good, but since we could never be with him we never found out.

One day Don Eli-ang coughed so hard that he turned into a corpse. What a drag. They should have caught those bugs and kept them in a jar, like Titing did with all the ones he found, and also little lizards and grasshoppers, but I don't think they even thought of that and they ate that poor guy all up, and he went and died.

They all cried a lot and we did a little too, but don't think it was so bad he died, because like that he would not have to cough anymore and he could sleep straight through all the time, and when we told that to the three daughters they said yes, we were right, now he was resting in peace and we were very wise little girls.

Their mamá had a mustache, although she was not a man but a lady, but really she did have one, but she did not have a beard, only a mustache.

One day I asked Mamá Chong:

—Why does Doña Amp-ang have a mustache if she is a woman?

And Mamá Chong answered me very serious:

—Child, we do not say such things!

But she didn't tell me why, and as I saw she was a little mad I didn't ask again, and I didn't want to ask Ne-ning either in case she'd get mad too, so I stayed without knowing.

Across from my house, which was on a corner, and for that reason was not on one street like A-ma-ling's but on two, on the part that was not the park (which was on the street Ruiz de Mendoza), there was living a fat and deaf man whose name was JoeyStreet because that street must have been his even though it had another name which was Incarnation, which meant it was always red, like a carnation.

With his family.

And Sundays after mass at the Brothers, A-ma-ling and I would get on a balcony and spy on his daughter, who was very grownup and had more than five hundred dresses. Or maybe six hundred.

Because we could see them piled up on top of her bed, and on the chairs where she put them after trying them on, while she decided which she would put on that day

My sister Ne-ning always told us:

—Lol-i-tang, well, pretty... she's not what you could call pretty, but she has a lot of style...

And of course we knew what that word style meant, style = dresses, which we saw with our own eyes!

I think Ne-ning did not have that style, because she didn't have five hundred dresses, but hers were much prettier than Lol-i-tang's, especially one that was a material called *piqué*, white with big fat polka dots and that we touched whenever we got the chance.

Even Lupeng told us:

That dress of your sister's is really pretty; I hope you'll tell her one day to lend it to me.

But I think she never lent it to her.

Probably Ne-ning didn't want her to stain it with ice cream or food.

I don't know.

About that style thing, Lol-i-tang had a lot of hats too, that were called Pamélas. I don't know why they had that name instead of hat or cap, maybe because caps are made of wool and hats would be like what grampa Edua-rding used and the pamélas were for sisters and their friends and other people like that, when they went to weddings.

Lupeng didn't have any paméla, but Ne-ning did, she had one that was like straw, almost yellow and with a black ribbon for when she had to go to a wedding, that she wouldn't even let us try on because she always had it hidden.

One day after high-tea, our snack time, we went into the girls' room, which was my room, and we saw Paméla on the bed, so we decided to put it on and make faces in the mirror: we were beautiful! Even though we couldn't see anything because it was over our eyes, that was the good thing about being two: though you couldn't see, the other one could tell you what she was seeing and if she said you looked so beautiful, well you believed her, that's why she was your friend, and you knew it was true.

As we were so busy, one of us putting on the paméla and the other one looking and telling, we didn't notice that Ne-ning had come in till she started yelling and screaming and getting really, really mad and told us:

—You've made me furious! Which was the biggest anger possible. —You two will find out! Mamá, Mamá, look what these kids did to my paméla!

Well, without meaning to we dented it a bit, and also not on purpose we got some streaks of chocolate from the snack on it, it was stuck to our fingers and that also was not our fault, because if Ne-ning would have left us Paméla instead of hiding it all the time nothing would have happened and we probably would have had clean hands...

But Mamá Chong didn't scold us at all, because she knew we were little girls, you're just a girl before you change into adulterer.

Between our two houses there was a precious garden, very big, with lots of trees, that was called The Upper Park, I think so people did not get mixed up and confuse it with the smaller one, the one that was Doña Margarita's called The Lower Park, and that had a gazebo where the musicians of the band played music every Sunday night in the summer, and also another kind of musicians played at the night parties called verbenas. This garden had some little houses called snack kiosks and many double benches of granite so the people could sit down.

All around the park it was full of stone benches, and in the upper part almost opposite A-ma-ling's house was the summer Casino called "Versalles," and it was where they had lots of dances for my sister and her friends and grownup adulterers in summertime, and also for their boyfriends or the ones who wanted to be boyfriends. It was like a beautiful garden and there were bars around it to keep out people who were not her friends; we liked a lot looking at who were inside dancing or talking or telling secrets. One day when we were there watching, my sister Ne-ning saw us and I think she got a little furious, because she said we were spying. Well get that! All we were doing was watching and laughing at how bad some of her girlfriends were dancing...

On the other side of Upper Park, but opposite my house, was another place for dances for people who belonged to the Casino, but it wasn't a garden, it was made of a white cloth and its roof too, it did not have tiles or anything on top. This was only used for very special dances, and we couldn't even look there because when they did them it was very late and we were already asleep.

It seems like they put those dance places, one across from her house and the other across from mine, so we would each have one and not get envious, but since we never asked anybody we didn't know for sure.

And then there were those little snack kiosks which were like bars but not real bars in buildings under the flats, but little houses made of wood and tin that only opened at nighttime in the summer. Well some opened in the afternoon too. There were three and one more that was not a kiosk but a churrería, right in front of my house, where they made the long straight jeringas and round churros, and many people went there every day and bought them for breakfast.

We liked the jeringas a lot more than the churros

Making jeringas seems very easy, but it must not have been.

First they made the dough, which was like a paste from flour and water and they must've put in a secret ingredient because once when A-ma-ling and I tried to make them along with Lupeng who was the one next to the frying pan, they came out horrible and we couldn't even eat them.

Next, they put that paste in a thingy called "*churrera*" and very carefully went making a snake, not a live one like in the fields, because this was dough, and then they threw it into boiling oil.

When the snake was all fried on one side, they took some long sticks and turned it over.

Then they were ready to cut and sell.

They sold them right away because there were always a lot of people saying "I've got dibs on that, my dibs, my dibs, next dibs," and they were *jeringas*, none of those "dibs" they were yelling about, but we heard them say that.

They didn't put tables or chairs next to the churrería.

But they did at the kiosks, folding chairs and tables, and if you moved around a lot or you climbed up one, sometimes they closed before you knew it and Sas! you fell onto the ground, and the dirt was hard! That's why we always had a bunch of skinnings and scrapings all over our legs and on our elbows....

We spent a lot of time in upper park because since they could see us from the balconies of both houses we could be almost alone.

And across the street from the park, on the other corner from JoeyStreet was the Church of the Brothers, which had another real name, but everyone called it that because many brothers lived there, eighty or a hundred, or a thousand, I cannot remember but I know for sure there were piles of them.

Although they were brothers don't think they looked much alike because some were very tall, others a bit fat, some blond, other pretty bald, but that happens in a lot of families, and though their mamá and their papá should have made a mold so they turned out the same, or almost, they must have forgotten and that's why they were different, even though they all dressed the same.

Those brothers became good again, but before, they must've been really bad and their parents had to be fed up and decided to go somewhere else, because we never saw them, but they were still alive; if not they would've been called The Orphan Brothers, which is what they called ones who didn't have parents.

A-ma-ling would say:

—Do you think the Brothers' parents are living in Portugal?

I said —Maybe, I don't know, could be. But in Portugal they don't know how to speak Turgaliuman. After having so many boys their mamá would be very tired, and on top of that, if they were so naughty and didn't obey their father... probably what they wanted was not to have to talk with anyone.

She'd say —And imagine, when they'd eat fried eggs with potatoes their poor mamá would have to fry eighty or a hundred, or a thousand to give each one, one. It would've been better for those brothers to take care of themselves. They wouldn't have been so naughty and wouldn't have bugged their poor mamá and papá so much!

We'd talk about them a while longer and when we were tired of that topic we'd leave the poor brothers in peace and concentrate on more important matters.

On Sundays, since we didn't have school, we could do a lot of things and they were all stupendous — we didn't even have homework!

After the weekly bath, and breakfast and dressing in the Sunday shoes and dresses, we went to the ten o'clock mass at the Church of the Brothers, which was very close to our houses, in fact right in front of mine and where all those naughty sons lived.

That church was very big and the most wonderful one of all the ones in Turgalium, because it wasn't scary to go into — what a difference from all the others that were dark and with saints that frightened you. In this one, everything was white, and of marble, and the Virgins and their kids were always laughing, especially when they saw us come in, so we always managed to get into the first rows so they'd look at us and wouldn't think we'd forgotten to go.

And lots of times we went alone! Well almost alone, because we let go of the hand of who went with us and went running so we got there before anyone else in our families and got good spots and didn't have some bighead in front who didn't let us see everything.

When mass started the priest came out in a suit of gold or silver, depending on was it summer or winter, and many altar boys, who were priests but a small kind, I think they didn't let them be priests until they were taller, and they talked or sang however they wanted, but during the mass we got bored, so we talked in soft voices, until somebody in front or behind said — Shhh, hush... be silent, we are in a sacred place, hush up, don't talk.

Then we stopped speaking a little while so they would leave us in peace, but after five minutes, when they were busy getting up and kneeling and sitting down, we talked again.

And living way up on that church, almost next to the bells, that were close to our "holidays dining room," were the storks who were also our neighbors, but they weren't there all the time because once in a while they'd go to Africa to see their families, who lived there.

Before winter they were all back in Turgalium and every stork family put themselves back in the same place as other times.

The ones who lived across from us were super nice. In the morning two stayed there, and then in the afternoon a few others would come for a while to chat.

And look, to be nice must have been a big job for them, because the rooks, who were so ugly and all black, really liked to give them a hard time. And besides, since they didn't know how to make good nests, well, not good or bad because they were just a disaster — as soon as the poor storks went to see their grampas and grammas or their cousins who could hardly fly, and had to stay in that town in Africa with other relatives— well those rooks got into the storks' nests and messed everything up, after all the work making them so big and precious... that's how bad those jackdaw rooks were.

But as soon as the storks got back from their trip, the rooks acted like they had been so well behaved, and I think they told them that they were there taking real good care of everything, and then they left, though actually they stayed pretty close but at least they weren't inside the nests.

After a month or so somebody brought the storks some huge eggs, like a meter or more, where the little storks were kept that would be their children, and one of the storks stayed quietly on top of the eggs and the other one went to get food at the stores in the country, worms and things like that which storks eat. I don't remember who brought the eggs. My brother Man-o-ling told A-ma-ling and me, but that day we were daydreaming and didn't pay very good attention and didn't want to ask him to tell us again so he wouldn't think we were some dummies who didn't understand anything.

And suddenly one morning two or three storkies showed up, who were so cute, and just like the big ones, but little, so they must have been bored inside the eggs and didn't want to stay there any longer even though it was cozy.

So now the whole family was together, though it seems to me they were kind of squashed, but very happy, because now the mamá stork could go back to her job bringing the babies from Paris, and the papá could also do other things, and in the meantime the two or three little ones stayed there watching the people walking along the street, because they didn't know how to fly or anything but they were entertained.

We spent a lot of time watching over them while their parents were gone because since they were still a bit dumb, if one accidentally pushed another one they could fall down to the street, far down, and get smashed, and that would have made us very sad.

But none of them fell while we watched over them!

And in the springtime they were learning to fly, oh what a thrill!

At the beginning they just made very short trips, to our balconies, or to JoeyStreet's house, but since they were copycats and wanted to do the same as their mamá and papá, right away they started flying around over upper park and lots of other places, and the whole family went out afternoons; some days they returned very late, almost at my bedtime. When I heard them return I felt calm and could go to sleep with no problem.

Next to A-ma-ling's house was City Hall, which was a precious palace, but look what a shame, no princess lived there. Just somebody called Mayor and a few others called Authorities, golly.

As we were neighbors they all knew us and let us go in, but it was a bit boring there, not like Doña Ma-rta's house, or the Telegraph offices, where there were many things to touch and look at, or TrickyJoey's bar, so what we almost always did there was spy on Mayor and those other ones, to see what they did, and that's that, and if they didn't like being spied on, well they had to take it, because for that I was their neighbor.

OTHER RELATIVES

We kids didn't have what they call furs cousins in Turgalium, they were all in Madrid, but Mamá Chong and A-ma-ling too had lots of them.

Because my gramma had a sister, Aunt Isa-be-ling who was alive, and a few brothers and a sister who were corpses since a little while ago.

So their sons and daughters were her cousins and she loved them all a lot, but none lived in my house, they were spread around in other streets, though they came "stoptby" many many times and talked for thirty-nine hours at least.

Besides these Mamá Chong had a lot of "*segun-cousins*" who were cousins but a bit less, but she was so nice and good that she loved them like the furs ones and always said:

—My cousin Bel-u-kang made me a precious shawl; today I'm going to the movies with my cousin Sal-va-dong; my cousin Con-ching this, my cousin whats-is-name, that....

Like that, all the time. Even if they were those Seguns, she didn't care. Besides, they all talked a lot, just like her, so naturally they were cousins. And since we didn't have any real furs cousins there, we acted like their kids were our cousins.

My gramma's sister was such a cute lady. But look how silly, that instead of living in my house she was in another with her daughter, Aunt Con-sue-ling, when those two sisters could have had a good time together.

When gramma lived with us I said to her one day:

—Hey, why don't you tell your sister to come live here? Since your bedroom is very big we'll put in another bed and that's that. Look, it's easy, just like Ne-ning and me in the girls' room. And we can call it the gramma sisters' room.

But she said no, impossible, because they liked to play different things and they'd be fighting all the time and besides Aunt Isa-be-ling had to be with her daughter just like she was with Mamá Chong and we were with our mamá and that's always what we do.

But I think it wasn't for that. It was so her sister wouldn't take her pesetas and her treasures, and she said the other thing so I wouldn't ask her again.

Because my gramma had a furniture that was called "The Strongbox" which was tall, tall - imagine how tall, it went almost to the ceiling.

It was pure iron, some parts a little green and others brown and I didn't much like those colors, but it was like that and you couldn't change it to pink or orange though pink would have been much more precious.

That's where she kept all the pesetas she had, wrapped up in little papers so no one could see them.

In the Strongbox, besides all those pesetas, she had the treasures, it seems to me they were necklaces and bracelets and everything, with lots of jewels and gems.

Nobody could open that Box, only she could, because it had a super secret combination with many numbers one after another, a hundred twenty-seven or like that, and not even my papá had learned them, and look, he knew lots of numbers, but also she changed the numbers many times in case somebody was watching her open it.

One morning when my friend and I were in her room, the one next to her bedroom, which was also hers, where she got together with her friends when they came to see her or for high tea, she took us by the hand and took us to where that Strongbox was, and told us:

—Don't tell anyone, but today I'm going to show you the treasures!

Oh gosh, how exciting!

Because she had never shown it even to Ne-ning.

She closed all the doors so no one could come in, put in all those numbers, and the Strongbox opened right up.

The door was very heavy, even more than the one on the icebox, and inside were many things, some in little boxes and others with little papers.

She went taking everything out, she put it all on the bed, and our mouths fell open because there really were some real treasures: the first thing she showed us was a very soft ball full of many colored pins. It was called "pincushion," a hard new word that I couldn't even ask Man-o-ling about because what we saw was a secret. There were so many that they were squashed together. We had never seen so many together, and some girls in our class had a lot.

Before vacation A-ma-ling and I had learned how to play the pins game, which was a stupendous game but quite dangerous, because you could get poked and get full of blood or become a corpse. Also, if you weren't very clever you lost them right away and wound up with none and that really was a drag because until your next allowance on Sunday you couldn't buy any more.

My gramma gave each of us three, and she whispered to me that when she became a corpse the pincushion would be for me, and even if Ne-ning got very "capricious" not to pay any attention to her and keep it myself.

Well, I'd prefer to have my gramma alive instead of that pincushion, but the truth is I would have liked to have both at the same time, but I couldn't, only when she was real dead I'd have the pincushion, so I said okay, I'd wait but I'd like better that she was alive and flesh and bone.

Then she gave me one more, take that! But only to me, without my friend knowing.

She started opening the little papers, and you can't imagine: in some there were pesetas, in others, bills of five pesetas, and in a few, twenty-five pesetas! And in the last two, bills of a hundred pesetas! Wow, we had never seen so many pesetas at once... That's why she didn't want her sister living in our house, in case she convinced her like Feipang did to us and took away everything.

We helped her wrap everything up very well and she continued showing us more treasures.

She had a very pretty white box and when she opened it, guess what! Huh? A pure silver rosary, which she used only on Sundays so it wouldn't get worn out. All the balls had many little holes, and she told us that was so that if any sins were in there, the Angels or I don't know who would come and throw them out. What a great treasure!

Then she showed us a photo of my grampa, but instead of being paper it was glass. She said it was very delicate and could never ever be in the sun, because if a sunbeam touched the picture it would erase, and that must never be because it was the only one she had of her husband, who was my grampa, and since he was a long time in the cemetery sometimes she didn't remember his face, but with this photo that was solved, because she looked at it for a minute at nighttime, and right away she remembered. We thought this was a very good idea because sometimes some people's faces got erased from us, though they were not our husbands. Having a glass picture was stupendous and we told her she was so smart.

When we wrapped grampa up so he was nice and dark, she took out a little blue sack, and I'll bet you can't guess what was there. You can't imagine: a white rabbit's tail, precious, so soft and smooth, and she let us touch it for a long time.

She told us that the rabbit had been her friend, and when a mean hunter killed it my gramma scolded him a lot and that mean guy told her:

—Come on grandma, so you will be quiet and stop bothering me I'm giving you the tail, which will bring you much luck, always, and don't cry because you are making me sick.

The rabbit was named Crispino, and my gramma told us he was so very good and smart too, he even knew how to draw an O around a coin, and that was hard because sometimes I heard Papá Bo-ling say that some of his students couldn't draw an O around a coin, and they were already adulterers; on the other hand Crispino, look how smart.

When the three of us were so cozy someone knocked on the door.

It was my gramma's hairdresser who came to make her chignon, so we rushed everything back into the Strongbox, she closed it and said the secret words, and we sat on the bed like nothing was going on and she said to the knocker:

—Come in, come in, I was waiting for you...

And she winked at us.

We couldn't see more treasures that day, but the ones she'd showed us were stupendous. Good thing nobody knew the secret combination and couldn't take them from her.

We went to play with our new pins and on top of that we won six more.

What a lucky morning!

SECTION THREE: SCHOOL

And in front of where the Brothers lived, but on the other side, there was our school, which was called *"De las Carmelitas,"* which was full of nuns; those were also sisters, but these were good sisters (more or less, because there were also some who were bad, and others were very bad), because their parents and brothers did go to see them many times, and bring them sweets, or a cake, when it was the saint's day of one of them.

We both went to the same school, which was very close to our homes, and we could almost go alone, but they would not let us do it because we had to cross the road, and a car could run over us, then we would have died, and that day we would not have gone to school, but we didn't like it at all, like they say, not at all, and that was not the one of "The Jackdaws," that was a super drag, and we would have been very sad or angry if they had taken us there.

Because our nuns, at least, wore very long black dresses, down to the floor, but then, around the head, and the neck and shoulders, they had a part that was white and that covered all their hair, because they had made a promise never to ever show their hair to anyone, and they weren't supposed to see their hair themselves, so they didn't know if they were blonde or brunette, or if they had curly hair, or long or how. I think they had to have a lot of lice stored there, because sometimes they were scratching their heads, but when I asked Mamá Chong she started laughing, I don't know why, and she didn't say anything, it must be that she knew about lice but she didn't want to tell me.

But the "jackdaw nuns" thing, that was terrible.

In front of my house, almost alongside JoeyStreet, lived a lady named Doña Ant-on-ia Dangit, it was a very bad name, those words you could not say, those of those stewps people, but the poor thing it was her name, and many times when my grandmother went to visit her, she would take me with her, although she always said to me: —If you have to answer something, you call her Doña Ant-on-ia, but without a last name.

She must have been ashamed to have a last name like that, and she would not want to even hear it.

But it was very strange because when I accidentally said Doña Ant-on-ia, Dangit, the two of them laughed a lot, I think old ladies are different. I don't know.

Well, this lady, suddenly one day decided that she wanted to have a school for herself, with many classes and many nuns, and a chapel with Virgins and, like, saints, and even with a priest for herself, I don't remember why that mania entered her, although my grandmother told me about it, but it did, and all the time she was pestering that she wanted to have many nuns, and everything else.

Her friends tried to convince her that this was silly, because my grandmother told me, but she must also be one of those spoiled ones, and she didn't stop until she succeeded.

She went to various towns and found none.

Finally she went to Salamanca, which was very far away, because they told her there were a few there, but they did not know what she was going to find.

When she went to the nun's shop, there were only some horrible ones left, all dressed in black like rooks, and I think they were pretty bad; besides, they were not sisters, they were nuns who were on their own and who had joined them.

So poor Doña Ant-on-iaDangit had no choice but to buy what there was, but she was very happy because even though she knew they were ugly, she had her school to herself....

As her friends told her not to be so greedy, what she did was put the jackdaw nuns to work, so that they could also teach the girls, like the Carmelites, but those dummies did not know how to teach anything at all, not even the EM with the A, and all they wanted was for the girls to become nuns too, so there'd be a big bunch of them.

We were very lucky to live so far from where they had their school, because if we had ended up there, what a shame.

At school our classroom was beautiful, with balconies that overlooked the nuns' garden, where they had many vegetables, like those you eat at home, but they were raw and on the ground.

In that garden there were always two nuns working, putting down soil and taking away soil. I think they weren't working, but playing, but they said yes, they were working, maybe they wanted to fool us all, but I don't know, and Sister Luisina did believe it.

Inside the class there was a very large black chalkboard, a crucifix, the table of Sister Luisina, who was the sister who we got when they passed around the nuns, and many large, round and low tables, with stools for all girls to sit on; there were eight of us at each table.

Sister Luisina was very old. She must have been older than my grandmother and A-ma-ling's grandfather Edua-rding put together, at least a hundred and something, and it seems to me that they had put her there so that we would not be bad, because we were very sorry that she had to be there, instead of going out to the street to play with her friends, or lying on her bed reading stories, but she was there with us, the poor thing, and look she didn't know much, okay almost nothing, because all the time she kept repeating and repeating the same things.

She was also very short, almost like us. What happened is that before reaching her table there was a step where the table was, like a platform, and when she stood there it seemed that she was taller than us, but from time to time she went down and was almost the same as us.

Besides being very old and very short, she must have been very dim, because every day she took her notebook, which was like ours, and began:

—Girls, attention: eM with a, Ma; eM with e Me; eM with i Mi...

And so on with all the letters, vowels and consonants. What a bore.

And then:

My mamá loves me, my mamá misses me.....

As if we didn't know that! What a silly nun!

But since I already knew how to read (which I had learned on my own with a book that my brother had, which was called the El Catón grammar, and also when I found very difficult words, I asked Mamá Chong or Man-o-ling), what I did all the time was talk to A-ma-ling, or the girl on the other side, and that's that. Or I pretended I was listening, or writing, but the truth is that I was thinking about anything else, like stories of the Chinese, or of the gods.

A-ma-ling knew how to read less than I did, because her brothers must not have had that Catón, and for that reason she could not ask them like I did Man-o-ling, and sometimes she would say to me:

—Shut up, they are going to scold us!

But I didn't pay any attention to her...

With that sister Luisina we went on an excursion for the first time in our lives.

Before that day, the nun stood up and said:

—The most important before any trip is this: Eat and un-eat, drink and un-drink. Don't forget.

We knew what were eating and drinking, because we did every day, doggone it, but about that un-eat and un-drink, we had no idea.

So when IsabelM came to get us at the school, the first thing we asked her was,

—Do you know what is eat and un-eat and drink and un-drink?

She looked at us both very seriously, and then we realized that maybe we had said a swear word, the kind like the stewps people, but it was strange, because our nun had told us, and the nuns didn't even say dang. She opened her mouth as if to speak and she began to laugh! Yes, to laugh and laugh and laugh.

We got very worried, in case she had suddenly gone crazy, and we tugged at her hands and the sleeves of her coat, so that she would stop laughing, but nothing, she kept on.

When she finally stopped, with many tears in her eyes from so much laughter, she explained to us that un-drinking and un-eating meant going to the bathroom and peeing and pooping.

My gosh!

And how easy it would have been for Sister Luisina to have told us!

But the nuns were very strange and never called things by their real names.

The truth is that neither of us liked going to school, especially in the winter, and since Papá Bo-Ling always said that he would rather have live donkeys than dead wise men, we devised a great plan to stop going many times.

(Well, it's not that my papá wanted us to be real donkeys, the ones who were at the fair, or in the vineyards, he just didn't want us to get sick and for Don Teodoro, who was our doctor, to come to see us. He would come to see us when we had sore throats or fever, and he would put a spoon in my mouth over my tongue, which he squeezed a lot, and then he would give me a piece of candy. No, what he meant is that he didn't care if we were a little bit donkeys, for not going to school and not learning letters, I think. My brother Man-o-ling explained to me what he wanted to say, but right away I forgot.)

When it was time for school, I wrapped myself up to my head and didn't even move.

As I did not get up, although my nanny came several times to call me, in the end Mamá Chong appeared to see what happened.

And I, with the smallest voice I could, said to her:

—I'm very sick, Mamá Chong! My throat hurts a lot, I can hardly speak, and my ears hurt too.

And she, seeing how serious I was, said to me:

—Look, chatunga, as it's very cold today, I think it's better that you stay in bed, maybe it's that you're going to get the flu, or you're starting with a cold.

And I, of course, very happy!

When a long time passed, and I heard that the clock of San Francisco struck ten or eleven o'clock, I woke up so fresh, and told everyone that I had already gotten well, that I was going to play in the park with A-ma-ling, who had done the same acting at her home.

I think IsabelM and Mamá Chong knew it was a lie, and that we weren't really sick, but maybe they were very sorry for us and let us think they believed it...

BAZOOKA BUBBLE GUM

One day that we were in class, one of the girls at our table showed us something wonderful: a packet of Bazooka gum that was like a fat round tube, which had little slits; if you counted you knew that, although it was a tube, it had seven chewing gums, one for each day of the week, but since they did not put the days, you could eat them as you wanted: You could start on a Sunday if you wanted and then on Monday you could eat another that was Thursday or Friday.

We had never seen anything like it!

Because the gum that we chewed was a round, red and hard ball and at first they were like candy and inside was the gum, but you had to be very careful not to accidentally swallow the gum believing that it was still the candy, and have it stick to your guts, because a girl we knew accidentally swallowed a few, and they had to perform an operation called "a pen deck to me": they had to open her entire belly until they found the stuck gum and took it out. Uff! What a pain.

That's why, when we had balls, we always watched.

—Let's see, where is your ball going? She asked me.

And I would take the ball out of my mouth, which then was no longer red but yellow, because all the red had stuck to my lips, and my tongue and teeth, I would show it to her, and then we saw that we still hadn't arrived at the gum, so we could continue sucking a while more, until the gum appeared.

A little while later I asked her the same question, like this all the time.

We weren't going to let those chewing gums stick to our guts and they would have to split us open...

That girl from the bazookas couldn't give us any, because she had them counted, and if she gave us two, then a week would have had five days instead of seven; imagine if you would run out of Saturday or Sunday, what a bummy thing, just days of school and uniform. A drag.

Since the discovery of the Bazooka tube, this became our most important thing.

We asked IsabelM to buy us one, even if it was for both of us. Nothing.

We ask Mamá Chong, the same. Nothing.

To Ne-ning and Lupeng: nothing.

To our grandparents: nothing.

Her uncles, nothing either.

Well, we teased all the older people we knew.

Or almost everyone. Maybe not everyone. But many of them, yes.

Then I had a great idea.

Every night, when we were in bed, and before going to sleep, we had to pray to Jesusito, the Guardian Angel and a few others, she did it at her house and I at mine, but we both had to do it, So I proposed:

—As they have not wanted to buy us the fat Bazooka gum tube, what do you think if we ask Jesusito and the Guardian Angel?

A-ma-ling thought it was perfect, and for the next few days that's what we did.

Every night, after the ordinary prayers, I would say:

—Please, Jesusito, please Guardian Angel, get me one of those Bazooka gums, if you bring it to me I'll be good, forever and ever. And then I even said amen, which was like it's over, but for the prayers.

And she, the same, for I had explained well what she had to say, so that she would not make a mistake.

Several days passed and those two did not pay any attention to us either, because the Bazooka gum did not appear, so we got very angry, and we decided that we were not even going to pray anymore. Well, what had those two thought? For once we asked them for something, and above all please, and they as if they were deaf, nothing, like the whole other family.

Every noon, when my papá came up from the office and I came home from school, I would sit on his lap, hug him and say:

—Oh my pappy! What a hard beard you have and how much I love you. Little no, a lot yes!

And he was super happy.

But that day that we had decided that we were never going to pray again, I was quite upset, and I didn't get on his knees.

My papá was very surprised, and he asked me what was wrong with me, so I told him everything, but everything from the beginning, and that I no longer planned to pray, never again, and that I didn't love either Jesusito or the Guardian Angel anymore.

My papá spoke little, well he spoke normally, but almost always it was Mamá Chong who was speaking, that's why it seemed that he didn't speak.

But when he did, he always said things that would serve forever, come on, for a lifetime, even though you were no longer a girl, but an adulterer, and that day he said to me:

—Look, chatunga, you have to have faith, because faith moves mountains. Ask Jesusito again tonight, but with faith, let's see what happens.

That night I said my prayers and then I said to Jesusito:

—Hey Jesusito, let's see if you can bring me that gum that I have asked you for many days, excuse me, I didn't know I had to ask you with that faith, but now I know, chewing gum with faith, don't forget it. And thanks. Amen.

And I fell asleep.

The next morning, as soon as I woke up, I looked under the pillow and, miracle! There was the Bazooka gum bar!

You can't even imagine my joy, the faith thing. It had worked! And you see, it was easy to say it, but of course when you don't know things, well so it goes.

And my papá always said things that were useful.

So I told A-ma-ling so that she would do the same, what had happened to me with that faith, and although her father did not have a stiff beard like mine, nor did she tell him that she loved him very much, she told him about it and at night she did exactly what I had done, and it worked too: Another packet of Bazooka under her pillow!

And look, I was willing to share mine with her, even if I ran out of some days of the week, but it was much better that way, right?

Since that day I have faith.

PRAYERS

When we were at school they made us pray all the time.

And look, that was huge nonsense, because we already prayed at night, and on top of that we went to Mass at the Brothers on Sundays, but our nuns were very pesky, and come on, nothing but pray and pray.

In class we said something called "Trisagion," which had to be said three days in a row, because if not God would get angry, so if we said it for two days and then Sunday came, it was useless and we had to start over, but it had to be like this: Three days and that's that.

At twelve it was "Angelus" time, which was when an Angel appeared to the Virgin of Victory, to tell her I don't know what, I think to remind her it was time to put the pot on the fire, because the Virgin had many things in her head, and sometimes she forgot to make lunch, so God decided to send her an angel every day, and that way she could not say that she had forgotten.

We looked everywhere to see if we saw the Angel, but nothing, we did not see him, but one day A-ma-ling and I decided to close our eyes, and then suddenly open them. And we did catch him! He had white wings, which reached from the part of the shoulders to almost the floor, a blue and white dress, hands together, he looked at us and left... When we told the other girls at our table, they did not want to believe it and they said that we had invented it, and that we were liars, that Angels cannot be seen, and many other things, but we did not care, we had almost seen it, because I had explained to my friend before how that Angel was, how he was dressed, the wings and all that, and that he did not speak, but that he smiled at the good girls, that you could only see him for a moment, if before you had closed and squeezed your eyes a lot, and she had done everything I told her, that's why we saw it, even if the others said no. And on top of that, Sister Luisina said that maybe we had seen it. Take that!

Besides all the prayers in the class, we also had to go to the chapel every day to pray the Rosary, and that was really boring, lasting many hours.

First, we had to put on some white tulle capes, which reached to our knees and were very precious, but they were not the capes that are worn in the streets, or those worn by bandits and outlaws in the movies. The ones we had were held on our heads with a rubber band, and sometimes they squeezed a lot, but we didn't care because we were so beautiful.

When we all had our capes on we would leave our class, which was almost the last on the entire hall, they would put us in line two by two, and they would not let us talk or anything, because all the time the sister was saying:

—Silence girls! Gather!

Although we didn't gather up anything, but she said it, and since she was so old we almost listened to her, but as soon as she went to another part of the line we talked all we wanted.

As we were the youngest of the school, they always put us in the first rows, and that was a drag because you couldn't fall asleep, but if you didn't get put in the very first row, you could sleep a little, and sometimes you also could pretend you got dizzy, from the incense or whatever, and then you could just sit with your eyes closed, and wait for the whole Rosary to finish.

And what I tell you about Trisagions and Rosaries and all that was not all, there was more, and it bored us a lot, but we could not say anything. Buff!!

With so much prayer it seems to me that we should be quite holy or Angels, but I don't know if it's like that holiness thing did not stick to me, because everyone was always telling me that I was very naughty, besides, no matter how much I looked at the part behind me, in case my wings were growing, I never saw anything, not even a few feathers, so I put up with it and stayed just a girl.

FIRST COMMUNION

And on top of that, when we were almost seven years old they prepared us for communion.

Every day, from January to May, we went to Catechism and we had to learn the Catechism (which was a book but it looked like a notebook, because it was very soft), the Ten Commandments and many other things, and Luisina came to ask all the time; if you didn't say it exactly, she almost started to cry, so we learned to recite that of "I renounce Satan, all his pomps and his works" and everything else letter for letter so she would not get sad.

Satan was another name for the devil. It was the name for when there was communion. Sometimes he was called devil, and other times Lucifer, and many more names, but it was the same person, what happens is that if you knew him well you could call him "Devil" or if you were a priest you called him Lucifer, so depending on who you were, you called him by different names.

When we learned about the renouncing I said to A-ma-ling:

—How many "pumps" do you think Satan has?

She didn't know either, but she answered:

—I don't know exactly, but it must be eighty-six million at least.

—And why would he want so many pumps? I asked her.

—It's like many break down and you have to have a spare, she told me.

—Well, we have two or twenty and have enough, I'm telling you, was my final comment.

So this thing about renouncing his pumps was not difficult for us, because our families had pumps to spare. It was very easy: you went to the hardware store and picked out the pump you wanted and that's that. I don't know why Satan wanted to have so many millions of them. It seems to me that devils are a little different from girls, but maybe not.

And the same thing with the "works."

It must have been that Satan had to build a lot of houses for all those who were going to live in hell, and it was always under construction, but since we already had a house, we didn't have to worry about any work.

Furthermore, we didn't have bricks, or cement, or a big brush, or a whitewash brush, and we didn't need any of that, and so we were not bricklayers but girls, it was very easy to give up building works! Let Satan keep them all, we didn't care!

The commandments thing was a little more complicated; some were very easy, like that of "You will honor your father and your mother," which meant that you had to love your papá and mamá very much, and as we did that every day, we had no problems.

That of "Loving God above all things," we also did, but not entirely because the chaplain told us that in God there were three, the Father, the Son and the Holy Spirit, who was a dove. I don't remember if he told me that they were all together or how they managed, but there were three of them.

To the Father, who was God, and who was like a very good grandfather, but who was in Heaven instead of in Turgalium, and who had a very large silk beard and a very long white suit, which looked like a bathrobe like that we put over our nightgown, but that he wore to be very comfortable, instead of other clothes, we loved him very much, and the Son, who was Jesusito, too, almost more than the Father, that's the truth, but what was the Holy Spirit was very strange, because before they told us that he was there we had never prayed to him, but when we found out we began to pray to him a little too, so that he would not get envious of the other two.

But other commandments were more difficult, especially one that was "You will not lie" it seems to me, that one was a drag.

Because I sometimes used to tell a lot of lies, unintentionally, they came out and as soon as they were out I couldn't keep them back even if I wanted to.

Every day a few.

And my friend the same, but less.

Her brother Titing was indeed a liar, much more than me, it seems to me that he was the one who stuck them to me, and got me into the mania of telling lies.

But for communion, I had to promise not to say even one a week, and there was no other choice, so I took a piece of paper, to write down and underline those that were coming out without my realizing it. When three or four days passed and I looked at the paper, I saw that there were a lot of lines, a lot, and it seemed to me that I had only told five or four lies. That method didn't work, so I stopped writing down; what I did was tell Jesusito at night that the next day I was almost not going to say any, and I was so calm.

And also the "You will not kill" thing, don't think it was very easy.

Because look, the mosquitoes bit me a lot, as soon as they saw me come, peck me, even if I was sleeping, and notice that in the girls' room Ne-ning slept next to the balcony, and I more to the inside, and in the summer when it was open they had to pass by before reaching my bed, but they did not mind having to fly for a while longer, they came straight to bite me and it itched all over my body, in my eyes, and on the fingers and even on the feet that were covered with the sheet.

I was very angry at these mosquitoes, and as soon as I saw one when I was awake, or was walking down the street, I would bash them and kill them, but they were very pesky and all the time pecking at me and they made me very angry and very mad, and even if they put DDT on me or anything else they didn't care.

Mamá Chong used to say,

—They bite you because your blood is so sweet.

And since I couldn't get it out, to see if it was sweet or salty, I had to continue with the pecks, but one day when I pricked myself a little and sucked on a drop, it didn't seem to me that it was so sweet, and when I told Man-o-ling that he suck too in case I was wrong, he told me no, that that was dirty and that he wasn't going to do it, and I couldn't ask anyone else because it stopped coming out.

And then there was that "You shall not covet the goods of others," which we did not know what it was, but that Luisina explained to us that it was that we did not have to love the things that other people had, and that commandment was also very difficult, because we wanted my sister's needle heels, and her lipsticks, and our brothers' books... Buff, that was one for sinning on a lot; in the end, I think it was easier not to know about the Commandments, because if you wanted to be very good you had to be thinking all the time, and then you had no time to do anything else, but if you wanted to do First Communion you had to learn them, so we learned them whole.

It was a lot of work, but we got it and on Saturday afternoons, since we didn't have Catechesis that day, my sister Ne-ning would ask us, to see if we had forgotten any, and we were never wrong.

We were ready to have communion!!

When May came A-ma-ling and the other girls in my class did it; not me, I had to wait until September, but it didn't matter much to me, because I went to see them in the Chapel of our school, and then I went to have lunch at many houses, because my other friends had also invited me, and although I did not wear a First Communion dress like them, I was also very beautiful, I even wore a velvet ribbon on my head and I had a great time, we played with many dolls, they showed me their gold medals and then I went home.

In our family we could not make the First Communion in May and I did not know why.

The year it was my turn, I asked my mother:

—Hey, Mamá Chong, why don't you let me have Communion the same day as the other girls?

Mamá Chong took me by the hand, led me to the living room and explained that she had had only one brother (which was the one who became a godfather for my sister), and that some very bad guys had killed him that same day in May, and that since then she did not like that date at all, because when First Communion was made it had to be a very happy day, but since she did not like that day, and she always got very sad, because she could not see or speak with her dear brother ever, never, again, she had decided that we would have communion another day and another month, and that's that.

I mean, I learned that catechesis with my other friends, but I had to wait until after the summer to be able to make First Communion, and that was many, many months. I was a little afraid that I was going to forget the Catechism, and all that about the commandments and the Lucifers....

I was a very entertaining girl, not very precious, not like my sister although she was no longer a child, a little short for my age, and everyone always told me that I was quite naughty, or a lot; all the time I just heard:

This girl is impossible, she only comes up with mischief!

This girl does not stop, she's not still for a minute, and what an imagination!

This girl seems to be made of lizard tails!

And so all the time...

The truth is that I don't know why they said that about lizards, because I was made of flesh and bone: the whole body and face were made of flesh and bone, and when A-ma-ling's bad brother taught us to take off the lizards' tails, because he said that if you plucked them off they would come out again at night, we learned to do it right away, because you only had to pick up a stone that was very smooth, the kind that were not called stones but slates, like the blackboards at our school but small, you threw it at the lizard when he wasn't looking, but not in the part of the head, it had to be in the other part, and then the tail stayed in one place, and the body and the head on the other, but no blood came out or anything; it was very funny because the tail, since it did not know that it was no longer attached to the body, kept moving and made us laugh a lot. But however much I looked, even behind my legs, I couldn't see any of those tails, but they really said that to me all the time. Maybe it was to bug me, but I don't know for sure.

So I really wanted to become Holy with that communion thing, and look, A-ma-ling was almost like that when she did it, she was holy only three or four days, then she became normal, but since mine was after the summer maybe it was different.

The idea couldn't be better, so I was looking forward to that date.

The day before communion, as was the obligation, I went to confession for the first time.

Like I said before with that thing about forgetting, that scared me a little. You had to get down in a confessional, which was a piece of furniture like a little house that had three parts: in the center it had a very large armchair that had to be very soft, because the priest spent many hours there, and he had to be very comfy, and on both sides there were things called the kneelers, so that the one who was going to confess would get down on his knees.

Further up, where the head reached, there was a grill, and that was where sins were said and the other heard them.

The priest, who when he was in that piece of furniture was called the Confessor, knew who was confessing, but I, until Titing told me later one day, believed that everything was secret, and that since you did not see that confessor, he could not see you either, you could only hear your voices, and also you had to speak very softly so that no one would find out, like those who were around waiting with their bag of sins, and whatever you said the confessor did not know who had said it. Besides, he could never reveal what they had told him, because if he did, he would go straight to hell.

When I made my First Communion there existed sins, and there was the devil and hell.

That was where Pedro Botero lived, with all his little devils.

They were very many of them, they lived in a very large house, which was far below the ones we and other people lived in. If you made a huge hole going down, I think you could see a chunk of hell, but we never did it, in case we slipped and stayed down there forever.

That Botero had all hell full of fire and then on one side, attached to the wall, he had many giant pots, some filled with boiling water, others with freezing water, and some little demons - who were the ones who were learning how to do all of the bad things, to be like Lucifer, their great boss - they were in charge of getting you into them, first in the cold ones, and as soon as you were shivering and very frozen, they would take you out of there and put you in the hot water ones, to torture you and annoy you and be getting blisters all over your body, full of pus and ugly junk; and don't think that the small devils felt sorry, no way, they laughed a lot while the poor people who had fallen into hell twisted around in pain and did nothing but say:

—Oh! Why wouldn't I confess? Oh! Why would I forget?

But there was no remedy now.

So that confession was very important.

Those who had wanted to confess but had not been able to, because they were in the jungle, or on a boat, or had stayed dead while they were sleeping, went to a place called Purgatory, which was in the middle floor, between Hell and Heaven, next to the Limbo of the peeing babies, and there they could confess in the evenings and then go up to Heaven and become Angels with wings.

But to confess you had to have sins.

Having many was very important because that meant that you were already very old. Sometimes when A-ma-ling and I were in a church and we looked where the confessionals were, if someone was confessing and took a long time, we got a little envious, for the luck they had, and how grown up they must be. When that happened we pretended we were praying, and we waited until we saw who it was, because we supposed it was someone very special.

Well, I went to confess and despite the precise instructions that they had given us in catechesis, maybe because of nerves, or because months had passed, or I don't know for what reason, the fact is that after saying the first thing, that was: "Ave María Purísima" (and that was written down on a piece of paper and I kept in my pocket just in case I forgot), when they answered "conceived without sin", and I said: "Father, I accuse myself of ... ," I did not know what to say.

Totally blank.

Desperation!

No sin. Nothing came to mind. And I was already a chatterbox at that time!

On top of that I was alone, without A-ma-ling, and I couldn't ask her anything ...

And stuck in that piece of furniture!

So I had to invent a lot of sins, because of course, going to confession, even for the first time, and not taking a long string of them was a very awful drag.

Since I had been baptized, I was not unfaithful, but there were all those years from that day, when I was a baby and didn't even know how to walk, until confession, and in all that time there was room for many, many sins, so I told the priest everything I could think of: "I have kicked my little brothers in the shins," "I have put on my sister's heels," "I have taken her lipsticks to draw with," "I have hidden the books from my brother Man-o-ling's collection," and many, many more, because once I started the sins came out and came out, and there was no way to stop...

At last the confessor ordered me something called "Penance" and gave me absolution.

And I heard him chuckle...

Maybe the confessor had been doubled up with laughter earlier, from so many sins that I had told him, but I don't know, and since it was secret I couldn't even tell A-ma-ling or Mamá Chong.

That Penance thing was to pray, and he told me to say an Our Father, but that I had to say it when I returned to my place, and on my knees, so that God, or Jesusito or I do not know who from Heaven found out well, and that I didn't forget, so I ran to the bench and prayed right away, just in case.

On top of that, it was the morning the day before communion.

Many hours had to pass before I could receive communion.

That was a problem because another confession could not be made. How was I going to manage to be without catching some sin that was loose out there, eh? What if without meaning to, I hit my two brothers who were always annoying me? ...and many other things.

What a dilemma.

But one way or the other, the hours went by, and no new sin stuck to me.

When it was almost night, sitting on the threshold of my friend A-ma-ling's house, as we did every night in the summer, I had the great idea that the best thing that could happen to me was that I die that night! So I would go straight to heaven !!

What happened though is that the matter of dying was not as easy as we thought.

We were looking at different options. I proposed to my friend:

—And if you stick me with a fork in many places, until I run out of blood?

But we didn't have a fork on hand; fetching one from the kitchen would have raised a lot of suspicion. Surely at that time they were already preparing dinner and some squealer would have told everyone and they would have known that we were thinking of some mischief, and that could not be because I had already confessed.

—What if you put my head in the pool, or in the bathtub, until I can't breathe and I'm completely corpse? I insisted.

But since it was at night the pool was closed, and if we both stayed locked in the bathroom for a long time, until the bathtub was filled to the top with water, someone from the house would notice. The plan would also have failed.

—And if I get on the bike, you push me a lot, I fall and dump all my brains on the ground? I insisted again.

But she was a little scaredycat, and that about seeing my head open, with everything inside shooting out on one side and another, and seeing my brains all sticky, it kind of scared her a little.

I thought and thought, I devised many similar things that would lead me to a quick death, but nothing, all my plans met with barriers, and also, the big problem is that there was not much time left, because that night I had to go to bed very early, to rest well and be ready in the morning.

So there was no choice but to give up on the quick death thing!

My only hope was to die in my sleep.

I imagined the surprise of everyone in my house when they saw that I did not get up, they went to the bedroom and saw me dead:

Oh, she looks like a little angel!

Surely she is already in heaven!

What a shame, on the day of her First Communion!

With those thoughts I fell asleep so happy.

But nothing, the next day when I woke up I was very alive, no hint of being a corpse, so I thought:

Well, what are we going to do? To continue living and that's that!

On the day of the first communion it was not possible to have breakfast.

It was necessary to keep a fast from the night before, until the thing happened. You couldn't even drink water, not even a sip.

If you broke your fast you could no longer receive Communion, and imagine how bad that was: everyone would know that you could not do it because you had eaten or drunk something, even if it was secretly, without anyone seeing it, because it would show in your face and the whole city would say:

—Oh, that's that bad girl, who couldn't even make First Communion! Poor little parents and her little brothers and her grandmother, they have to live with her!

In other words, even if you were getting dizzy with hunger, without breakfast. Horrible. But if you could not, well, you could not and that's that.

It was time to get dressed, oh how exciting!

My communion outfit was gorgeous.

I had inherited it from my sister Ne-ning, because then the communion dresses were used for all the girls in the family and although I, unfortunately and due to age difference, never could inherit almost anything from her, this time I was going to do that.

It was white organdy with lace and frill edges.

It was always kept in a secret place, in a flat cardboard box, high in an armoire where none of the children could reach, so I had only seen it in the photos of Ne-ning's first communion, and the day that they took it down from the top shelf of the armoire to take it to wash and iron, it could not be done by even Mamá Chong, nor by any of the maids: It had to be some nuns who were hiding in a convent who did it, because it was made of very delicate and very precious stuff.

Titing told us that the Virgin of Victory taught those nuns how to iron the girls' First Communion dresses, because she knew how to iron stupendously, but it was a secret, so they could not tell how they did it to any person who was not dressed as a nun, and that one day a villein disguised herself as a nun, entered the convent, and began to watch how they were washed and ironed. She was writing it on a piece of paper when the Virgin, who was on the roof, realized what the villein was doing, blew very hard and lifted her nun's dress, and the others who were there realized that she was not one of them, they punished her and put her in a corner with her eyes covered, and although she cried a lot they did not remove the blindfold, come on, so that she would not be naughty and not copy.

That morning, when it was time to get dressed, my dress was beautiful: it had been washed, ironed, and frilled and looking at it was really wonderful; being inside it, I can't even tell you.

Besides the dress, I carried a small bag that was made of the same cloth, but that was at the waist instead of hanging over the shoulder, and there I could keep all my money. A missal had covers of mother-of-pearl and the edges of the pages were gold. It had many things written, it seems to me they were prayers, but it was only to carry in the hands, I did not even have to open it.

I also carried a rosary of gold beads. We only used that for the day of communion, then it was kept in its box, which was also made of pure gold, and we did not see it again until some other child in the family made First Communion.

And a medal that had the Virgin on one side and on the other was my name, but not in full because it did not fit, only the first letter and the day it was, September 8.

And white patent leather shoes! which were special and only used on very important days.

In my hair, as it was short, they couldn't make curls on me like they had put on some of my friends when it was their communion, but I didn't care because I had a little hood made of the same material as the dress and they wouldn't have shown anyway.

We went to church, we got on a bench that was lined with velvet, my Papá, Mamá Chong and I in the middle, I took my First Communion with my parents first. Ne-ning, Man-o-ling and all the others who were there did it later, because it was not their first time. I got very tired, I got a little dizzy (I think from hunger and from all the kisses they were giving me). And finally we returned home and I had breakfast! I was already a little holy, although when I looked at myself in the mirror I looked the same as before, I didn't even have a silver ring on top of my head, well, it would be inside, so that other children who were not yet holy would not be envious...

At that breakfast there was only the family and A-ma-ling, who was my close friend, because the other friends came in the afternoon.

Then they took off my nice dress, so that I could play and not get dirty or with smudges, because I had to wear it again when my friends and other people came to have lunch, and I could play with my friend so calmly, and look at all the remembrance papers, which was where they put all that about who I was, in which church the Communion had been, the day and many other things on one side and on the other there were paintings of the Virgin, Jesusito, or all those who already were in Heaven.

A-ma-ling and I hid a few of the most precious ones, so that no one else could take them later, and when we were putting them away, Feipang came to us and said:

—Either give me twenty, or I'll tell Mamá Chong! If you don't give them to me, they're going to take away that First Communion from you, and you'll see! I need them urgently for a business.

So we gave him twenty and we were left with only one each, but look, we had no choice but to put up with it, he was so annoying and tattling.

At six o'clock all my other friends from school began to arrive, friends of my brothers, a few relatives and neighbors, and all together we were able to have chocolate with spongecake, tarts and many other things, but I was not even hungry, I just wanted to be playing with my new things and talking to my friends.

I was very lucky, because they gave me a lot of gifts: fairy and Celia books, a case full of colored pencils, a doll that opened and closed her eyes, and when I picked her up said "Mamá" because she believed that I was her mother, the silly, notebooks with dolls to cut out, and a lot of money! More than a hundred pesetas, I had never had so much money together.

At nine o'clock, very tired but very happy, when everyone had left, I was finally able to go to bed to sleep. On top of all, that night I did not have to think about dying!

And okay, if I became dead it didn't matter.

Botero and those were not going to catch me!

ONE HUNDRED PESETAS

One hundred pesetas, which were called twenty duros, was enormous capital for a little girl. In order not to lose them or that any of my little brothers, especially Feipang, would cajole me and get hold of them, I gave them to Mamá Chong so she could keep them and give me some when I needed it.

Communion day ended without incident. Now I was good. Now I was Holy. Let's see if it lasted.

And the hundred pesetas? What happened to them?

I'll tell you:

For a long, very long time, every time I wanted something, though not extraordinary, but costing more than my weekly allowance, I would go to Mamá Chong and ask her:

—Mamá Chong, can you give me five pesetas on account of my twenty duros, please?

And of course, Mamá Chong gave me the money.

Thus passed many months and it seems to me that some years also; I kept asking on account and Mamá Chong giving me, until one day when Titing was at my house, playing with my little brothers, he heard me and said:

—Mamá Chong, it seems to me that Ma-ring has been asking for money on account for a long time out of one hundred pesetas.

Surely you have already given her much more than double!

How disgusting, what a bad boy!

Who was he to go into our business?

For that reason, and for many thousand other things, I always tell you that he was a disaster drag, more than bad, and that I did not want to get together with him.

And Mamá Chong, who had never written down what she was giving me, and neither did I, decided that maybe she had given me a little more than what I had deposited, but that it was not fair to suddenly run out of anything, so she proposed the new "deposit" would remain at thirty pesetas, and that from that date we would figure the accounts to the letter.

What a love of a mother!

There will never be one like her!

From earth to heaven: a big kiss, Mamá Chong.

MIRACULOUS FISHING

Every year, when the saint's day or birthday of the Blessed Joaquina arrived, we had quite a few parties.

That Joaquína was the lady who founded our school. She was not even a Saint, she was something that is in the middle, between those who are people, come on, flesh and bone, and the saints, and they call them that so that everyone knows that soon, it may be the day after tomorrow or the next, they are going to turn into saints and they can now go to Heaven.

In Turgalium there were many such blessed women in the churches, which Lupeng told us about; they were ladies a little old and quite ugly, who were there all the time, nothing more than praying and praying, on their knees. They didn't even go home at night, or to have a snack or anything, ever; they just wanted to pray, what a bore, but it was what they liked to do, and also to be saints soon it seems to me that they had to be blessed for a while.

Well, on Joaquína's day, although we had to go to school, our nuns left us free and we didn't even have to go to classes: we could be in the playground and gym all the time.

Most of the time. Because first you had to put up with a mass, which was called "Solemn Mass" and it lasted at least sixteen hours. Luckily Amaling and I acted like we prayed and sang, and what we were doing was talking, but without looking at each other, we only looked to the front, and that way Sister Luisina and the other nuns did not catch on.

In the yard, that day, there were many games, and we were also together with the older ones, who helped us girls jump rope, do cartwheels and everything.

As there was a big tiled basin in the center of the patio, when the saint's day of that Blessed of ours was going to arrive, what they did was empty it, but not so that we would not fall in and drown, they did not care; no, it was to do something there called "The Miraculous Fishing."

The first year we were very excited to see what it was, because everyone was always talking about that miraculous fishing, but we did not know what was done there.

A girl at our table had told us that her sister went fishing every year, which was great and a lot of fun, but that we had to bring a lot of pesetas.

The week before the party a very tall nun came to our class (although she was dressed the same as the others, she was much more important, because all the others, and even our mamás, called her "Mother," and that even though A-ma-ling and I knew that she was another sister, and that the others were not her daughters, but we did not say anything so as not to bug), and she told us that the day before the party we all had to bring two unwrapped gifts for our Founder, that we should not forget, but in case we forgot, they would give us a piece of paper to give to our families, but we had to bring them without fail.

How greedy that Blessed! Two gifts! Well, what luck, the day of her Saint she was going to find a million or two things ...

My friend and I brought some precious gifts. We would have liked to keep one of them, at least, and we almost did, but in the end we gave Sister Luisina all four and that's that.

The morning passed between mass and games, and when we were going to go to eat, Mother came again with a loudspeaker to tell us that in the afternoon it would be the miraculous fishing, that we should not forget to bring money to be able to fish.

As we had both already spent our allowances, we asked Papá Bo-ling and Don AngelB, Dona Mart-ing, my grandmother, her grandfather, well, everyone we caught, but don't think that we achieved a lot, between the two of us we had nine pesetas, although that was better than nothing.

We went back to school after lunch, and in the afternoon the playground was much better than before. There were a lot of candy stalls, others where they sold cakes, others with ribbons and many other things, others with comics and princess stories, well, everything and, finally! the basin full of packages!

That was where the miraculous fishing was going to be done, the fish would be underneath, but we didn't see them, I'm sure they were swimming so calmly, because with all the noise they might not even be able to sleep a little siesta.

A-ma-ling and I started to look first, to see how it was done and she said to me:

—I'm going to see if I catch a shark, I'll make a pool in my garden, we can tame it and teach it many things, and then we'll charge a fee to enter if others want to see it.

—And you don't think it would be better to catch a dolphin? Because remember that sharks have very sharp teeth, and maybe they'll accidentally bite us, and we'll lose our heads, I told her.

—Well, a dolphin or a whale, I don't care, whichever comes first.

In order to fish, you had to ask a nun who was there for a fishing pole, and it was not a cane pole like the ones used by the fishermen at San Lázaro pond, no way, these poles from school were very ugly: it was just a stick with a string, and the string had a hook on the other end. What junky poles, but they really were like that.

And on top of that, they wouldn't let you if you didn't pay two pesetas, and they were only good for fishing once, you couldn't even be fishing all afternoon, as normal fishermen do; in miraculous fishing, if you caught something you had to return the pole immediately so that another girl could fish, and go somewhere else.

If you wanted to fish again you had to get in line. And give another two pesetas again....

We were looking for a long time and nobody caught any fish. Only packages wrapped in newspaper.

As we did not want to get out of the front row, so we could see when the dolphins and sharks would arrive, but we also wanted to know what was in the packages, I told my friend:

—Look, stay here and don't lose the place. I'm going to see what they got in the packages, and if you have to push because someone wants to sneak in, then you do it, or a pinch and that's that, but don't let anyone take this good spot away from you.

She said okay, and I slipped out of all the mess that was there until I reached the line of those who had already fished.

I got behind one that had a very large package, because I was sure that there would be some good fish inside, or a fat sardine at least, which got into there to be very warm.

When she opened it I was stunned: No fish, not even a small one! After removing all the papers, the only thing there was was a box of colored pencils.

As she was one of the older ones, whom I knew a bit, I said to her,

—Look carefully at all the papers, surely the fish is hiding there!

And she laughed.

And laughed some more.

Well, what a silly, on top of that I was giving her such good advice.

But it is what she did.

I waited another while and kept looking at others who were opening packages.

But no fish showed up, just ordinary things, like gloves, a bunch of plastic flowers... okay, total nonsense.

I went back to A-ma-ling, who by then had already changed her mind, because she told me:

—Look, since dolphins and whales weigh a lot and it will take us a lot of work to bring them to my garden, I think the best thing is that we catch twenty or twenty-four shrimps. We'll put them in a can with water so they can swim a little while, and then we make them a small pond and then train them.

—Well, it seems like a good idea, but when I was looking at the ones who caught something I didn't see any fish, nor any shrimp. The only thing inside were other things, I replied.

—Nah, that's because they haven't had any luck, like we're going to have, you'll see, was what she answered.

So we continued there a while longer. But we were getting a bit bored and we went for a walk around the candy stands.

As there were many things we wanted to buy, we decided to spend almost all of our pesetas and save only two to fish the shrimps, and that is what we did: We bought ourselves a very precious story, about a princess who was locked up in a castle and then a prince got on a white horse and saved her, for the two of us, mint and strawberry candies, caramelized almonds, two wonderful lollipops and many other things, and when we ran out of money we went again to miraculous fishing.

We had to stand in line for a long time, I think five or six hours at least, but in the end it was our turn.

The nun asked us for the two pesetas before she gave us the pole. Well, what a suspicious one, like we were going to keep the pole and the pesetas! But she really did that....

My friend told me:

—Hey, it is better that we hold the pole between the two of us, so we have more strength when we take out a huge fish, just in case the shrimps are hidden in a corner and we don't catch them.

—Okay, I said, —we do it like that and that's that.

The nun, whom we had never seen before that day, and I think she was a bit mean and unpleasant, gave us a shout and said:

—Come on, you two, it's for today! Stop talking, there are many girls waiting!

What a dope, even if she was a nun!

We took the pole, we saw a huge package and I said to A-ma-ling:

—Since we don't see any whales or dolphins, we are going to try to catch that one. The shrimps must be in there. You will see how happy they will be to be with us.

She agreed and we caught the package with the fishing pole.

We went between the lines that the other waiting girls had made, and we got to a quieter place so we could open the package.

We were a little nervous, that's the truth, and suddenly it occurred to both of us that we did not have a can to put the shrimps in, or the anchovies or whatever came out, so we went to look for one before opening the package.

Luckily we ran into one of the nuns who were always in the garden, we did know that one and we knew she was good, so we asked her:

—Sister, could you lend us a can for a while? We need it very urgently, but we will return it to you immediately.

She told us that at that time she did not have a can, but she did have a large glass jar and that she would leave it with us.

When we had the jar, we went to a corner to open the package.

We were both very eager to see our fish appear, but since we had everything prepared we calmed down and began to open it.

Papers, papers and, come on, papers.

Nothing appeared there!

Finally, after I don't know how long, a sugar bowl appeared! Can you believe it? Not even a small shrimp! How disgusting.

My friend started crying, lots of tears and tears, but I said to her:

—Look A-ma-ling, don't cry, at least we didn't try to find names for our shrimps yet! Imagine what would have happened if we'd already done it!

She then stopped, because she knew I was right.

We went from the schoolyard to our houses, we decided that we were never ever going to return to any miraculous fishing, that the nuns were liars, Joaquína was a swindler, and that we were not planning to bring any gift again, not even a single one, and that's that.

But there we were, without a dolphin.

And the only shrimps, we had later; they stayed on a plate, a little dead and with pink sauce, and we couldn't train them.

What a pity!

THEATER

One day the nuns at our school decided that they were going to do a play and that all the classes had to participate, even ours, which was the littlest girls.

Our school was very beautiful, it had many classes and many girls of many different ages, some very young like us, and others who were the oldest.

We were many, but no boys, because we were all girls, the boys were in other schools, and they were not allowed in for even a moment, so that they would not kick us in the shins, or scratch us, or teach us bad things, because that was what they did.

The school had two floors:

At the bottom one was the chapel, the big patio where we went for recess and for gymnasium, other rooms I think were for washing clothes, making meals and storing many things, and the classes for the girls in white.

In the courtyard there was a large tile basin where the "Miraculous Fishing" was made.

On the floor above which was the top floor there was a part that was secret, because there lived all the nuns and the head of the nuns who was called The Mother, but she was not really a mother like ours and those of other people.

When you went upstairs there was a glass door and a very large room, almost like the hall of my house, and you could never go to the left side because that was the house of the nuns, where they ate and took baths and went to bed, and I think they also had to pray a little there, and you couldn't enter because it was very forbidden.

That same side was also where the inmate girls rooms were, but not together with the nuns, and they did not have to wear nuns' suits but uniforms, because they were normal girls who lived there because they were from other towns where there was no school, and their mothers brought them to ours so they could learn many things.

But if you hung to the right, all our classes were there, and at night the classes were empty because we went home.

So we had many kinds of students: there were the inmates, the half-borders, the normals and the white ones.

So many.

The first three of us had navy blue uniforms, with a pleated skirt and a white stiff collar, Gorilla shoes and socks. The older ones were allowed to wear stockings to make them warmer, but not us, just socks. And we also had navy blue coats.

And to go to the Chapel where we made many prayers and many Masses, we put on the white tulle cape.

While we were in Sister Luisina's class, we had to put on a smock over the uniform, so that it wouldn't get stained, but we didn't care because they were quite beautiful, pink and white, with squares and had a large pocket to put stuff there, like chalk and things.

The girls in white were in the classes downstairs and they were not allowed to join us, although they were very good and very nice, but their parents did not have much money and could not pay the nuns, and that is why they were not allowed to wear uniforms like ours, only white coats that they put on over their ordinary dresses, so that everyone would know that they had not paid and that they were poor. And in the Chapel the same: they just put an ugly black veil over their hair and that's that.

Besides, they were always in the last rows, but don't think they could fall asleep if they got bored: their nun was always looking at them, and if one of them closed her eyes a little, she would give her a very fat pinch. And they threatened to kick them out of school.

It seems to me that the ones in white weren't taught many things, but they couldn't say anything because when the nuns were handed out they got one of the grouchy ones, and if they said something they would hit them with a ruler on their hands, or they would throw them out of the school.

When A-ma-ling and I came across one of the girls in white we would always stop to say hello, but if there was a nun nearby we couldn't say anything, so they wouldn't punish us too. And we didn't like that, because even if they were dressed in different clothes, we knew that they were the same as us, and that under the white robes they were also made of flesh and bone like us, but the nuns were that strange....

Well, well, this time the nuns said that we were all going to perform, even the ones in white, so my friend and I were very happy that, finally, we could talk to the poor girls.

Those of our class were going to be the little angels that were around the baby Jesus (which was a child that they had lent to the nuns, because they didn't have any of their own, and look, they had a lot of rooms in the school, they could have asked the fat stork and she would have brought them many), and would sing a song saying how happy we were that he was born and stuff.

Since they had recently brought my brother An-dong-ni, A-ma-ling and I pretended it was ours and the song came out perfect, not like other girls who forgot their words all the time, and then the sister Luisina got a little angry with them.

We had to do a lot of rehearsals; every day after writing the letters and numbers, come on! again rehearse and repeat because our nun wanted us to look great and very perfect.

The day of the performance finally arrived!

It was going to be in the afternoon, and we all really wanted to do it, and for our parents and our families to see us so beautiful.

We got on the stage in the auditorium: from up there we could see everyone. Many people had come to see me: Mamá Chong, my papá, my sister, my brother Man-o-ling, my grandmother with her sister Isa-be-ling, (who was already also a bit old, and quite friends even if they were sisters, I think it was because they wanted to see me and throw chocolates on stage; my grandmother had blonde hair and green eyes, and Aunt Isa-be-ling had brown and her eyes were blue, but they really were sisters), Aunt Con-sue-ling with her three daughters, Aunt Ma-li-ya Ter-e-sing and Uncle Sal-va-dong, Mar-u-xing and An-dong, the three sisters who lived downstairs from us, well a lot of people I knew, but Feipang was left at home because Mamá Chong didn't want him to start doing business, or fall to the ground if it got into his head that he wanted to be a little angel too, because that couldn't be: He was a boy and all angels had to be girls and if he couldn't, he couldn't, and that's that!

They filled more than a whole row!

And they all had gift packages for me, because I was the artist; Titing had told us the day before that they always bring many gifts to the artists, to make them very happy: chocolates, sweets, flowers, dolls and everything, but then we had to give him half of the chocolates and sweets so that he could try them, and check that they were not poisoned, because a friend of his did not give his brother half one day that he was an artist, he ate everything by himself, he poisoned himself and became a bit corpse.

Luckily they opened his belly in a moment, they took out all the poison and he was able to stay alive.

But when we told Ne-ning about it, she told us not to pay any attention to him, that it was one of his lies, a big fat one, and that if we gave him one it was enough, that he was a cheat and what he wanted was to keep our sweets.

A-ma-ling's family filled two rows too, with lots of her cousins and her uncles and other people from the tile factory and stuff, and they all started clapping as soon as they saw us up there.

The show began.

We were in the center, a bit crowded by the other artists who were behind and were taller, but in a wonderful place because we saw the Child Jesus very well. And the Virgin too.

We started singing our song and it was turning out stupendous, when suddenly I really wanted to pee.

What could I do?

For me to get off the stage was impossible. Everything was full of angels and relatives of the baby Jesus, and the nuns would have been very angry.

So I held it and kept singing.

But when more time passed, I couldn't stand it, not even jumping around, or putting my hand so that the pee wouldn't come out.

Buff, what anxiety!

And while I was thinking about what I could do, without even paying attention to the song or anything, suddenly my pee came out of me!

And not a little bit.

Very much.

A big puddle on the floor boards of the stage.

Nobody noticed, well A-ma-ling yes, and since she was my friend between the two of us we tried to push the liquid to the other side, so that if some nun noticed, or the Virgin Mary who was next to it saw it, they'd think the baby Jesus did it.

So we couldn't even pay attention to the show anymore, the only thing we both wanted was for it to end immediately. My panties and socks were soaked, they made me cold and I wanted to go home.

After a long time we left the stage.

No one had seen me!

When they saw the stain they would not know I had been the one, I would not have to go to jail, which I think was where they put people who pigged up theaters, so I went where my family was, and I told Mamá Chong in her ear that I wanted to run home.

Everyone wanted to kiss me, give me the gifts, tell me that I had done very well and that I was a very cute little angel, but I did not care about all that. I was wet.

When we finally got to my house, they washed me, changed my panties and socks, and I was able to be in my nightgown and warm slippers. I went to the parlor where my mother was with some more friends of hers and I told them:

I don't want to be an artist !!

Thus ended my first stage appearance, and the last in my life.

SECTION FOUR

OUTINGS & WALKS

Not all of our wanderings were at her house or mine or in the park Paseo de Ruiz de Mendoza or in the one of Doña Margarita, a lady who was green and still and was in the center of her park with a lot of children around, because she was very good and bought them food and pants, if their parents were very poor; she was a good friend of my grandmother (and that even though my grandmother was not also in a statue, but since she wasn't envious she didn't care, she also had much more precious hair, that's the truth), but other times we went out for a walk with the nannies, to have a picnic in the country, or simply "out."

SPONGE CAKE

One day we heard IsabelM say to my mother:

—Mamá Chong, today I have been with the Cakies. You have to go to their house because now the garden is beautiful.

As soon as we were alone, our machinations began:

—Do you know who the Cakey ladies are? A-ma-ling asked me.

—No, no idea, I don't have the slightest idea, but they must be ladies made from the nuns' cake, was my reply.

—And if they're made of sponge cake, how can they wash their face and hands without getting soft? she went on.

—Very easy (I replied) —They must have glass eyes, and to wash their face and hands they will use a rubber mask, and rubber gloves as well.

—And when they have to shower, huh? she insisted.

—Well, it's very easy, they put on a raincoat and some rubber boots and that way they don't fall apart, was my final answer.

But that matter had us very concerned, and what we wanted was to be able to meet those ladies Cakies and see what they really were like.

As my brother Man-o-ling knew everything about everything, because every week with his allowance he bought some books which told all the world knowledge, and in which, on the second page, he always placed his two names, his two surnames and a signature (it seems to me so that Feipang would not take them and sell them since, although he was much smaller, he always wanted to play tricks on us all, but I'm not really sure), we decided that the best thing was to ask him.

So the first time I saw him alone I asked him:

—Hey Man-o-ling, do you know where the Cakies ladies live?

But he didn't know either, though he offered to ask Mamá Chong and tell me later.

In the end we managed to find out, and you see, her house was on the way that we sometimes went with the nannies, when we went for a walk to the well on the Cáceres road.

And all the time without knowing it!

That same afternoon, when it was time for a walk, the nannies wanted to take us to another place, but we screamed and gave so much trouble that, in the end, they took us to the road we wanted.

When we were getting closer to the house we were both very nervous, we would finally meet some ladies made of sponge cake! It seemed like a story, but it was real life itself! Uff, what a thrill!

When we got to the gate of the house, sitting in their beautiful garden and smiling at each other, what we saw were two ladies of normal flesh and bone. What a disappointment! What a cheat, so much work to find out where they lived and then it turned out that they did not have any part made of cake! Not even an arm or an ear! And why were they called that then? We felt very cheated by those stupid ladies who didn't even smell like sponge cake.

It was a tremendous upset and we spent the rest of the afternoon very angry.

MAGIC BELL

Sometimes we would go for a walk with the nannies to the duckling pond, which was really called the San Lázaro Pond.

That saint was very good and when they told him one day: "Lazaro, get up and walk," as he was very obedient, he started walking and walking all the time and never stayed still, and since he was the owner of the ducks too he always had them moving from one place to another. It seems to me that neither he nor the ducklings would even go to bed, because if they were asleep they would have to stay still, but I don't know any more because at night we weren't around.

On the way to the pond we passed the house of some people who were also very rich, even more than Luisito's family, because they must have had about a hundred twenty thousand pesetas, or more, and that was much more than what the others had and as they were so wealthy they had a different door knocking way from all those of us who weren't very rich. It was a "door-bell"!

That bell, when you pressed it, if you put a pin or a fine needle, it kept ringing and ringing all the time, it could be ringing for fourteen years, according to what Titing told us, but maybe it sounded a little less, because that bad brother always said a lot of lies.

We only saw the lady who lived there once.

She was ugly. Very ugly. She looked like a monkey.

And from then on it became part of our conversations:

—A-ma-ling, do you remember what Man-o-ling read to us from Our Children's Book? I asked her.

—Well of course! Do you think I'm dopey or what?she answered, very indignant, because being a dopey was an insult of the worst, if you were like an idiot.

And I: —Well, it seems to me that that lady's grandfather was a monkey.

—Or maybe he was a chimpanzee, who are much fatter, she told me.

And I again:

—And how do you think he got to Turgalium?

—It seems to me that he must have lost himself in the jungle and when Tarzan saw him, he was very sorry because he was crying a lot, he brought him here and then he stayed forever, so he could be the grandfather of the monkey lady.

I said to her:

—How many bananas do you think they eat a day?

And she would answer:

—Buff, a lot, seventy-four at least.

So, when in one of our houses we heard that there were no more bananas, we knew that it was because that woman's family had been very hungry that day, and they had eaten all the bananas that were in all the stores in Turgalium. Look, we weren't dopey!

THE LORD OF HEALTH

Before reaching the pond we sometimes passed a very scary place called "The Lord of Health."

You can bet we got trembling there!

It was like a church, but small and almost normal, if you didn't pay close attention.

And look, it was next to some very beautiful gardens.

Those gardens were not like Doña Margarita's or the park's, all in a row. No, in those, which were also from San Lázaro, there was a path in the middle, like a street, but it was not called a street, and then on both sides, many stone benches for the nannies to sit down, and put there the bag for snack time, and there they talked about their boyfriends and that; there were lots of plants and flowers and ground to play with and we really liked going there and playing with other girls, skipping rope and blind man's bluff and all the other games that we knew.

But if we entered the chapel, there the problems began.

As you entered, to the left and to the right, on the walls, they had everything hanging: hands, legs, ears, noses, hearts, guts... Everything you can imagine. Terrible.

Because when people had something that hurt, they would go there and say:

—Lord of Health, if the pain goes away, I'll bring you a hand!

Or a foot, or whatever hurt.

So as soon as it stopped hurting, as they had made a real promise, it seems to me the kind like Word of Honor, they had to cut off their hand, or their nose or whatever, cover it with wax so that the blood would not drip and stain the entire church floor, and leave it there for everyone to know that they had kept the promise.

Titing also told us that he had seen someone whose eye hurt, and that he had to tear it off later to take it there.

But for us, even though we saw that they were loose parts, we were scared in case they got tired of being there and decided to put themselves in any other body, because Titing told us that had happened many times: One day he was there with a friend of his and some guts of those that were hanging insisted on placing themselves on his friend, and since then he had many problems because even though he ate a lot, his second guts would remain empty and make a lot of noise, even when he was in class and everyone looked at him.

And well, a few guts, okay, because they stayed inside, but imagine if a nose or an ear stuck to you, what a drag of a disaster, having to go down the street like that...!

In other words, to avoid problems, we tried to enter that place as few times as possible and only went when the nannies got very tiresome and wanted to pray for something about their boyfriends or their family.

SAN LÁZARO POND

And we arrived at the pond.

With so many stops, sometimes in one place and others in another, it was almost time to have our chocolate bread for a snack.

In many houses, such as ours and A-ma-ling's, the remains of food and the peelings of potato and tomato and garlic and many other things that were the edges of meals, were thrown into a special bucket that was called the Swill bucket (I don't know who that lady Mrs. Swill was, but she must have been quite filthy because her bucket always smelled terrible), and then Fai-tong would come in the afternoon and take everything for her piglets to eat, who loved all that and got very happy and very fat.

But not the bread.

If there was leftover bread it was ground to prepare coated steaks or breaded croquettes, or cut up into little pieces to make Extremadura *migas with chorizo.*

Well, those little pieces on the crumbs tray, we always took some handfuls down to the pond to the ducklings, because they loved them and they were very happy when they saw us arrive.

And the poor ducks had to come running, because in that pond there were also many carp and tench and although what those two eat is mud, which was called silt there, they were so selfish that they also wanted to eat the bread.

Luckily, if Titing was with us, he would drive them away in a minute, because he would start throwing stones at them and they would scram, and they would go to the bottom of the pond to continue eating their mud and forget the bread.

When it began to get dark we went back to our houses.

THE TILE FACTORY

Another of our favorite outings was to the tile factory.

There were a lot of floor tiles plus kitchen and bathroom tiles at that place.

Besides, we could go there in any season, it didn't have to be summer or winter.

It was a very big, huge place and there was always a lot of noise.

We could hardly ever go but only when we started being very, very bothersome and asking many times to please take us, Uncle Edu-ar-dong (which was another brother of IsabelM and was the boss there), said:

—Come on girls, today I will take you to the tile factory, to see if you could earn your wages!

We ran out, we held his hand and with him we both went so happy.

Making tiles was not that difficult, don't believe it, because in reality what you had to do was choose a mold that was square or others that were long, put a very ugly paste, which was called cement, which was gray and very pasty and in these molds it was forbidden to add any color, you needed to wait a while until it was a little dry, then put another iron mold on top that had many marks and many drawings of leaves or flowers, or stripes and things like that. Afterwards, you let a gunk or potion fall from a tube that was above and when you pressed a button very carefully all the colors came out, but not together. You had to choose the one you wanted and you put a bit of one color in one part, another of another color in another and so on all the time until everything was full.

We liked the ones that were pink and blue better, but we also used other colors sometimes.

When we had finished, we had to put that aside and wait another long time, flip everything over as if you were making a potato omelette and that's that.

The first time we made tiles, we got very wet and dirty, even our hair, and it seems to me that everyone was laughing a bit at us, although they covered their mouths so we wouldn't see them, but later on we were just like the other workers: we only splattered a little on our dresses and hands and beside that, one guy that was always around, left us some big smocks that came down to the ground, and although we were very ugly, we were totally covered, but with them we could hardly walk....

We made a lot of tiles, but as each one was different, Uncle Edu-ar-dong said that they weren't useful, or that they weren't good for selling, that we could keep them, look how lucky.

What happened is that we had to wait until they were completely dry so that they did not squash while we took them home, I don't know, two or three years at least, and although Uncle Edu-ar-dong was terrific and he wanted to give them to us, the truth is that we never took any of the ones we made, because we couldn't wait there that long, but we didn't care because not all the girls could boast of having made tiles, and when we told the others about it everyone from our table in class was left with their mouths open and they also wanted to go, doggone it, but as I said to A-ma-ling:

—Don't even think about telling them where the factory is! Look, if Uncle Edu-ar-dong gets mad and won't take even us again!

And she was very obedient in that, and never told the others.

PAQUITO

One morning when my friend and I were sitting in the big park, we saw many people, at least ninety-four, all men and dressed in Sunday clothes, with very shiny and clean shoes, standing at the door of the city hall.

We went to see what was happening, because we liked to find out about everything, look, we were not baby girls, come on.

The first was a man a little fat, short and quite ugly, who was wearing a suit like the ones that the men in the Civil Guard barracks wore, only in another color, with many medals and crosses and other things hanging, but not like the necklaces that are put around the neck, because he had all of that pinned on the sides of the jacket. He had four hundred or more, and they must have weighed on him a lot and maybe that's why he had gotten so short, but I don't know for sure.

Behind him were the Mayor and the Authorities and they all looked like they were very happy to be with him.

When he saw us and although we had not even spoken, he said:

—What nice girls! What are your names? How old are you? Do you live in this city? And why aren't you in school now? Do you know who I am?

Although he was a bit tiresome asking so much, we told him that we were A-ma-ling and Ma-ring, that we were six years old, that yes, that we lived here, one in the house next door and the other opposite, that we didn't have any idea who he was because we had not seen him before and he was not our neighbor, that since we lived nearby we had only gone to look for a while, and that day the nuns had left us free because someone very important was coming, but we did not remember what that important person was called.

When we told him that he started to laugh and laugh, and from so much laughter he started to cough and to cough a lot, and he almost fell to the ground and became a corpse, but then he became normal and began to tell us things.

He said his name was Don Francisco, but that we could call him Paquito.

Well, we didn't care what his name was, but since we had a lot of education we told him okay, that we would call him that.

Paquito was a little taller than us, but not much, maybe that's why he wanted to talk to us instead of "the Authorities," who were all very tall and would have to bend down when they spoke to him, but we said that in a soft voice, so that he wouldn't hear us in case he thought we were laughing at him.

He raised a finger, took each of our hands, and immediately some of his aides came with a bench and a few cushions and the three of us sat there together.

We liked that raising the finger very much, it had to be a secret language like talking with the pee, and then we saw that every time he wanted something, Paquito just raised his finger and someone would bring it to him! He didn't even have to speak! What luck! But although in the following days we tried to do the same, the truth is that no one paid any attention to us when we raised our fingers and they did not obey us, it would be because we were girls instead of a man, even if he was short.

Paquito told us many things, and although we were a little bored with so many stories, we let him talk and talk so that he would realize how polite and how good we were.

First, he told us that he was born in Galicia, that it was a very far away place and there it rained a lot, that there were many fairies and witches and gnomes and everything, that one day he would take us there so that we could see them. They weren't in towns or cities, just in the woods, but if you went after a quarter past nine, they were all having dinner.

I said to Paquito:

—Since we have to be in bed at that time, can you tell them to get together a little earlier? Maybe for a day they don't care.

He told me that yes, not to worry and that he would speak to the boss, who was called Doña Meiga, and that one day they would do it earlier.

Later he told us that he loved his mamá very much, the same as happens with us, because she was very good and prepared their meals, everything that he and his brothers liked, and taught all of them to pray the Jesusito at night and she wrapped them up well when they were in bed, well, well, that also happened to us, although we lived elsewhere.

I don't think he loved his papá very much, because when we asked him about it, he changed the conversation and he only said that he lived somewhere else.

As in his town there were many ships and a lot of sea, he told us for that he decided to become a sailor or a ship officer, I don't remember which of the two, but that when he went to talk to the one who commanded all those, he told him:

—Look, Paquito, you are not going to be a good sailor because you get seasick and also you can't swim, and you are a little short. Get into the military and there they will give you a horse and you will see how high you are going to be and how well you are going to have a good time in wars.

That also seemed like a very good idea to both of us, because as he couldn't wear needle heels like my sister Ne-ning, he would always stay the same, very short, and on top of that he would have a horse for himself, not a donkey, what luck !

So he got into that military thing and he went with his horse here and there looking for wars and he said to us that he had a great time, that he was very tall, and that he could see everyone very well from above.

After going to many towns in Galicia and Valencia and many other places with his horse, one day when he was in Málaga a friend of his asked him if he had gone to Africa, where the Moors lived, and Paquito said no, but that he would very much like to go.

The problem was that neither he nor his horse knew how to swim, and to get to Africa they had to cross the Mediterranean Sea, which was very deep, much deeper than the Turgalium pool in the grownups' part, but his friend took them to a shop and they bought some great swim floats. His was blue and had a lot of painted things: starfish, shells, a lot of sand... And the one for the horse was also very beautiful, and they were both very happy with their new floats.

Of course, to put the float on the horse, they had a terrible time, because that horse was a bit of a donkey and would not allowed them to do it, and then Paquito did not know about raising his finger, but in the end they placed it and the two of them and the friend went to the beach from there to make the trip.

They swam and swam for a long time and finally reached Africa.

As they had not taken more than a little bread and chocolate for the trip, when they got to the other side they were very hungry, so they went to a bar so they would make them some fried eggs with potatoes and chorizo, but since they did not know how to speak African they could not order it, and they had to eat a very strange thing that the people there ate called couscous and that meal disgusted them both, but the horse did like it and ate five platefuls.

And they didn't even ask for dessert lest they get another pig slop!

When they finished eating they went for a walk around and he told us that yes, the truth is that everything was full of Moors.

Those Moors just said "Khamalahí khamalahá" all the time, and although it was very hot they had a lot of clothes on, and the women even had rags on their heads and none of them wore shoes, they were wearing slippers called "sandals," but he told us that they were not made of sand, which of course we knew, that they were made from the camel's hump, and that he did like them very much and that he liked them so much that he bought seventeen pairs for himself to be very comfortable, and a few others for his mother.

While he was telling us all those stories, "the authorities" must have been really bored waiting, because they were in a nearby shed drinking some wine for a long, long time, but Paquito didn't even realize it, he was having so much fun with us.

So Paquito, his friend and the horse were walking around there, and they met a few who were also from Spain, who told them how things were in Africa.

The Moors were quite bad and above all very rude, and they did nothing but wage war and fight all the time, some with whoever, and others with the poor Spaniards, who were less, because there were oodles of Moorings.

So when Paquito had been there for a few days, he decided it was better to catch a few Moors, get to be friends with them and see what would happen, because with so much fighting he didn't even have time to take a nap and he was very tired.

He remembered that in his hometown they made something called "Hotpunch," which was a very stupendous drink, and that when people drank from that they got very happy and wanted to dance and be silly, so he left for the marketplace, which was like Thursday in Turgalium but for the Africans, there he bought a very large pot, made many liters of Hotpunch and invited many Moors who were fooling around without doing anything, to try it.

Well, he told us that they all liked it very much, and that although they could not speak Spanish or Turgaliuman or anything that we who are not Moors speak, they began to tell him Paquito, Paquito! and to throw themselves on the ground and tell him that they would always be with him, and that he was their leader and many other things, because his friend who did know that khamalahí khamalahá stuff told him so.

It seems to me that the other Spaniards who were there were a little envious that Paquito had so many Moors with him all the time, but as we told him, well, they should have made them one of those drinks, come on.

And Paquito told us that he had to teach them many things, because those Moors did not know how to do anything at all, they did not even wash their faces or iron their clothes, they ate with their hands and they were kind of piggy, but that he, with a lot of patience educated them a bit, and also taught them to speak Galician.

When he was telling us all this and many other things about the Moorings, one of the Authorities came to our bench and said:

—Excellency, if you do not object, we should continue with the visit.

It seems to me that Paquito did not like much that he came to bother us, because he raised another finger and immediately two Moors who were hiding behind a tree came, and with very fat swords called scimitars, they cut off his head and our suits were almost smeared with the blood that ran all over his neck, but the Moors put the body and head in a cardboard box and took him away running.

Luckily the other authorities did not realize it, because they would have been very sad and angry at the same time, and maybe they would have gone home and then what were we going to do with him all the time?

When the two Moors took away the one who was already a corpse, Paquito was able to continue telling us his story, and although we were already a little tired and bored, we stayed still just in case, in case he also would get angry with us and his Moors cut something off us, because even though he said they were now very polite, it seemed to us that not so much, but okay.

As there were many Moors fighting with those from Spain and they were quite brutes, and they hurt them a lot and put their guts out, and sometimes they took out their eyes and cut off their ears so that they would not hear anything, Paquito got together his Moors and he told them to go talk to the boss of the others, and to tell him that he was getting a little fed up with so much silly fighting, and that he was not going to invite them to Hotpunches ever again as long as they continued like this, but if they stopped fighting then he would give away his horse to them and also make them a Galician pie.

The Boss Moro and his soldiers, who were called "Mess-a-Moors," were super happy and that same afternoon at snack time they stopped fighting, they went to eat the pasties and drink Hotpunch, they had a great time at the party and the war was over.

So Paquito was left without any war, which was what he really, really liked, and the truth is that he was also getting tired of having to make pasties and Hotpunches all the time, because all those of the mess-a-moors liked them very much, and they ate and drank them right away.

But his friend, who was also one of those soldiers, but not one of those who had been given a horse, came to see him one day when Paquito was in the middle of a big job making the dough for the pasties, and was all covered in flour, and he told him as a secret that in Spain there was going to be a very big war, but not against the Moors, nor against those of Portugal or France, that it was going to be Spaniards against Spaniards, because they had gotten very angry, and that they were going to kill each other.

Then Paquito was very happy: He would finally stop making pasties and let the Moors get along without them! Let them start eating that couscous stuff again and leave him alone!

As the war had not yet started, Paquito took the opportunity to go shopping, because he wanted to bring some gifts to his relatives and close friends, and he also wanted to buy a few necklaces for his wife because she liked them a lot, and since the shopping ended soon, he dedicated himself to teaching his Moors to behave, swim and fight in the style of the Spaniards.

When he and his Moors could swim stupendously, they stuffed a few pasties in their backpacks, the Moors grabbed their scimitars, and they all went to sea again, this time on their way to Spain.

When they got there, the war had started half an hour before, and Paquito went to a barracks where all the generals were sitting and said:

—Now I am a little tired because I have swum a lot today, but within a few hours, as soon as I am showered and change the uniform, I will be ready to go into combat, so what I want is for you to tell me if you would like me to be the boss in the war, because if I command I will finish with this nonsense immediately, because I have brought many Moors, but if you are in chargedo, I don't know what will happen.

Some of the generals, especially those who were very tall, did not want Paquito, who was quite a short guy, to be the most bossy, but in the end they all told him that well, okay, he should lead the war for a while and afterwards they will talk again more calmly depending how things were at the war.

Then he decided that he was going to be called "El Generalísimo," so that they would not confuse him with one of the other generals, who were also called Paquito.

That war was pretty stupid, like all wars, and some of a team called "the reds" fought against others who were "the blues."

Paquito told us that he was in the blue team, and that the reds were disgusting and a real drag, that they burned the churches and killed the nuns, and that they had no idea of fighting, that they only knew how to throw stones and break things, that they had neither uniforms nor bombs, nor almost anything, and that sometimes they were even more brutal than his Moors, and look, those were very brutal, even we had seen it when they cut off the head of that guy next to us, and that other reds from other countries had come to help them with airplanes and pistols and many other things, and also that they were liars, because they only said bad things about him and the other blues and that we should not pay attention when they told us all that — as if it mattered to us, come on.

He told us that they were fighting for three years, and sometimes it seemed that the reds were going to win, and other times the blue ones, I don't know why they got those names instead of the pink ones and the apple green ones, which are colors a lot more precious, but it seems to me that those soldiers did not know how to choose beautiful names for their teams, and since all that had happened a long time ago, even if we had told Paquito to change the colors, not even he could do anything anymore, and in the end the blues won.

The other poor people, the red ones, had a terrible time, because Paquito wanted them to turn blue and since they didn't feel like changing color, for that Paquito got a lot angry and put them in jail where they could only eat bread and onion, I think, or bread and water, I don't remember because I wasn't there, and when the prisons were full and there was no room, he killed those that were left over with a knife or a shotgun, well, or with something and we didn't like that at all, because the war had already ended, he had told us himself, and on top of that he was already the most bossy of all because he could have left the others in peace, but no, maybe it was that the being a brute thing stuck to him, like to his Moors, and he could not help it, and he told us that many Spaniards had left Spain, that he was not going to let them in again, come on, if they left it was their problem, and that if they would try to get in again without his knowledge, then they were going to find out, and that they better stay where they were, that he had to do a lot things and to inaugurate many reservoirs so that there would be water, and that the streets could be washed and all the blood that was stuck from when the war could be removed, and also he had to go to visit all the towns, and also had to see if the policemen had cleaned their pistols, going to parades and bossing around, that was why he had won the war and that the others could just go be bugged.

And suddenly he asked us:

—And tell me girls, what are your families like, blue or red?

As my friend was a bit embarrassed to speak, I was the one who answered him:

—Look Paquito, I don't know, because my brother Feipang, when he's very angry, turns red, and my little brother An-dong-ni sometimes if he is very hungry and cries a lot, he turns blue, and the rest of us are flesh-colored, but one day I will ask everyone and tell you, okay?

And he said good, stupendous.

With so much Mooring and so much war it had already gotten very late and we had to go home to eat, because if we were late they would scold us, so we said goodbye but he did not want to let us go, and he asked us if we could accompany him in the afternoon to a jewelry store, so that we could help him to choose a very precious necklace for his wife, but we told him that we had to do homework for school and that we couldn't go, even though it was a lie, but we didn't want him to keep telling us more of that stuff, he had already pestered us enough, and we went home.

When I got upstairs, my brother Man-o-ling was reading a story about the Vikings, who I think were almost as brutes as the Moors, or similar, only that the Vikings were taller and with blond hair. I told him everything that had happened to me that morning, but my brother didn't believe it, and on top of that he told me that I was a liar and that I was constantly inventing things, and that what I needed to do is go and wash my hands because they were going to call us to eat right away.

Well, worse for him if he didn't believe it!

In fact, it was a little bit silly to believe the stories of the Vikings instead of the Moors, even if they were big and blond instead of short and a little dark, puaff!

TELEGRAMS

A place we loved to go into was the Telegraph and Post offices, which were located in the downstairs of my house.

I don't think it was a single office, they were two, and each had a chief, but Papá Bo-ling was the supreme head of the two, the boss who bossed everyone.

As soon as you passed the door of the scary lions there was a hallway, where you couldn't look much either, because they had put tiles on all the walls, but not the pretty ones, pink or orange or such; the ones that were there were of very bad creatures, and Man-o-ling told us that they were mythological figures, but we did not like them at all, and what we did when passing through that place was to close our eyes tightly to not even see them, in case they would come out of the wall and hit us with a big smack.

Then there was another larger room, which was also a hallway but there the walls were wall, without those bad critters, and there our stairs began and before reaching the stairs that went up to our floor there was a door that was where the postmen worked and I think they also lived there, but I'm not sure because at night I was in bed.

Some of them were very good, and when we entered there they let us fiddle with all the packages, and look at the stamps of the letters that came from far away places like India or Peru, and one of them even didn't care that we put letters in his big sack, that was huge because he had to put in many packages and at least two thousand letters every day, and it weighed three hundred kilos or more. One day we tried to lift it between the two of us and we couldn't, imagine how heavy it was.

But some other, like Mr. Peñ-ong, was very unfriendly and was always telling us to leave, that we were doing nothing but bothering. Well wow! Like he believed that office was his, what a silly! Luckily Fel-i-crung (who was one of the daughters who lived in the middle floor of my house and who worked there, but not as a mailwoman, she just sat next to a small window, and when someone came and he wanted a stamp, she gave it to him real fast, and on top of that she was so good that she stuck it on the letter and that was that, the letter would arrive anywhere in a minute) - luckily she always called us to her side and let us see all her stamps, and we could touch them and everything, but we always had to keep our hands clean. We didn't even go near Don Eli-ang's office, because of those microbes, but we heard the poor man coughing. Not even there they left him alone. What bad and pestering bugs....

But although we had a good time there, where we really liked to be was in the other one, in the telegraph office, which was much better and larger than the post office.

First there was a room where there were always many people sitting around. They were the ones who had to fix everything that broke and stuff like that.

But they did nothing.

Just always talking, telling things and secrets. Well, one day when we asked them, they told us they had to wait until they were told that the lines were down, and then they ran to pick them up.

But we did not believe anything, what a lie, we were girls, but not dumb, come on, like the lines were going to fall, Ha! All the lines that A-ma-ling and I made stayed very still on the paper, but we said yes, good, as if we had believed it....

That room was full of messes, bicycles, ropes, chairs and a lot more junk, but even though we didn't like it we had to go through there to go to the best of the whole floor: The Equipment Room!

The equipment room had everything: Morse typewriters, which was an even more secret language than Pee's; some little pots, filled with a very sticky glue, and with a wheel through which the white tape that was the one that had the secret message was passed; teletypes, typewriters, and the best of the best: some blue papers that when folded looked like a small envelope, and that were telegrams.

Since my papá was the boss, we could go in there almost whenever we wanted and we had some free time, but we couldn't look at what was written in the telegrams, it was secret, and if someone read it they would take them to jail.

And look, that was really silly, because once, without wanting to, we looked at one that was open there, we read it and what it said was just: "Arrived well stop Will write stop."

Well, well, that wasn't such a secret either, but we didn't tell anyone, not even my papá, in case he had to take us to jail....

One day they even gave us two of those blue papers and they taught us to fold them, and also some pieces of white tape, but the kind that had no letters, and we glued them to the telegram, and as that day Titing, my friend's bad brother, had been bugging us a lot, we told my sister to help us write a secret message, to scare him.

She had to try a lot, until it was exactly how we wanted. First she wrote it on a separate piece of paper, so as not to mess up the telegram with crossing out, and when we finally liked what it said, she wrote it in capital letters, so no one could tell it was her.

The telegram said:

"Mr. Titing Frogmouth colon as you have been super bad early tomorrow comma very early comma we will cut off your head stop if you want to save yourself apologize to the girls stop and you also have to buy them a package of sunflower seeds goodbye stop stop."

We folded the telegram as they had taught us, we put the address on the top when it was like a little package, and we asked Pon-Ching to please take it to that address.

And the three of us died laughing at how scared Titing was going to be!

Pon-Ching met Titing on the upper park, gave him the telegram, and left.

In a little while, the two of us, who had been looking at everything from behind the statue of Doña Margarita, walked over and said hello.

He started running away and said, —I'll be right back. I'm going to the Plaza to Miz Manuela's stand, I have to buy something. Don't move from here!

We didn't say anything and as soon as he disappeared, we had a fit of laughter.

So the telegram thing worked! Luckily we still had one in reserve....

In less than half an hour, when we almost hadn't had time to play La Semana, he appeared very nice and said: —Hey, excuse me if before I did a few naughty things, but just so you can see how good I am now, I've bought you this big pack of sunflower seeds.

Amaling and I thanked him, grabbed our seeds, and took off.

That time we really pulled a fast one!

LITTLE MOUSEY PÉREZ

One afternoon, after school, when we were having our snack on the Paseo de Doña Margarita, which was the lower park, we saw a girl friend of ours with a hole between her teeth.

We both really liked being in that park, because there were many palm trees, many plants and many flowers, and in the middle of all that was the statue of that lady, which was not the one with real flesh and bones, who I think was in her home having a snack with my grandmother, so calm, talking about stuff, like my friend and I did.

The statue was not the whole body. They had only put a little chunk of the body, down to the waist, it didn't have a skirt or feet, but it was quite beautiful, although green.

Around it was a pond with water and then a border so that the water did not mix with the soil on the ground.

A-ma-ling and I loved to get on that border, jump and get to where that lady was with a few orphaned children, who were not flesh and bone, they were made of metal or iron, I don't know, and as the orphans loved her very much, they were always hugging her.

But do not think that taking that jump was easy, it was very difficult, if you did not do it well and perfectly you would fall into the water and you would get wet shoes and socks, and a hunk of your legs, almost to the knees.

Titing showed us how we had to do it, but one day when our older brothers were there they said never to do it again, that we had to wait until we were older, at least eight or nine years old. Buff, what a drag, how could we wait so long? Impossible, with everything we always had to do.

So we ignored them and as soon as we were there and no one was looking at us, we tried.

Well, that day that we were both trying to jump, that girl appeared, who was a little bit our friend, the one I was telling you about before.

We both stared at the hole and A-ma-ling asked her: —Hey, what's happened to you, why do you have a hole instead of a tooth?

She looked at us at two, put on a very big smile and said:

—It's that my milk teeth are falling out, but it's super stupendous because Mousey Pérez came last night and left me a bag full of gum balls and five orange candies, come on I'll give you one each.

We took the sweets, thanked her and ran to my house to ask someone who was there, what was that mouse and why he had not come to our houses.

When we got to the door we met Ne-ning, who had secretly gone to the mailbox on the street, to send a letter to her boyfriend Cheng-Chu, and we told her Holy Word that we were not going to tell anyone, so she became very friendly.

As we climbed the stairs I said,

—We met a girl who had a hole at the place for a tooth and she said it fell out because it was milk. But look how lucky, then someone called Pérez, who was a mouse, came and gave her many things. Can you write to him, or send him a telegram, or call him or something, and tell him that although our teeth are made of teeth and not made of milk, please bring us some candy? Also tell him that we don't mind giving him some tooth, okay?

My sister must have been very happy because she laughed, took us by the hand, entered the girls' room, sat us on one of the beds, and she faced us on the other and explained: —The teeth you have now are called milk, but they are not made of milk, they are made of bone just like the ones you will have later, which are teeth for life. Those teeth are very small and that is why they have to be changed when girls are growing up. When one falls out, what you have to do is wash it, put it under the pillow and that night Mousey Pérez comes, takes the tooth and leaves a gift in return.

Well, we were much calmer, because the true truth is that neither A-ma-ling nor I knew where to buy those teeth made of milk, and it must also be very difficult to eat with them, imagine, soft things maybe, but just imagine you were eating a breaded cutlet and your teeth crumbled while you chewed... Such a drag you could not bear it.

But we saw another problem: How were we going to get out the ones we had, leave holes, and be able to leave them under the pillow, eh?

So from that day on, what we did was touch them all the time.

My friend used to tell me: —Touch my tooth a little, until it moves, but very carefully so that no blood comes out or makes me a corpse.

I pushed on hers and then she did the same with mine.

But our teeth were very fixed and did not move at all.

Finally, one day when I was eating a ham sandwich, I suddenly noticed that one of the teeth did move. What a joy!

I ran to her house and told her to do the same.

That day they gave her another snack, but she kept pestering until IsabelM made her a sandwich like mine and then it happened exactly: two front teeth began to move, what luck, on top of that I had been the one who had told her the secret, but okay, she was my friend and I put up with it.

From that moment we were all the time poking our teeth to see if they finally fell out, but nothing, they did not.

The next Sunday, while we were spying on our neighbor who had so many suits, my tooth almost fell out. We went to Mamá Chong to show it and she told us: —It's on the verge, it's hanging by a thread. Now please be very careful, so you don't accidentally swallow it!

A-ma-ling was a bit envious, that's the truth, because since she had two moving, she thought she was going to be the first, but hey, luck is luck, as I told her, and above all I was the one who had told her the secret, so she was silent and did not protest.

At noon, while I was eating, it finally dropped out of me. And it didn't hurt or anything, just a little bit of blood and that's that.

We washed the tooth, which seemed much smaller than when it was stuck in with the others, maybe it had shrunk when it fell, and Ne-ning and I put it under my pillow.

I went to my friend's house, so happy to have a hole in my mouth even though my tongue did nothing more than keep wanting to go into that place, a real drag, and I showed it to everyone in her house. Everyone was very happy except Titing, who told me:

—You're so ugly! Now you do have to be careful and always keep your mouth closed because if you open it, even to talk or eat, or laugh or something, a grasshopper will enter that way and it will devour all your insides.

But Lupeng said not to pay attention to him, that it was one more of his lies, and that I could do everything as before, and what a lying kid, and many other things that I do not remember.

We spent the whole afternoon moving her teeth but nothing, they didn't fall out.

That night I was very nervous because I wanted to see the little mouse, but my sister had told me that he was a bit shy, that he only appeared if you were asleep, that if you pretended to be asleep, he would stick his head a little out of the doorway and leave, and so I asked Jesusito to make me sleep a lot, that other days I didn't care, but that night it was super important that Mr. Mousey Pérez saw me snoring.

I must have slept deeply because when I woke up it was daylight, and almost time to go to school.

I looked under the pillow: my tooth was still there and a piece of paper next to it.

Oh gosh, what had happened? Maybe my brother Feipang had said something bad... Even if it was a trifle...

Ne-ning came over, took the paper, because even my hands were shaking, and read:

Forgive me for not leaving you anything, I have no chocolates or any treats at home, today I am a little sick and do not want to go out to the candy store to buy them so as not to get worse, but tomorrow without fail I will bring you something good. Don't forget to put the tooth back there. So sorry. Signed MP

Buff, thank goodness!

Because I was already thinking that one of my brothers must have been telling him something, and tattling on me about something naughty I had done, but no, thank God it was just that he was a little sick, poor thing.

As soon as I got to class, A-ma-ling asked me:

—Did the Mousey come? Did you see him? What did he leave for you?

I told her about the letter and that I had to wait another day, but that I didn't care because Pérez the mouse was for sure not a liar like her brother, and that he would take the tooth and leave me something.

I showed my whole table the hole and they got quite envious, but to calm them down my friend and I told them the secret of the sandwich: it had to be ham, if it was something else the tooth is not going to move, and that then they had to touch it many days, in the morning and in the afternoon, if they could, push a lot with their tongue, and that's that, they were going to drop one of them too. And then we were able to continue painting numbers, which was what we had to do that day.

But since we hadn't spoken softly, Sister Luisina came to our table to see what was going on and I had to show her the hole too, but hey, while I was doing that I didn't have to write the numbers, and the others at my table neither, so I didn't mind.

That afternoon A-ma-ling and I could not be together, because my grandmother was going to take me to the house of her friend Doña A-ning, who lived in the Plaza right in front of the horse, and her maid Fe-mi-sang was going to make croutons to soak in chocolate, so as soon as I got home they took off my uniform, changed me to a dress of the ones I used to go out in, and we left.

When we returned it was a little dark, but my grandmother and I were looking at everything very entertained and it took us a long time to arrive.

We heard a lot of screaming and a lot of crying and we didn't know what was going on, but when we got to the living room we saw Mamá Chong, IsabelM, Ne-ning and Lupeng. They were all around my friend, who was the one having the tantrum.

I ran to her side, so she could tell me why she was crying like that, like a baby girl, but she had so many tears that she couldn't even speak, and it had to be Lupeng who told me.

—This afternoon your friend had a small accident: When she was having the snack, one of her teeth fell out and she swallowed it!

Golly gosh, that was a great disaster! And I who had been so calm eating croutons! I felt a great sorrow, that kind where you cry, but I held on, I went to where A-ma-ling was and I told her:

—Look, don't worry, if the little mouse comes tonight and leaves me something tomorrow we will share it and that's that. And shut up, because everyone is going to laugh at you!

And she got quiet.

That night, when I was in bed, all I wanted was for poor Mr. Pérez to get well, take my tooth and leave me something, to give half to my friend, so I fell asleep right away and all night.

In the morning my tooth was missing: under the bed there were two packages and another letter!

I called Ne-ning so that she could help me read it very quickly, we opened it right away and this is what it said:

"Since I know that yesterday you had a huge displeasure, here are some things and I hope you are still good girls. Signed RP "

What a thrill!

I didn't even want to open my package until I saw my friend!

When I saw her at the school door, I gave her her package, I showed her the letter and told her everything it said, because I had memorized everything.

We opened our packages and look: Chocolate bars, strawberry candies and even two gold coins, the ones that had chocolate inside!

We were super happy, we went into class, and that's that.

CINEMA

There were two cinemas in Turgalium.

Every night Mamá Chong and my papá went to see movies, which is what you do when you go to the cinema.

Sometimes the two of them went alone, sometimes with their friends or with my mother's cousins, who also always wanted to go.

But I had never gone to the movies.

And neither did my friend.

That's why many times I asked my mother:

—What was the movie last night like? Were there many princesses? How many fairies did it have? Look, come on, tell me....

But it seems to me that she didn't like those movies very much. She preferred others and when she saw on the poster that a movie theater was showing one of princesses and that, she went to the other.

A-ma-ling and I wanted to go some day, but they never took us.

Finally, one Saturday afternoon, while we were cutting out paper dolls, my sister Ne-ning came to where we were and said to my friend:

—Tomorrow afternoon, after lunch, I will take you to the movies, to the children's session; tell your mamá that you will stay for lunch with us, so we don't waste time.

Because the movies were always at night, almost at the time we had to go to bed, but on Sundays they played one at four, so that all the children could go and that is what was called the children's session.

We were so happy and stopped cutting, because we had to prepare everything, think about the dresses and shoes that we were going to wear, talk about the film, well, a lot of work and maybe we'd make a mistake, and cut off their legs or their heads or wrists.

And what we wanted was for all those hours to pass, that the day would end and the other would come running, but even though we looked more than a thousand times at the cuckoo clock that was hanging on the wall, the next day never came.

On Sunday morning, when Feipang found out, he also wanted to go with the three of us but, although it took us a long time, in the end we just convinced him and we had to give him our whole allowance, but we didn't care, because it would have been horrible to have to take him, and with our pesetas he was calm.

We met Titing on the upper park and he told us that he had seen the poster in the Plaza, that it was going to be a very ugly movie, that we'd better stay at home playing games, and that he was going with Ne-ning, that we could go another day when he saw that there was a beautiful one and many other things, but we did not pay any attention to him, as though he was going to fool us. Ha! We were not dopes.

Even though lunch was seafood soup and croquettes which we loved we were so nervous we could hardly eat and kept asking —What time is it? Is it four already? Do we have to leave now? Come on Ne-ning, run and put on your high heels.

Imagine how disgusting if just for eating we ran out of time, they closed the cinema and we were locked out on the street.

But that didn't happen, we were really lucky that day.

The time came. We put on our scarves and overcoats, got our tubes of sunflower seeds, and went real happy, holding her hands, to the theater called "Gabriel y Galán Cinema Theatre"* because it belonged to those two brothers and they put that names so that everybody would know it was theirs. First, the two of them used to watch the movie alone, but their mamá told them not to be greedy, and to let in other people, donkeys or cats or dogs no, just people who lived in Turgalium; and since they were good and obedient they paid attention, and that's that.

* see *Notes on Chapters*

It was quite close to my house, in front of where Cheng-Chu lived, in a huge Palace that had been owned by a King or Queen a thousand years ago, but since they no longer used it, they loaned it to those brothers.

Before entering, you had to climb quite a few stairs, not as many as those in my house or A-ma-ling's, but many.

My sister bought the tickets, which were papers that put the name of the movie, the time and many more letters, and they let us in.

We both kept those papers as a souvenir, although they were already a bit torn, and look, we told the guy at the door to be careful, but he replied that if he did not tear them, he would not let us in, so we told him okay and we entered.

That cinema was beautiful. It had many parts and A-ma-ling and I began to look at everything, although my sister and a guy called "Thusher" were rushing us and they wanted us to go to our seats, but as I told my friend:

—Let them hold on for a moment, look how long we've had to wait, so many years, well now they can leave us in peace!

And we kept looking, take that.

In one part of the cinema, on the floor, there were the seats, which were made of pure velvet, all connected together, not like the seats in the houses that could move around and it was very easy to take them to another place, to any room, or next to the balconies to watch people go by, or paint, or whatever. It seems to me that they had stuck them together like this so that they would quietly sit there.

They called that "The Orchestra," Ne-Ning told us, look at that silly name, because it was not an orchestra with violins and bugles, and the things that the orchestras have, there were only armchairs and in the middle a corridor for people to walk past, but since my sister was not one of those liars and she had never told a lie, we believed it because it was surely true.

Around that orchestra, making a very wonderful circle were "The Mess-a-Nines," which were also armchairs, but not at all a mess because we later went to touch them and we saw that they were also velvet, very soft and very good.

As my sister and "Thusher" were getting to be a big pain, pulling our sleeves and behind us other people pushing us, we went to our seats so they'd leave us in peace, but we kept looking at everything.

In the middle, also hanging around the orchestra and above the nine messes, were The Boxes. You could not go up there, it was forbidden and only some who had bought them a year before entered. They were very cute, like small rooms more than like cardboard or wooden boxes, but they only had three walls and on the other side no wall, so that those who were inside could see the film and so they believed they were at home, in the living room or in the closet. If they wanted they could invite their friends, but they all had to be adulterers — girls were not allowed because maybe they thought they were dopes who were going to be crying all the time, but I don't remember if my sister told us or not.

I don't know how those boxes could be floating in the air and without falling, that was a very mysterious mystery, but there they were, and look, inside there were some fat people, the kind that weighed eighty-five or one hundred and four kilos, but they didn't collapse. Surely the boxes must have been stuck onto the walls with some large nails, or glued with glue paste, which was the one my friend and I used, and with which you had to be very careful because otherwise you would have two fingers together forever. A girl at our school table accidentally glued three fingers and had to take them off with a saw, it hurt a lot and she got many liters of blood, which she told us herself.

At the top, almost at the ceiling, was "The Roost," which was where the villeins and others who were a little bad would put themselves, to make a lot of noise and throw things at those below. They were a drag and "Thusher" was scolding them all the time, but they didn't pay any attention to him.

We started to eat our seeds, because that was mandatory in the cinema, if you didn't have seeds they wouldn't let you in. Even if you didn't want to, you had to do it, which Titing had explained to us well. Because he had told us very clearly:

—You always have to go to the movies with a good tube of sunflower seeds. If you say that you have them hidden and it is not true, you can get ready for what is going to happen to you. If you die at that moment, the devils come, they grab you by the hair and drag you to the street, they leave you lying there and you die forever and ever.

But we were very calm, because Ne-ning had gone to Miz Manuela's stall in the morning and had bought us two large tubes.

The lights were turned off and the movie finally started.

But it wasn't the movie we wanted!

It was something called the "Headlines," what a cheat, there was that Paquito who was making us dizzy for a whole morning, telling us about the Moors of Africa and all those stories, only that in the Headlines he was not with the Moors, nothing more than he was walking with other people and saying:

—This reservoir is inaugurated!

Well, it's boring, as if we cared about that...

After a long time the lights were turned on again and A-ma-ling asked my sister:

—When is the movie really going to start?

—Right away, but you have to be still, now Thusher is checking that we all have seeds, she answered very softly.

So we held on and waited another thousand hours.

They turned off all the lights again, so that the cinema would stay like nighttime. And finally the movie began!

It was "Snow White and the Seven Dwarves." Precious.

And on top of that, Lupeng had read us the story, so we knew everything that was happening and what was going to happen, with the bad witch and the apple and the dwarves, who were very good, and the prince, well the whole story, but we cried a little when poor Snow White fell asleep and was not able to wake up.

Look if it had happened to us, how disgusting!

But since we weren't princesses or had stepmothers, we could be very calm....

When everything was over, the lights were turned on again, we put on our coats and went outside.

Ne-ning kept asking us:

—Did you like it? Wasn't it a beautiful movie? Come on, now the three of us are going to get lemon cakes at the sweets store Basilio's, for a snack before we go home!

Of course we liked it! It was very pretty, and we were never going to forget it, but I said to my friend: — From today on, don't even think about eating an apple! Just in case....

And she agreed.

FIFTH SECTION: SPRING

PALM SUNDAY

More or less when spring came, Holy Week came too, and we had vacation again at school!

On a Friday the nuns got sorrow.

We didn't know what sad things they were, but they said:

—Today is Friday of Sorrows.

And they would send us home for almost two weeks. What luck!

The first time we heard it, my friend and I thought they were talking about a friend of theirs whose name was Sara, but another girl at our table told us no, it was because they had gotten very sick, with a lot of pains, I think in the belly, and that since they could not be in any class, we had better go home, so that those pains also did not enter us.

Sister Luisina seemed to have many of those, because she made a face, like old and scrunched up more than ever, but I did not ask so as not to bug her.

So... free to do what we wanted! How great.

The next day A-ma-ling and I, with our mamás, Ne-ning, and Lupeng went to Shops Street to buy new things. It happened like this:

It was because we had to buy at least one new thing for each one of us.

And why did we have to buy something new?

Well, because Ne-ning, the night before, had told me a very important thing:

"Debut something new Palm Sunday, or lose your hand for sure one day."

I almost couldn't sleep that night, and besides, I hadn't even been able to ask Mamá Chong if that was true, because she had gone to the movies with Papá Bo-ling, and when I asked my nanny and also my brother Man-o-ling, they didn't even want to answer me and then I got put to bed, and I couldn't get out of there until the morning, but as soon as I got up, and had breakfast, and they put my clothes on, I went to my friend's house to tell her because I was very worried.

And they had told her that too! I mean, it was true.

We asked IsabelM if she could take us to buy something, and she said yes, we would go to Shops Street, but first she was going to call Mamá Chong so that we could all go together, and that's what we did later.

And the thing is that everyone knew that Sunday was Palm Sunday, and we had to show off something so as not to be left with only one hand, because that was a drag, and you could almost not do things, not even button your coat.

From our houses to the shopping street it was very far, it took us at least five hours or more to get there, but we didn't care because we had nothing to do that morning; Mamá Chong and IsabelM would stop every minute, to talk to a friend who was walking on the other side, or to see something, or for I don't know what, and meanwhile we had time to run a race and return.

Ne-ning and Lupeng, they weren't friends like us, just neighbors and sisters of ours, so at first, when we were still going past the theater, they hardly talked much, because they weren't close friends and couldn't tell secrets, but as it took us so long, by the time we finally got there, they had become very good friends and were having a great time.

Lupeng warned us,

—Let's see you behave yourselves, even if it's just for a day.

Well! ... Not even if we were tiny little girls! What a dope.

Shops Street was called that because it was where all the shops were, or many; well, there were other streets that also had stores, but they were for food, steaks and sardines and that, but the stores that we liked were in the one called that.

When we finally arrived there were a lot of people looking at the windows, going into the sweets stores, to buy lemon sponge cake and pies and pastries and things for dessert and tea time.

Because as all of us who lived in Turgalium were very fond of sweets, there were two bakeries on that street, Basilio's, who I think was always very tired, because he had to bake his cakes at night and he couldn't go to bed, or sleep not even a minute; if he fell asleep the villeins would come and eat them all; and he was always sitting at his brazier table very cozy, and doing nothing more than watching while people chose their sweets; and the other sweets store, which belonged to a lady named Mrs. Úrsula Go-a-wei, which was open a lot but those who came from Las Huertinas and Madroñera and La Cumbre, and from other towns believed that they could not go in there, because the sign said U. GO-A-WEI, but we knew that we could go in, because that lady was a friend of our mamás, and whenever she saw us she gave us café o-lay candies which were very soft and very rich, and besides, Señora Go-a-wei had red hair. She was not a redhead as they sometimes called my mamá, her hair was really the color red, and we loved that, because she was the only person in the world who had that color. Before, she had it normal, I think blond, but one day when she was baking a cake and was in a hurry, a can of paint fell on her head, it spread all over her hair and it stayed that way forever, and it was never put back like before.

Every time we saw her, A-ma-ling would say to me:

—As soon as I'm twenty-seven, I'm going to tell Go-a-wei to put something from that can in my hair, and also on my shoes, and you'll see how beautiful I am going to be.

And I didn't say anything to her so she wouldn't get angry, but I liked her better with her blond hair....

The pharmacies were also on that street, the one belonging to the So-lís, whose daughter was at our table at school, and another that had a lot of salt, it seems to me, that of the Sal-ta-zars, and in those was where they sold aspirin, and cough syrup, and calcium-20, and many things for when you were very sick, and there we only liked to go in to buy Jua-no-la licorice pills, and some candies that when you sucked inside, they would sting your whole mouth and nose and throat. And An-dra-da's store, which had chairs and tables, and things like those that are put in the rooms, and So-li-ta's store, which had many notebooks, and pencils, and books, and newspapers and that was where the Three Wise Men went for the toys, and for the things they brought us on Three Kings Day, (I am pretty sure the Kings got them there, because when we didn't see them anymore in the window, sometimes we saw other children with them the next day); and there were also two shoe stores on that street: the one belonging to the Ci-van-tos, who were very close friends with Mamá Chong and my papá, and we knew them a lot, because they were the godparents of my little brother An-dong-ni, and the other, which was of some people that I think maybe gave you a cane when you entered there, the Cane-a-la-da. One store, although it was open, was the one belonging to I.M. Klost or something like that, but I'm not quite sure of that name; there were also two stores where they sold gold and diamond rings, and emerald necklaces, and earrings and watches, and all of that, which were called jewelers; the first was of some who surely had very long beards, at least five meters, that reached down to the ground, the Bir-dos, and the other was of some who must have been sometimes bent over, who were the Cur-ve-dos, or a name like that, I do not remember exactly; and at the beginning of the street, at the top that was attached to the Plaza, there was a store with materials with which you could make dresses and sheets and bags, and lots of other things that were made of cloth. They called the owners of that store the So- leens, and I don't know why they were called that, because they were a bit fat, but hey, that thing about names in Turgalium was always very strange, and when you got one of those, you had to put up with it.

But we didn't go into any of those stores, or any of all the others, because we went first to La Giralda, to see things and choose.

Before the Giralda there was a store that A-ma-ling and I loved. It was called Ro-drí-guez Stores, Materials and Ready to Wear, and it had two very large mirrors next to the door that reached up to the ceiling, where we could make faces, stretch our mouths, wink our eyes and do a lot of other nonsense to make us laugh, but that day we couldn't do almost anything, because our sisters gave us a jerk and ran into La Giralda.

They bought us both beautiful socks, of a kind that had many little holes and were called "openwork socks," and which could not be used in the winter, because the holes were very cold. Mine were white and hers were pink. Now we could be calm because we had something to debut when we went to the procession.

And that although in the afternoon something happened to us that almost made us lose a hand the next day.

We were at my house playing, and when we passed by Mamá Chong's room we saw the package with the socks and my friend said to me:

—Hey, if I try on your socks and you try on mine, that's not canceling debut, right?

It seemed like a great idea to me, so we ran to her house to get hers, to try on without anyone knowing.

When we got there we had to search a lot, because we did not know where IsabelM had put them, and look how easy it was, they were in a place called "The Reception," which was silly to call it that, because it was not for any reception, it was only used to pass through, and as soon as we saw them we took them and again we crossed the upper park, we went up to my house, and we got the two packages into the room with the fireplace where there was no one.

We already had our socks in hand, we were taking off our shoes and the ones we were wearing, when Feipang came in with a friend and said:

—Get out of here immediately, I have a business to do!

And the thing is that even though he was smaller than us, he was very bossy, and if you didn't obey him he would get very angry, so we left and decided not to do the try on in case someone else caught us.

On Palm Sunday we went to a very beautiful procession, with Jesus Christ riding a little donkey walking through all the streets, and we all debuted and showed off new things, so we did not see anyone without any hand, not even their fingers were missing.

We also all had twig bouquets and palms, so they could put holy water on top, which was almost like normal water, but you couldn't drink it, and it was the kind that was in the churches so that we crossed ourselves when we entered, and it seems to me that they would bring it from heaven early in the morning to the Plaza, they would throw it in the fountain, and then those from the churches would go with a bucket and take some away.

When the olive twigs and the palms were well soaked, they could be put on the balconies, and you could remove what was from last year, but you could not be without an olive twig bouquet or palm bouquet for a minute in case the Demon came, or some of his little devils. Every time the demon was going to enter a house, if there was a bouquet, he would bump into it, get hit by a good punch, and he had to run to hell again. But to let those in the house know that he had come, he left a brown stain somewhere in the bouquet. My brother thought it was a stain because he blasted a pooper, but I don't know exactly that.

When we removed the bouquets that were on our balconies, they had a lot of stains, we were counting them until we had to go to eat, and we didn't even have time to get to the middle of the bouquet, we didn't know how to count more, that's the truth, because there were a lot of stains, but we stayed very calm, because in our houses, at least, no demons had been able to enter, so there!

And now Holy Week was beginning.

It was almost like one of the other weeks, but it was holy.

On Monday, Tuesday and Wednesday we could do our normal things on vacation: jump rope, read and draw in our notebooks, go for a walk with other girls, or be in our houses playing house, or with our dolls, or cutting out dresses to put on the paper dolls, which was very difficult, but we loved it, and we almost did it ourselves.

HOLY THURSDAY

But on Thursday we already had a lot of work again because it was Holy Thursday.

And that day, and those that followed afterwards, we had to be very good, because that was when some very bad people had killed Jesusito as soon as he got older, when they already called him Jesus Christ.

In The Book of Our Children he taught people called Jews, who were drawn very ugly and had very long beards, but in their hair, on the part of the ears, they had beautiful ringlets and we really liked those ringlets. I thought maybe they were Jews because they made a lot of jewelry, like I said, like on Shops Street, but I am not sure how that works.

In the morning we could play, but when we finished eating, come on again! and change our clothes again, have our hair combed and make us beautiful, because we had to go to something called "The Offices," which was like a very long mass, and had nothing to do with those "Thoffices" at A-ma-ling's house or going to some office like a post office but was in the church, and it lasted eight hours or more, and many people took a nap for a while, but not us, because we were almost in the front row to see everything well.

Since Ne-ning and Lupeng had already become a bit close friends, from the day of shopping, they were the ones who took us to San Francisco, because for that The Offices thing you had to go where you were supposed to, and if you lived on one street you went to San Martín, and on other streets, then to San Francisco, and you couldn't go to the other church because if you went, a policeman would pick you up and put you in jail, which Titing told us the night before, and told us that a friend of his had tried to enter San Francisco one year (and San Martín was his turn), and a very angry policeman came, put many chains around his neck, on his hands and also a fat ball on his feet, and he took him to jail, and he was still locked up there, and they gave him only stale bread to eat, and dirty water to drink. His mother went to see him every day, but they wouldn't even let her in, and she had to see him through a very tiny window full of spider webs, buff, what a disgusting thing.

The Offices thing was different from the other things that priests did on normal days, and even though in Turgalium there were many churches, that could only be in those two places, and that's that. And thank goodness for the two of us, and for everybody from our houses, that we had to go to the same church because otherwise, what a mess!

Ne-ning and Lupeng were wearing black dresses, and on their heads something called "La Mantilla," that was like a very large and very black veil over their hair, and so it would not slip off they had stuck in huge combs, but so carefully that they would not go down into their brains and make them corpses.

They were both gorgeous and my sister had let Lupeng wear some of her needle heels, so they were both very tall, although Lupeng didn't know how to walk with them as well as Ne-ning, that's the truth, but we didn't tell them because, as those days we had to be very good...

We arrived in San Francisco, and after a lot of squashing because everyone wanted to enter at the same time, The Offices began.

We did not like it much, come on! stand up! sit down! and get on your knees all the time, they did not give us a moment's peace, because you had to do that, if you made a mistake Ne-ning or Lupeng gave us a pinch that hurt a lot, and on top of that, you couldn't cry or anything so that those around you wouldn't think you were a baby girl; but then, when we were a little bored, there came a part that we really did like: they put twelve men sitting at the altar, they quietly told them to take off their shoes and socks, they put a basin with hot water in front of each one and a priest came and told us that he was the representative of Jesusito, or of Jesus Christ, I can't remember which of the two, he got down on his knees and, holy cow, wash everyone's feet!

I think some of them were a bit ashamed, because their feet were very piggish and very black from so much filth, but the priest told them that it didn't matter, that he was going to leave them very clean, and that's that.

Luckily we hadn't brought my brother Feipang, because since he had this habit of throwing himself on the ground and taking off his shoes when he got angry, his feet were almost always dirty, and the priest would have had to spend at least an hour rubbing them with soap, as his nanny had to do every night, and then I don't know how many more hours that Offices would have lasted.

At last they finished and we all went to my house because we had to have the snack of chocolate with churros and hurry up because the procession was soon.

Ne-ning and Lupeng did not even have time to eat a churro, poor things!

As soon as we finished, we were out on the street again, but this time with Mamá Chong and IsabelM, hand in hand so as not to get lost among so many people. And with the bad brother, uff.

At least my two little brothers stayed at home, because it was already very dark and they had to be in bed, naturally.

Man-o-ling and AngelMaring also had to parade in the Procession, but they did not wear a mantilla or comb, they wore black robes to the ground and then a white cape, and on their heads, a very tall hood that covered everything and it reached very high, at least twenty feet.

With those hoods you couldn't know who was inside, but the one who was hiding there could see you, because the hoods had two holes for the eyes and another for the mouth, so that they could breathe and did not drown right away, and they also had to carry a very fat candle lit all the time.

If it accidentally went out, someone would come and give them a hit on the back that hurt a lot, so they had to be staring at it all the time, just in case.

A-ma-ling and I told our brothers to signal us as they passed, but Man-o-ling said that it was forbidden to speak when you walked lined up, it would be better to put a ribbon on the candle, so we would know it was them.

We and our mamás were at the door of San Francisco, in a great place to be able to see everything very well, but some villeins came pushing us, and until they were in front they did not stop, well, what rude behavior! But we did not say anything about that; we had to be good on Holy Thursday.

The first one they carried out they said was Saint John. I think he was very happy, because he was laughing all the time.

But we saw that it was not really Saint John, that he was already dead and in heaven; it was one that looked like him and was called "the image of Saint John," it was made of wood and wearing a very lovely outfit, and it had many lighted candles and many flowers around it, and Titing told us that when the real Saint John saw that image he said that he liked it very much, that it was almost the same as him, only that it could not speak or eat or anything, so that he could be very calm in heaven, while the image went through the streets in processions.

Then came another image that scared us!

It was of María Magdalena, one who was a bit bad, I think, like the ladies who lived on the steep Cuesta de San Andrés, and we thought she was a little crazy and that she hadn't even combed her hair for a walk in the procession. Her hair was all full of tangles, and since it was quite long, it looked awful. And a slightly dirty dress too.

It is known that the Magdalena of flesh and bone, which I don't even know if she was a Saint or one of those Virgins, had to be doing something like the bad women and she had not had time to go see her image, not like Saint John, who had come down from heaven in the morning to see his, but of course, if she was busy, what could the poor thing do...?

When she passed by us, she looked at us a little, and we started to tremble, what a fright, at least we were able to stoop down behind the villeins, and thank goodness they carried her off right away, because she really scared us.

Then an angel came with a cup in his hands and with Jesus Christ kneeling.

And that image was really pretty!

The Angel had a blue dress with all the edges of gold and silver, and the cup was also of pure gold. And huge wings to fly up to the sky in a moment. Titing told us that one day he had gone to heaven eighty-three times, and that he had not gotten tired at all, that he had not even stopped to eat a French omelette, because he had so many errands to run, from Turgalium to Heaven and from Heaven another time down, he couldn't even stop, and the poor guy always had a lot of work.

But that night he was there with us and so happy.

Jesus Christ had a very sad face, it seems to me that he already knew that something bad was going to happen to him, so the Angel kept saying to him:

—Don't worry, drink a little from my glass, you'll see how we'll get away from those Jews who are a drag!

But Jesusito didn't believe it, because he knew more than the Angel, ha.

And then many more images followed, but we were already a little sleepy because it was very dark, and we almost ignored them, what we wanted was for the mantilla veils and the pointed hoods to appear, and that's that.

When the hoods began to arrive, everyone fell silent, only the Music Band and the drums could be heard, which made a lot of noise.

A-ma-ling and I stood on tiptoe to see if we could find our brothers, but since there were at least five hundred and forty hoods or fifty-nine or more, it was extremely difficult.

We were looking and hunting around when one of them, as he passed us, said to us in a very evil voice:

—You can't hunt around in processions.

And he kept walking so calm.

And we stopped looking for Man-o-ling and AngelMaring, in case they hit us with the stick....

At that moment, the mantillas appeared!

That was really nice, they went in a row, on each side of the saints and they were all gorgeous, but our sisters were the most beautiful and, as soon as they saw us, they said hello but quietly, and they even sent us a kiss! since they were not going to punish them like they did to the poor hoods....

After those ladies and big girls and many priests with the Authorities, the procession ended for us and we ran home.

Because the procession went on and on: they had to go to walk the images through all the streets of Turgalium, for all those who did not enter San Francisco, or in the surrounding streets, to see them, but since we had already seen everything, well, we didn't even have to look out from our balconies and we could go to bed.

GOOD FRIDAY

Friday they told us that it was the most important day of all that Holy Week, because it was the day that Jesusito was killed, and we all had to have a lot of sorrow and a lot of pain.

As soon as I had breakfast I went to A-ma-ling's house to see how much pain she was in, because nothing hurt me anywhere, not even a little, and I asked her:

—Hey, does your belly hurt? Do your ears hurt? Does your head hurt?

She told me that no, that nothing hurt either, and that she was not very sorry, but if they asked us, the best thing was to say yes, that we had a lot of sorrow and enormous pain, so that the adulterers would not get angry with us.

So we did.

Every time that morning someone asked us how we were doing, we just said:

—With great pain and great sorrow.

And that's that.

It seems to me that those who asked us did not care how we were, that they only asked because it was the custom, or because of education, because when they heard us they only said:

—What two good girls!

And that was something different from what we heard all the time, naturally.

In the morning that day we were cutting out paper dresses because we had a lot of new ones, a whole notebook, which my sister Ne-ning had bought for us, and in the notebook there were also shoes and boots and bags and headbands and everything, so we could put a lot of different outfits on our paper dolls and change their shoes, until we started to fool around and put sandals on them with a winter coat, or a tank top with some rubber boots, and since we started laughing, we had to stop doing so many silly things.

On Good Friday you could not eat anything that had meat, or something with meat broth, not even in secret or even if no one saw you, it was a sin of the ones that sent you straight to the kettles of that Pedro Botero.

Nobody could ever eat meat on any Friday of the year, that was a very fat sin, and it couldn't be done, but those of Turgalium were allowed to, because we had something called "The Paper Bull." Man-o-Ling had read it in one of his books and it was true, and he told us about it, but on Good Friday they took that Paper Bull away from us, so, in all the houses that day we had to eat chickpeas with rice, and then fish, and that was also quite tasty, but that was a day you really wanted to eat ham, or a steak with potatoes, or something that in ordinary days you might not like so much, but if you couldn't, you couldn't.

And, as soon as we brushed our teeth, again, come on, and change to go to The Offices again!

That day, as we had gone the day before, we already knew what they were like.

Well, no.

That time they were different, they did not wash anyone's feet or anything, but it also lasted many hours, and people prayed and cried a lot, and we also cried a lot, so that they would not think that we had no pain or sorrow from that, and when we were crying, suddenly we were really sad, because the priest told us that they put Jesusito on a cross and put a spear in him, they had also put a crown on him, but not that of kings and princes, the one they put on him was made of thorns, which pricked a lot, so his whole head got full of blood and scabs, the blood got into his eyes and he could hardly see anything, and on his feet and hands they tied him with some very fat ropes, and on top of that they put some very large nails so that he could not get off the cross, or escape, or anything.

And then they put some others on crosses on both sides, I don't remember if they were gypsies or villeins, but they did tell us that one of them was terrible and did nothing but stupid things, but the other, whose name was Barra I don't know what, he was a bit good, although he had stolen a few things in a store, and I think that a chicken too, and he immediately became a good friend of Jesusito, and told him many secrets and many things about his family, about his school and from his town, so Jesusito told him that later, as soon as he finished everything on the cross, he could go to his father's house for a snack or a drink, and that since that house was heaven, there was plenty of room and it was possible to stay to live there, and Barra was very happy and said okay, he would go later.

The other guy, he did not invite him or anything, because he was so bad and an awful drag, so, heck with him. Take that!

And then he died.

Under the cross, which was thirty feet high or more, were the Virgin and Saint John and that Magdalena, and a few other people, all crying and screaming and quite angry at what they had done to him, on top of how good he was, but a lot of those other people were such a drag.

Saint John was not like when in the procession, he was very sad because they had killed his close friend, look, imagine if they had killed A-ma-ling, I would have a very great sorrow, and the same would happen to her, so we understood him very well, but we couldn't go and say anything to him because we were on a bench a bit crowded by other people, and if we left maybe then we wouldn't find Ne-ning and Lupeng, so we stayed still.

That Magdalena did nothing but pull her hair, and look very furious, I think she even wanted to spit on some, and then we realized that that's why the day before she had been so angry, so sloppy and so ugly, because maybe someone had told her something about what was going to happen, and we decided that from then on we weren't going to be afraid of her, and that's that.

And the Virgin was the one who had the most sorrow of all, of course, since they had stabbed into and killed her child - imagine how Mamá Chong or IsabelM would be if they had done it to us... Thank goodness, none of those Jews lived in Turgalium and we could be calm.

As The Offices lasted so many hours, we did not even have time to return home for tea time snack, take that! Another procession began immediately and, on top of that, that day there were two, one that was the normal one, and another very late at night that was called "The Silence" and those who went had to be Dumb or a Mute or, if they were ordinary people, they had to sew their mouths with a thread so that no word escaped them, not even one.

Mamá Chong had never been able to go to that procession, because she liked to be talking all the time, and she didn't want to sew her mouth, but Papá Bo-ling did go for many years and told us that it was very beautiful, that only Jesusito was in the procession, and dead.

We believed that they kept him in an uncovered trunk so that everyone could see him, but my father told us that it was not a trunk, that where they had placed him was called the coffin, which was a difficult word and we had to write it down and everything, it seems to me that not even Man-o-ling knew that word, how difficult it was, because it wasn't coughing like it sounded, which was very difficult but we knew because Don Eli-ang was always doing that, and since we learned it, we could use it all the time to put those who were corpses there, even if they were normal people, not from heaven.

With our mothers we went back to the same place as on Thursday, to see everything very well, and that day we did not let anyone sneak in front of us, for that we had arrived early and we had not even had a snack.

In the Procession, all the same people came out that the priest had told us about when the sorrow thing, so we already knew the whole story, we didn't even have to cry, well, in the end we did cry a little when we saw the Lord nailed to the cross and with a lot of pain from all the nails stuck in, but we got over it right away, because we were watching for the hoods, and for those who were dressed in veils of mantillas, and we could not be crying and looking at the same time, right?

And that day our sisters could not even give us a sign that they had seen us, because since they had to go to The Silence later, they decided that it was better not to speak in that first one, so that when they were in the other they would already know what they had to do and not make a mistake, so we were left just wishing.

And there was no bugle band either, just drums, because they told us that all of us in Turgalium were in mourning and no songs could be heard, so we got a little bored, we were hungry and what we wanted was to go home and that's that.

HOLY SATURDAY

On Saturday, although it was called Holy, we no longer had to be super-good, just a little good, but if you did something that was what they told us was naughty, nothing happened, Buff, what a rest! so many days in a row being super-good was tiring, and it was a lot of work.

The first thing that happened that day was that one of his students gave Papá Bo-ling a live lamb, so that Man-o-ling could take him for a walk in the Plaza on Sunday.

He was so cute, white all over and he was very happy to be in my house, although they put him upstairs, in the rooms on the terrace, so that he would think he was in the country, although there was no grass or anything there, but that was better than to be in a flat, at least.

Then we both had to go with our sisters, to buy espadrilles.

And we needed them for the Chíviri, the big celebration in the Plaza.

Because since our feet didn't stay the same all the time, and they got bigger without us realizing it, and since we weren't

Chinese, the ones we had from the other year didn't work for us anymore, and besides, they were ugly because they had gotten all piggy dirty with stomps, so Ne-ning and Lupeng took us to a store for them, and then to another to buy black ribbons to put on them to hold them on so our feet would not come out.

Lupeng kept saying:

—Oh brother, we don't get a break from these two for a single day! Let's see school start and we can get some peace, because they've got me fed up!

And Ne-ning: —They're horrible! Let's see how they behave today, but I don't trust them one bit...

Well, look what a couple of dummies, and we hadn't even done anything yet that day.

We bought the espadrilles, went to the other store for the ribbons and returned to my house, to have them attached to the espadrilles.

This was a very difficult operation, because they had to pass the ribbons on one side of the fabric, which was on the top, to the other side that was below and through many places and with a lot of work, and they had to do it for many hours very carefully, but when I told Ne-ning why didn't she glue them on, she laughed and said that I was impossible.

So we got bored and went to play with the little lamb.

And then we went to her house to change the dresses of some rag dolls that Lupeng had made for us.

Mine had brown wool hair, because she was dark like me; and A-ma-ling's had yellow hair, so she was blonde. And they both had very long braids, not like us who didn't have braids.

Some girls in our school did have braids and they were gorgeous, but as soon as our hair grew a little longer, Ma-no-long, my papá's barber, cut it off right away, and we couldn't even have ponytails, it was so short, but our dolls, as they had such long hair, even if it was not hair like ours but wool, we could do everything for them: sometimes we made them a braid, other times two pigtails and at the end we put some precious bows; other times we made them a top bun, like my grandmother's, other times we left them all loose; every time we played with them, we put different dresses on them and their hair another way and that is how they looked like different dolls.

When we got tired of that, we went to see the folk skirts that we were going to wear the next day, and before you knew it, it was time for each of us to be in our homes for dinner and sleep.

EASTER SUNDAY

Sunday finally arrived, which was no longer holy or anything like that, it was Easter day, Chíviri day, and we could go back to being normal. We didn't need to be wonderfully good!

It was the day we put on the folk costume dress: the kind called refajo or the other kind, pollera, along with an apron of silk or velvet, embroidered with sequins or beads, a purse almost always the same colors as the refajo, a black silk shirt with long sleeves, and on top a kerchief called "a thousand colors," but it didn't have that many, because once A-ma-ling and I started to count them and there weren't so many, but even though we told our mamás they said that we had to call it that, it was much easier to say that than if you said sixty-three color kerchief or whatever it had, less of a mess, because since kerchiefs were different in each house, you didn't have to count the colors and say "well my kerchief has nineteen colors," or twenty-seven or whatever, and in that they were right.

Other girls wore not a black blouse but a white shirt with embroidered straps and a bodice on top, and then they did not have to wear a scarf.

On the inside we wore white breeches, stockings, which were very scratchy, and esparto grass espadrilles.

And on the ears, some very nice and large pure gold earrings, which had the same pattern to what we had to have on the neck:

the Burgaño, a necklace also made of pure gold balls and in the front a thing like a bug called burgaños, which are daddy-long-legs, very bad and bite, but the ones they put on us for Chíviri didn't bite, because they were not real and were not alive.

Since neither Ne-ning nor I had ear holes, we couldn't wear those pretty earrings, or anything else. Papá Bo-ling didn't want us to be like the African Kaffirs, who put a lot of things on their faces, and on their ears, and in their noses, and everywhere, and he never wanted us to get holes drilled, so, although we would have liked it, we couldn't and couldn't.

When I got up, my sister Ne-ning was already wearing her refajo folk skirt and most of the rest, and mine, along with all the other stuff, was laid out on the parlor table.

My sister's skirt was yellow with black sewed on, all made of felt and it weighed a lot, I think it was seventy kilos or sixty-two. Mine, which had been my sister's before, was green with white sewed on, and it weighed nothing more than a little bit, and both were very pretty.

Also, our kerchiefs had belonged to my grandmother, or my great-grandmother, I no longer remember, and we had to be very careful not to tear or stain them, because Mamá Chong said they were very valuable and very old.

Ne-ning helped me to dress and immediately my friend came with her brothers and sister to get us.

And we all went together to the Plaza, even my brother, the little one who didn't walk very well and had to go very slowly, but we didn't care because that way we could talk about our things.

Ne-ning and Lupeng were already close friends, like us, and held hands. It seems to me that they were copying us a bit but hey, we let them.

Man-o-ling led the little lamb with a red ribbon, so that it would not get envious, because my three brothers had on very lovely kerchiefs, also red, and it was around its neck, but not too tight so that it did not choke.

AngelMaring and Titing also had them, but my brothers were more handsome, which even Don AngelB said when he saw us all on the street, and look, those were his real children and my brothers were only neighbors, but the truth was the truth.

Very many people were in the Plaza, three hundred and fifty thousand or five hundred and thirty at least. If we had counted them, the count would have lasted till the day after tomorrow, and we also didn't know how to count up to so many, there were tons of them.

And all singing:

At Turgalium at Easter time what can compare with this?
Ay, Chíviri, Chíviri, Chíviri, ay, Chíviri, Chíviri, chon.
Outsiders come pouring in like so many slippery fish!
Ay, Chíviri, Chíviri, Chíviri, ay, Chíviri , Chíviri, chon.

And much more, but A-ma-ling and I only knew that little piece.

Feipang told us that he had to leave for a moment and that he was taking the little lamb so that it could look at everything very well.

My sister warned him:

—Oh God, be very careful with him, so he does not get lost. Look, Mamá Chong wants it to stay with us and then when it has a family they will take them all to Las Viñas. Come back soon, we are not going to move from here until you return.

He told her not to worry, he was coming right away.

So we keep singing, dancing and having a yummy time.

A long time passed and Feipang did not return.

Nothing, he did not return.

My sister said,

—Why don't you two go see if you can find him? As there is so much noise here, it may be that he does not know where we are. But don't get lost too. We'll wait for you here, next to the fountain.

My friend and I said good and we left.

We walked around and immediately saw my brother, very happy but without the lamb, what could have happened?

We asked him where it was and he didn't want to answer. He said that if he told us, later he would have to repeat the same story again and that that was very tiring, and I don't know what and I don't know which, he didn't feel like telling us. But he came up to us and said:

—Even though you are stupid, I'm going to give you a peseta each, so you can see how good I am, and clam up.

And mind you, I was older than him! How bossy!

But we took the pesetas and went to the fountain.

As soon as she saw us arrive, Ne-ning came running up to us and asked my brother:

—Where is the lamb? Didn't I tell you to be careful? Come on, let's all look for him, because since he's the only one with a red ribbon, we'll recognize him right away.

And Feipang, who was a lot younger than her, came out with a very powerful voice and said,

—You're a little upset. Calm down. Look and shut up.

(That's what he said, and Holy Word that I'm not making it up: all our mouths hung open that he knew how to say it and on top of that, to my sister, who although she had become his godmother was very bossy too.)

He reached into his pocket and pulled out a gold watch with diamonds all around it! And besides, a very fat packet of pesetas.

Ne-ning got very nervous and we all started looking around, in case the guards came to put him in jail, and look, what were we going to say to Mamá Chong? What a problem, but he sat so calmly on the edge of the fountain and told us:

—Well, me and the lamb were walking around (and that couldn't be said, it was forbidden: you had to say the little lamb and I, because only the badly educated said it the other way, but although they all scolded us if we said it wrong, Feipang said it if he wanted and nothing happened), looking at all the things and we met a very nice gypsy who told me: "Hey Feipang, what a good lambkin you have; that would be very good for me today, because I have to make a lamb fry for the country Turn picnic, can you trade it for something?" Then I looked and saw that he had this good watch so I said:

—Come on, I'll trade it if you give me your watch and ninety-three pesetas, and he said okay and we closed the deal.

But my sister was still very worried, not knowing what we were going to say to Mamá Chong when she saw us arrive without the lamb; Man-o-ling was very sad to have been left without it and even An-dong-ni looked like he was going to cry, so many pouts he made, but Feipang ordered us:

—All for home, we have to eat!

And we went down.

A-ma-ling and her brothers went to their house and the four of us climbed the stairs in great fear. Feipang no, calm as a cucumber.

As soon as Mamá Chong saw us arrive, she asked us:

—Did you have a good time? Were there many people singing and dancing the Chíviri?

Before anyone could answer, Feipang went to her, gave her a big kiss, took out his watch and said:

—Mamá Chong, since that lamb kept saying baaa baaa baaa all the time, and it was going to make you dizzy a lot and upset you and make your heart very bad, I traded it to someone for this precious watch for you. For sure you like it!

And what do you think my mamá did, scold him? Well no, she gave him another kiss and said:

—You are the most wonderful son in the world, always thinking about his mamá!

So we shut up, we went to wash our hands before eating and that's that.

And he kept all those pesetas. And on top of that they didn't scold him or anything!

TAKING A TURN

On Sunday and the next two days in the afternoon, as soon as we finished eating, we had to go running to the San Juan field to do something called "Taking a Turn."

Others went to different places.

Well, it was called the Turn, although nobody had to spin around, or to wait in line, because what it really was, was walking out to our countryside with a snack and being there for many hours, singing, dancing and eating again, and that's that.

And instead of having the same snack as every day, they made us potato omelettes, breaded steaks and sandwiches of many things.

The field of San Juan those days, as it was not fair time, was not full of cows and donkeys and piggies, there were only people of all sizes, because many families went there with everyone, grandparents, aunts and uncles and even babies, who couldn't even eat the breaded steaks, but they took them too. Maybe it was so that they wouldn't be left alone in the house and they would start crying a lot, I don't know.

We took ours, we got a great place and the nannies put a tablecloth on the grass so that the bugs wouldn't come to eat our things.

Because the ants and the beetles and grasshoppers and all those loved the snacks we brought, and they were waiting to grab something, but Man-o-ling said to all of them:

—If you even think of getting onto the tablecloth, I'm going to make a smishing-smashing that will teach you!

Titing said that my brother had not said that word, that it was another, but we heard it very clearly. Besides, he was a liar, so it was that word.

A bunch of ants who were waiting on the edge of the tablecloth pretended they were looking at the picture on the cloth, the smart alecks, but we all knew what they wanted: eat whatever they felt like and then dirty up the rest, which is what they liked to do.

We had a great time and when we got home it was late at night and we were very tired.

On Monday and Tuesday we did the same, because we still had vacations, but when we got back from the Turn on Tuesday night, we found an urgent telegram from the nuns: Their tummy pains had passed and we had to go back to school, right away, the next day!

Well, well, and we thought they would last forever and ever....

Don Teodoro must have given them a good syrup.

SECTION SIX: SUMMER

ICE CREAM

We liked all the seasons, but one of the favorites was summer, and also the season that had Christmas, which I think was in winter.

In the summer time, since we didn't have school, we could do a lot of things all day.

As Mamá Chong had something every month called "*myrents*," which meant that some people who used some of the houses she had, gave her money to use them, in the summer, in the afternoon after siesta, when A-ma-ling would come to pick me up, my mamá would tell us:

—Girls, go to TrickyJoey's and buy a pack of Six-in-One, they paid my rents!

We would quickly grab the pesetas, go down the stairs, cross the park and the street and enter the bar shouting:

—Joey, sell us a 6-in-1 pack!

And as soon as we had it, we would take the same way back again, well this time much faster so that the Six-in-One would arrive without coming apart.

Because the Six-in-One were frozen chocolates, inside they were vanilla and outside chocolate. You had to know, because if you thought they were some normal chocolates and you waited a long time to eat them, then they got all smushed together and were not chocolates and not ice cream, and not anything.

Mamá Chong would open the box and she gave us two each and she kept two others.

And the thing is, my mamá was not like other mamás, who were very greedy and kept the whole box of Six-in-One. Not her. She always shared it with us.

Also, in summer was when my house made ice cream and popsicles.

At A-ma-ling's they didn't make them, I don't know if because they didn't have an ice cream maker, or because they didn't know how to make them.

On the day they made ice cream, we all got together, even if at other times we weren't very friendly.

They always made just two kinds: meringue milk ice cream or custard ice cream.

The meringue milk was quite easy, and even we could have made it, but they would not let us go near the fire, in case we burned ourselves or like that, but we watched how they made it, and we knew it was very easy: first you put the milk in a saucepan, with a lot of sugar, a cinnamon stick and a lemon peel, it was stirred with a wooden spoon, and so on all the time until it was well boiled, and then, when that potion was a little cold and was no longer hot, it was all poured into the ice cream churn and it came out ice cream.

For the custard ice cream, it was different but also very easy: you had to separate the egg yolks, and that really was the most complicated, because no egg white could be left, and then you put in lots of sugar and milk, and that was boiled too. So, it looked a lot like custard pudding, but we couldn't eat it even though we liked it a lot, because it was for making ice cream.

The ice churn was a gadget that seemed just wonderful to A-ma-ling and me, not to mention to my little brothers: it had a round metal part, like a can but without a lid, and that was where you put the liquid before it became ice cream, then a hollow place to put crushed ice and big salt, and that could not be mixed with the other, because then it would not come out ice cream, it would be total pig slop. Titing tried it once, and when we tasted it, we didn't like it at all, yuck, disgusting.

And on the outside it had some wooden boards, which were held together by iron hoops, or I don't know what.

And then, on top, there was a crank that connected all that, and that when it moved it made the liquid go round and round, and little by little it turned to ice cream.

What we liked the most was turning the crank, but Feipang and Titing got very angry, they shoved us and almost did not let us, but A-ma-ling and I found out that if we pinched them, they let go of the crank and went to tattle, and meanwhile we could stay at the head of the line, hah! we were girls but not dopes!

What happened is that the ice cream did not come right away, and when we cranked a while we got bored when some minutes went by and still the ice cream did not come, so we left, to play with our dolls, and we let the ice cream come when it would come.

The popsicles were much easier to make: you put orange juice, or milk with Nesquik, in some little plastic things we had, and some wooden sticks, and put them in the ice box, in the part where the ice was, and that's that.

There was nothing to do, just wait a while and then eat them.

Other times, especially if it was Sunday, Mamá Chong would buy some blocks called "Triflavors" and she would cut them and put them between two waffers, and they were like the ice cream we bought outside on the street. Ooo, how delicious!

SWIMS

In summer, when it was super hot, which was almost every morning and afternoon, we also had another entertainment: swimming.

Sometimes we went to the pool with some of the brothers, but we didn't like going with Titing, who was awful, and he spent all the time wanting to sink us in the water, so that we could drown, and that way he could go without us. He'd say to me:

—Come closer, I'm really, really not going to do anything to you!

But since I knew he was a big liar, because his whole family always said "This child is such a liar, he is very tricky," which meant that he was much more than a liar, the most liar that can be in the world, I paid no attention to him, and didn't go near, because I knew it was a fat lie ...

But he'd come from behind and, come on, sink me, and I swallowing water.

So we liked better to bathe in a tin bathtub that Lupeng put on the little terrace for us, next to their kitchen. We felt so good and cool there, telling each other stories and getting tan! And besides, IsabelM would cut a tomato in half for us, put salt on it and we'd eat it up, getting ourselves a little slopped up, but it didn't matter because we were in the water.

Other times we would go up to our large terrace, the one that was above our floor, we sprinkled ourselves with a watering can, and we had a yummy time, which meant better than fine, because there my sister Ne-ning was frying herself, and she was so busy getting tan, she didn't even have time to scold us so we could do whatever we felt like, but careful not to splash her because she didn't like that; maybe she thought so she wouldn't get moles where the water hit her....

Mamá Chong would tell her from downstairs:

—Please Ne-ning. Don't take so much sun, you're going to get sunstroke!

But she didn't care, she turned around, put on another layer of a cream that was orangish, and kept on frying.

As one day she had told us that she had seen a movie about blacks, with a few missionaries who were in Africa to make them white or like white people, and that they were beautiful, it seems to me that she had decided that she was also going to be black, and that's why she did it.

A-ma-ling was very fair, although she took the sun for thousands of hours she never got tan, just a little red. I, on the other hand, was like a gypsy, maybe that thing about my godfather had stuck to me even though he never came to see me, and as soon as the sun touched me a little I would get super dark, but since I had not seen that movie from Africa, well, I didn't want to be a black girl like Ne-ning, but to stay like one of the regular girls.

JUNE FAIR

And at the beginning of the summer there was a fair called "The June Fair," because it was in that month, and it was when we showed off the new dresses, the shoes, the esparto espadrilles, and all the other things.

It was a stupendous fair, with lots of little gadgets and the witch's train, where as soon as you were not careful she would hit you on the head with a broom.

The witch had a green face and a huge schnozola, like Don Nestor's, who was a friend of my father's, and I think also of my friend's father; that man had the biggest nose in all of Turgalium.

About Don Nestor, Papá Bo-ling always told me:

—Once upon a time there was a man stuck onto a nose....

And if you think about that, it was a very strange thing, because noses are stuck to men, to women, to children, come on, everyone, even the dogs and cats and many animals, but not the birds, nor the snakes, those kinds don't have noses, and although it was the other way around, my dad said so, because it was a poem, and he laughed a little while he had his cigarette Jean in between an upper tooth, which was broken off, and a lower one; it seems to me that he had split that tooth in half to be able to smoke no-hands on purpose, but I never asked him, so I don't know if that is true.

One day A-ma-ling asked me:

—How do you think Don Nestor's handkerchief is to wipe his snot?

And I, who knew him more than she did, because I saw him many times talking to my papá, said right away:

—It's not a handkerchief like ours, or like all other people's. It is a huge bed sheet. And of many colors.

And from that moment on, every time we met that man, we would pay close attention to see if we saw the sheet, but he must've kept it hidden because we never saw it....

Well, as I was saying, besides the witch, the Ferris wheel, and the pink cotton candy (that was called that but it was not the cotton for cuts and scrapes, but could be eaten), there were also bumper cars, which were small cars where you got on and crashed a little with other cars, because all those who were there, they were children and they didn't know how to drive.

We liked them quite a bit, but as soon as we saw that Titing was in one, we no longer liked riding them, because he would always hit us head-on, and that was very dangerous because you could fly out of the car and someone would accidentally run you over and he would cut off a hand or a leg, and then you were good and crippled or lame because they couldn't be glued back in place, and that was very complicated, or you were just left very corpse.

PEPITO

The June Fair, on the other side of the rides, was called the field of San Juan, and that saint must also be quite rich, because his field was huge and was full of all kinds of animals, but not wild ones, that were kept in the circus, but of the others that were called domestic: cows, bulls, dogs, cats, sheep, goats, pigs... And donkeys! many donkeys of all sizes.

Francisco, the Guardian at Las Viñas vineyard, had a donkey that had no name, it was only called a donkey, but it was terrific, and not like other donkeys owned by other people which were very disobedient, and that is why when someone was a drag they were told: "Don't be a donkey," which was like an insult worse than a fool or an idiot, and we didn't like it at all.

And I wanted to have a donkey!

Since I was always telling A-ma-ling stories about Francisco's donkey, and she wanted one too, we decided that we would go to the June Fair and buy one for ourselves.

But we didn't know how much a donkey cost, so we went there to ask.

They wouldn't let us go alone to that part, but Aunt Lurdes, who was Uncle Edu-ar-dong's wife, took us because she was so good.

Aunt Lurdes was really called Lourdes, like the water that came in little bottles, and it was miraculous but you couldn't drink it, just put a little on your outside, as did IsabelM when the half needle was giving a lot of the trouble, but all people called her Lurdes, so that it would be known that she was a person and not water.

Well, it was three o'clock, and when we saw one that we liked a lot, I asked the gypsy:

—Good morning. Could you tell us how much your donkey costs?

And he told us:

—My donkey is terrific, his name is Pepito and he is like a son to me. We even sleep together and he never kicks me! I'm selling it for sixty pesetas, but I can discount it to you to for fifty-eight, and say no more.

We were very happy to have found a donkey as good as Pepito, because he didn't even kick, not like my brother Feipang, who when they put him to siesta with me was always kicking a lot, and he was not even a donkey, but a brother, but the problem is that we had neither sixty nor fifty-eight pesetas.

After talking a bit between us, we said to him:

—Mr. Gypsy, could you keep Pepito for us until we have the money?

—Yes, I'll reserve it for you, he replied.

We went so happy again to the rides part, because we also knew that although Aunt Lurdes was an adulterer, like Mamá Chong and IsabelM, she was not going to say anything to anyone, come on, she was not going to squeal, and that way none of our brothers (especially Feipang or Titing, who always wanted to spoil our business) were going to get ahead of us and buy our donkey.

We decided to save all our pesetas, from allowance, from saints' days, what my grandmother gave us, what Dona Marting and Grandpa Edua-rding gave us, I mean everything, even if we couldn't buy any sweets for a long time, and we knew that between the two of us, although it was very difficult and a lot of money, we were going to get it.

But we had some other problems, because one of those days A-ma-ling asked me:

—Do you know what donkeys eat?

I didn't know either, but I told her I would ask Man-o-ling, who understood everything, and as soon as I saw him at home that afternoon I asked him:

—Man-o-ling, can you tell me what donkeys eat, and what is the food that they like the most?

He laughed and said,

—Wow, you're so silly sometimes! What do you think they're going to eat!? Grass and just grass.

And then I was much calmer, because if they ate French omelettes, or churros, or things that we ate, where in the world could we have gotten them, eh. The grass thing was very simple because we had A-ma-ling's yard, where there was so much, and no one ate it.

From that day on, we started saving and preparing a little house for Pepito.

But everything was secret, top secret.

We only told Lupeng, and she gave us "Holy Word" that she would not tell anyone.

And you already know that of the three promises, Word, Word of Honor and Holy Word, this last one was the best, and if you didn't keep it, you went straight to hell, so we were very calm.

The following months, although we did other things in the meantime, we dedicated ourselves to saving our pesetas, and preparing a good house for Pepito, so that he would be very comfortable and not cry for not being with the gypsy.

IsabelM, when she saw us bustling around in the garden, was very happy to have us around. But sometimes she would ask us:

—Girls, what have you got up your sleeves?

Because we had a lot of work; look, we had to make the house, and also, without anyone realizing that it was a donkey house, prepare a bed and a pillow, find lots of stones to put around the house, so that he would not escape, or someone would steal him, and many other things.

Lots of work.

The next year, when the June Fair came again, we had everything ready: the house and the money to buy Pepito.

As we were older, they let us go to the San Juan field with Man-o-Ling and AngelMaring, and we didn't even have to hold their hands, well, just when crossing the streets, but all the other time we were loose, because we were already seven years old.

We got there, and while our brothers were busy looking at some very funny pigs, who wanted to have a race, and since they were very fat, their hams were heavy and they fell all the time, we went to look for the gypsy man.

Finally, after walking around a few times, we saw him.

He was alone.

No Pepito by his side.

So we went up to him and I said:

—Good morning. Do you remember us?

He looked at us a lot, shook his head a little, took off a black hat that he was wearing and that was the same one from the year before and answered us:

—Well, no, I can't place you right now.

Immediately the two of us, speaking at the same time, said to him:

—Don't you remember that last year we told you that we wanted to buy your donkey, Pepito, and that you told us that you were going to keep him for us?

Then the gypsy suddenly remembered!

—Where is Pepito now? we asked him right away. We have the money ready.

Because we carried the fifty-eight pesetas in a small bag, which Lupeng had made for us so that it would not get lost, or no one would take it from us, and we had it in a very tight hand where it could not get out.

We had never had so much money, we too were a little rich.

The gypsy told us:

—Ah! Very good. Pepito has gone to a place for a moment because he had to go to the bathroom, but give me the money and I'll go find him right away and I'll bring him to you.

We took the pesetas out of the bag, he counted them, he was very happy, he took them and left.

And we both stood waiting for him to come back.

And we waited.

And waited.

And waited.

A long time passed and Man-o-Ling and AngelMaring, when they were fed up with seeing the pigs, came over to us.

They wanted to go back to the rides part of the fair, but we couldn't leave there!

So we kept waiting and when there was no one left there, neither people nor animals, our brothers, who were a little angry, well, pretty angry, took us almost by force and said that they would never take us to the fair again, that we were very tiresome girls and didn't know our own minds, and much more.

And all that, though they were the good brothers!

But, look, we couldn't say anything, because everything was a secret, and it was better that they scold us and get angry than to tell them that we were waiting for our Pepito!

And as soon as we got to A-ma-ling's house, and half crying we told everything to Lupeng, she laughed out loud and could only say:

—But you two are silly! But what a pair of dummies! If I didn't see it, I wouldn't believe it!

And it seems to me that sometimes, although she was quite good, she did not understand us much either.

CIRCUS

And with the June Fair came the circus!

The circus was like a very large round house, but it was not made like the houses in which we lived: it was made of cloth! But it was made of a very hard cloth, not like our dresses, skirts, or coats, and it had blue and yellow stripes, and the roof instead of tiles was also made of cloth, I think that they had made it with many umbrellas so that if it rained, no one who was inside would get wet, and the wild animals and the people would not catch a cold.

The circus was also in the field of San Juan, between the fair of the rides and the fair of the donkeys, the sheep, the cows and all those that were animals, but not the wild ones, get it? - the normal kind.

My friend and I had never been to the circus, so when IsabelM and Mamá Chong decided to take us, we were very happy, it seems to me that Lupeng had told them about the donkey Pepito, and they knew that we were very sad after all that we went through.

When we were eating, my mamá told Man-o-ling and me

—Kids, tonight we three are going to the circus with A-ma-ling and her mom, so you have to have a good siesta because we'll go to bed very late!

We went to bed as soon as we finished dessert, and although we did not like to take a nap, and we always protested, that day we did not say anything and I closed my eyes very tightly, to look like I was asleep, in case someone came to check up.

When the time came they fixed us up. I wore a very beautiful new dress that was almost white, but not quite white, and it had many fat butterflies of many colors that were flying around the cloth, and some Pirelli sneakers with which I could walk and jump, as if I were barefoot, they were so soft.

My friend also wore a dress, but hers had no butterflies but lots of red and white squares, and her sneakers were red.

We were both gorgeous!

But we almost did not go, because my brother Feipang as soon as he found out that we were going to the circus, since we were not going to take him, he took my littlest brother out of his crib and had him on a chair to tame him, to teach him to talk, to put on his clothes and all that, and he did not want to put him back, so he got real angry when he was taken from him, he stood in front of the door to not let us out, and until Mamá Chong gave him a lot of chocolates and convinced him to be good, he did not move from there. Luckily we still had time!

Around the circus there were a lot of people lining up to buy tickets, but we didn't have to go there, because my papá had bought them before, so we went in without having to wait, and that was great, because we would have been bored a lot to be in single file for so long.

A-ma-ling's bad brother told us that the inside of the circus was called "the Big Top," although we both knew it was a lie, because tops are made out of wood with a metal point and a string around them, and the boys in the park throw them on stone or cement and try to split open and ruin another boy's spinning top. We didn't see any tops in the circus, not even the smallest ones, but since we didn't feel like fighting with him, we told him that well, sure, it was a big top, so that he would leave us alone.

And we were in the front row!

What a good place! That way we didn't have any big heads in front.

My brother Man-o-ling and AngelMaring sat at one end, and Mamá Chong and IsabelM at the other to be able to talk, which was what they liked the most, and they left the two of us in the middle, with her tiresome brother, but since we were so happy to be there it didn't matter much to us.

After waiting many hours until all the people were in their seats, the show finally began.

First a man came out who was the head of all those in the circus and explained that we were going to have a fantastic night, that we were going to see many wonders, and we were going to have a great time, but that some parts were very dangerous and we had to be very quiet and still; well, while he was talking some clowns were circling around him, goofing around and teasing him. I think they were quite rude and that's why they behaved like that, and the poor Boss had to put up with them and pretend they weren't there, but the others came to bother and bother, and on top of that they went over to our row and wanted us to talk and move around too, as if we were also their kind.

My friend and I paid no attention to them, come on, but Titing immediately started jumping and hopping, and the Boss of the circus told him that if he didn't stay still, he would send some policemen to take him to jail, and he had to sit.

Then many drums sounded, barrrumm, darrummm, tam, tararam, they turned off the lights and only left a few in the center, and some very pretty girls came out, wearing white dresses full of pearls and diamonds, and sneakers also with many pearls, beautiful, they were like girls but they were grownups, only very short.

The four of them were on top of some white horses, and at the top, next to the head where the horses have long hair, with that hair they had made braids, so that it did not get into their eyes and they were more comfortable.

And besides, they were much more precious than the other ordinary horses without braids, such as we sometimes saw in Turgalium.

And those girls not only rode like other people ride, no, they rode the other way around, they stood up, they flipped around like somersaults... Well, they did a lot of things while their horses went round and round, I don't know how they didn't get dizzy, the girls or the horses, but all eight were very happy, and they smiled all the time.

Man-o-ling told us that they were from TieLand, which is a country that is very far away, and that everyone there knew how to ride horses that way, and that they also knew how to do many more things, that he had read it recently.

We did not know that there was a TieLand place, it must be where they made the ties that our papás put around their necks, so that their shirts do not open up, but that day we learned it, and we would have liked to be from there instead of Turgalium, because we would have such beautiful dresses, and also a horse each, but we did not say anything out loud, because it was not possible to speak.

While the horses were in the ring, the clowns stood still and stopped fooling around. It seems to me that they were a little afraid of being kicked....

When all those tie girls left, they played the drums and the music again and the Boss of the circus came out again to explain to us what was coming next.

That Boss knew a lot, and explained everything much better than Sister Luisina, and besides, he did not repeat, he only said it once, and that's that, and we all understood.

Again, as he spoke, the clowns come through, bugging.

They already had us a little fed up, but we looked the other way because we didn't even want to see what a drag they were, and we told those behind to do the same, but they were laughing a lot and they ignored us, okay.

The next were some called acrobats and that looked like rubber: they bent in the middle, they jumped and put their heads on the ground, they caught their feet with their hands, but from behind... Buff! how difficult, and then they made a tower with all of them, one on top of the other up to the ceiling, even our necks ached from looking up, and the last one, who was a little boy, when he was at the top, waved to all of us. He took a huge jump and hit the ground and didn't even break his leg! And then his mother came, or his grandmother, or I don't know who she was, but she was an adulterer, not a girl, and gave him a chocolate bar, told him that he had done great, but to say goodbye again, because he had to have a bath and put on his pajamas to go to bed, it was already very late.

But we had taken siestas and were not sleepy, even though it was at night, so there was no problem.

Mamá Chong told us that they were a family, and that they were all from Brazil.

We both knew very well from "The Book of Our Children" that this was another place very far away, much further than Las Huertas, because to get there you had to ride a boat, because if you were swimming it would take a long time, and also at night, you couldn't even go to bed because there were no beds, and even if you wanted to put a very narrow bed, or a sofa bed, they would sink to the bottom, but since we were not friends with the acrobats, we couldn't ask them how they got here.

The Boss came out again and told us that the lions and tigers would come out immediately, and that they were going to put some iron things to protect us, because they were very wild, and that since that day they had all been very busy setting up the circus, they had forgotten to buy raw meat, we should not move because they were hungry.

All of us, except Titing, listened to him because we did not want to end up inside the guts of some lion or a tiger, and with raw meat around, how disgusting, but that brother of A-ma-ling I have already told you he was a big drag, and he kept moving and getting up from his seat, so annoying!

When the bars were in place and we were safe, the lions came out through a tube they had put in.

There were five of them, it seems to me that they were brothers, or first cousins, because they looked so much alike.

And the tamer came out with a huge whip and the lions immediately sat down on some benches, because they didn't want to be beaten, look, they were lions but not dumb.

The trainer made them do many things, even dancing, and we all liked everything they did a lot, and when we thought they were going to go home, the trainer said:

—And now, Ladies and Gentlemen, boys and girls, the most difficult yet!

He went up to one of the lions, the one who was closest to us, told him to open his mouth and he put his head there!

We all shouted with great fear, but the Boss of the circus came out and said:

—Silence! Let no one say a word! This stunt is extremely dangerous!

And we all covered our mouths so as not to say Ay!

The tamer spent a long time with his head inside the lion's mouth, and while the other four were getting closer, they touched legs and began to sing, well, they did not sing very well, that's the truth, and since it was a pretty silly song, from when they lived in the jungle, we all laughed a little, but softly so that the tamer wouldn't end up a corpse.

When the lions went down the tube, they didn't remove the bars because the bears were coming!

Those were also a family, Papá Bear, Mamá Bear, and a little bear, who was still wearing a diaper.

The three of them lived in a very cute little house and as we had read the story of the three bears, we knew everything that was going to happen, so it was very nifty, and when the girl came out, who they later told us was also a tamer but small size, we all applauded her a lot and she did the trying the chairs, and the soup, and the beds and everything in the story and we liked it a lot, because those bears from the circus even spoke like people, although you couldn't much understand them, but okay, they were bears.

After the bears, when they had done everything and I think they were a little tired, two tigers from "Malaysia" came. What a scare, because those were really bad! All the time, nothing more to say than grrrrrr, grrrrrr, grrrrrr and look at everyone with a very angry face; their tamer did not want to put his head in their mouths or anything, he just told them to behave well, that they were in front of a lot of people, and not to do foolish things, because if they did he would take them back to Malaysia and see how they would manage then, but don't think that they paid much attention to him - but we already knew that they were not very obedient.

And finally they removed the bars and out came: The Elephants!

They were very big and that day they were very happy, playing and jumping and filling their trunks with water from a basin that was in the center, and giving a shower to all of us who were there, especially those in the first rows, oh what a riot! And since we all laughed a lot, come on! more water and more showers! Mamá Chong and IsabelM got their heads so wet that their hairstyle was wrecked, and their perm almost disappeared, which was something they did to mamás at the hairdresser, so they would have their hair very curly and very beautiful, but they did not care because they were also laughing with those elephants, and they said that Pep-i-tang Va-re-lang would put the curls back on them the next day, the important thing was to enjoy things.

The elephants played for a long time, lifting up their front legs, kneeling because I think that that year they also had to make their first communion, although they did not have nuns, nor did they go to our school, but it seems to me that their trainer wanted them to know how they had to behave in church and be good.

We would have liked them to live in Turgalium, but they couldn't because they had to live in the circus, so we put up with it.

When all the animals had left, a voice came out of a loudspeaker and said:

—Ladies and gentlemen, boys and girls, dear spectators, we hope you are enjoying tonight, now we will have half an hour of rest!

While the animals were performing, the two of us had come up with a plan: we wanted to work in the circus, and live in a cloth house, and be every night in a different town, so we told our mamás that we had to go out for a moment, but that we'd come back right away.

Since they were talking, and talking, and talking about all their things, and nannies and meals, and all that, they almost didn't pay attention, so we ran out right away, in case they stopped talking and told us to stay in our seats.

We went outside and asked someone who was there:

—Do you know where the Boss of the circus is? We have to see him urgently.

That man pointed out a big wagon, which was in the middle of a few smaller ones, and we went there.

The Boss was having dinner when we arrived, but he saw us right away.

—Good evening, girls. Are you enjoying the show?

We told him yes, a lot, and that we wanted to work in his circus, and live with them, and travel to all the towns, to La Cumbre, to Zorita and Madroñera, and if he could hire us.

—Well, well, he said, —well, imagine, right now I need two girls for one of the acts. Do you have permission from your parents? I just need a signed paper and without that paper you cannot work here.

As we did not have the paper, we asked him if he could wait until the next day, because our parents were not in the circus with us, but that as soon as we got home we would ask them and that's that, and he said well, that he would wait until a quarter past nine in the morning, but we must bear in mind that it was a very dangerous job, which might not last long.

Well, we didn't care. When that one was over they would put us in another one, by then we would surely convince him...

We said goodbye until the next day and we went back into the circus.

A little after we sat down, the show began again.

The clowns, who had been so silly before, came out onto the floor and just clowned around, look, silly stuff, which is what clowns do.

Okay, come on, up and down, and if this and if that. Everyone in the circus was laughing, but we didn't like it at all, nothing.

As they could see that we were not laughing, one of them, the tallest and who seemed more serious, but who was also very silly, super silly, came up to us with an accordion, and played some very sad things, and sang and played, and spun his head around and many other things, to see if we laughed, but since they had behaved so badly before, we ignored him, come on, so that they would learn to be more good and be still for a while, doggone it, and we turned around and didn't even look at him, ha, who did he think he was!?

The clowns left and the Boss came out again to announce the next number: The monkeys of the jungle! and when he saw us, he winked at us and said:

—Dear audience. This number is dedicated especially to my two new friends, who will start working with us in this circus very soon! And he pointed to us, and also bowed.

They all looked at us then. We got very red and very embarrassed, and we did not know what to do or what to say, so we stayed still.

Mamá Chong stopped talking and asked me:

—What did that man say, that you are going to work in his circus? Don't you want to live with me, with your brothers and with Papá?

And she began to cry some very fat tears.

I didn't want her to cry, but I wanted to work in the circus, so I told her what we had done during the break, and that the Boss had given us a job if we brought him the paper, and if she could convince my papá to give me it, but she, come on, cry and cry, and everyone looked at her very sad, and my brother Man-o-ling said what a bad girl I was, that he was not going to get together with me anymore, nor be my Brother, nor read to me about the gods, nor anything else, and that he was not going to take me to the Plaza anymore, to Miz Manuela's stand, nor where the popsicles with three colors, and many other things, then he looked the other way very angry with me. And that was the good brother, imagine if it was one of the other two...!

And A-ma-ling, also suffering the same story with her mamá and her brothers, because IsabelM caught the tears too, and she was also crying many liters, there was even a puddle on the ground and none of the two could stop.

So they would calm down, we said it was a joke, that we we were not going to go with the circus people, and that was that!

Luckily the jungle monkeys came out and they stopped crying and we all got back to our old ways!

The monkeys were very funny and there were a lot of them, at least thirty-nine or forty-three or more.

They did not know how to speak like people, but everything was understood. They were wearing very nice pants and red velvet jackets, with buttons of pure gold, some lace-up shoes that they had bought for that night, and we all laughed a lot, and the tiresome clowns got in between them and they didn't even let them do their cute monkey things, come on, bug them and bug them, but then the monkey that was oldest, it seems to me the great-great-grandfather, went up to one of the clowns, and gave him a pinch in the face and a kick in the shins, and the silly clown had no choice but to run away, and the other one, who had seen everything, also ran away. Yea! they got what they deserved for being such drags!

The monkeys finished their performance after a long time and a lot of laughter, and the Boss came out again, who had changed his jacket again, and now he was wearing a tiger skin, I suppose of some old tiger who no longer wanted it but I'm not quite sure, and he told us:

—Tonight you are going to see the best trapeze artists in the world! They have traveled from Italy to offer you the best of their art. They will act without a net or any protection. With you, the Langostini Quartet!

My friend asked me:

—Do you think they are lobsters like the ones in La Molineta?

But I didn't know, so I asked my brother, who was still a little mad at me, and he told me to stop talking nonsense, and that we should keep still... what a way to answer me....

The Quartet ran out onto the floor, who were three brothers and a sister, all dressed in green, with suits that shone a lot, they even had green hats on their heads, and green sneakers; they looked very handsome but they were people, they weren't lobsters, but they were called that strange name, not like us who had ordinary last names; maybe in Italy they didn't have those lobsters and that's why their father and mother did not mind calling them that.

They went up a rope and in a moment Wow! they were at the ceiling!

And from there they began to go from one side to the other, to flip in the air, to fly from one end to the other, and they really went like monkeys from the jungle.... Then they put another very thick rope from one of the platforms to the other and the sister langostino got on a small bike, like my brother Feipang's, and began to go from one side to the other, while two of the langostino brothers hung on a cloth going around many times, and the other left over langostino played the guitar up there, without holding on or anything.

We were all very quiet, with our heads up and without moving or anything so as not to distract them, and I think then they got tired of going around the ceiling and doing all that, because they got down on the floor again, they told us they were very happy to have been able to perform in Turgalium, that they would come back soon and that *arrivederci*, which meant goodbye, but in Italian language, and they blew us many kisses.

The Boss came out again, and again the clowns were going around bugging and being silly, and he announced to us:

—Dear friends, for our last number this evening we are going to witness something that is going to make your hair stand on end! Hold your breath, because our next artist needs all his concentration to perform. He has had some problems lately, and the ones today are the last two girls he has left, but fortunately soon we will have some substitutes (and he looked at us again). With all of you, The Great Igor the Evil!

The drums sounded again and Igor appeared, who told us he was Russian or Ukrainian or something.

The assistants brought a round table top like the ones for the braziers, but this was all silver and had two figures drawn and each side of the figures had many rings, and they stood it up supported so that it would stay and not roll away .

Igor came out, who did not look like a Russian or anything, but like any man, just like those from Turgalium, although he was dressed differently: he had a suit all made of gold and his trousers and shirt were sewn together, I don't know how he had put it on, probably he stayed very still and some seamstress from the circus put it together. He was holding two girls like us by the hands, I don't know if they were his daughters or his nieces or what, because since they didn't go to our school, we didn't know them.

The three of them bowed a lot, and immediately Igor led the girls to the board, put the rings over their feet, over their hands, and around their necks, so they couldn't move, even if they wanted to pee or something, and left them there very still, while he went to get a box that he had on a table.

He opened the box and showed us all what was inside: very large knives with a very bad and very dangerous point! Oh, how scary!

And he started throwing his knives at the poor girls, who couldn't even move!

First he threw them looking, and though they stuck very close he didn't prick them or anything, but then he turned around and started throwing the knives backwards, and that was really scary, because once he almost hit one on a leg, and the poor thing just kept saying to untie her, that she wanted to go home, that she had to go. And she was crying and crying, but Igor seems to me like he was a little deaf or something, because he didn't let her go.

The drums sounded and then Igor said,

—Now the hardest yet

He put his head on the ground and his feet up and told his assistant, who was a blonde with very straight hair and very beautiful, and wearing white boots like the fairies do, to pass him the knives.

He started throwing knives very quickly, come on, one after another and another, and every one of them stayed on the edges of that round thing, but when he was going to throw seven knives at once, he suddenly began to sneeze, I think he did it without wanting, he jabbed the two girls in the heart and in the belly, and they were dead in no time.

As soon as he realized what he had done, he began to whimper, and the blonde also whimpered, and Igor saying that he had done it without a bad idea, and that he asked them for forgiveness and many more things, but the girls could not even talk because they were super dead, so I don't think they had any idea.

All of us who were in the circus were very sorry for those girls, but we didn't say anything to Igor in case he got angry, and threw a knife at us too.

The Boss of the circus came out for the last time, now wearing a very black suit, and told us that he was very sorry for that terrible accident, but that things were like that sometimes and not to worry, so we listened to him and we all got out of there.

When we were in the street, my friend and I looked at each other and, without saying a word, the two of us decided that we no longer wanted to be circus artists, better to be ordinary girls, and that's that .

And we went back to our houses because it was already very dark and we had to have dinner.

PLAZA

In summer we also went many days to play in the Plaza, and there we could buy treats, the day we had our allowance, or the times we had gotten pesetas, even if they were not allowance.

As our older brothers went there almost every day, we knew that if we got very aggravating, super aggravating, and we told them to take us, I think they could not stand it anymore, and they would tell us yes, okay, that we could go with them.

Until we got there we had to hold their hands because they thought we were going to get lost, but as soon as the Plaza appeared we let go, they went with some friends who were waiting for them, and they left us at the candy stands, and although they told us not to move from there we did not pay much attention to them, but we said yes, so that they would go and leave us in peace.

The Turgalium square was very big and beautiful, it had all the floor made of stones that were called "ofgranite," not of tiles as in our houses, because those stones were much harder, and if you fell you would get scraped, but neither A-ma-ling nor I ever fell.

All around there were many Palaces, and though neither the King nor the Queen lived in them, they had them there if they wanted to come to spend a day, or a whole week; before they did come many times, when the Palaces were not there, and they had to stay to sleep at the Inn of Señora Justa, which was a rotten place, and they had to sleep with the horses and donkeys and chickens, but as soon as Pizarro found out how uncomfortable they were, and how little the animals allowed them to sleep, he went to Peru, took many chunks of pure gold that the Indians had lying around, put them in a very huge bag, and they brought it to make a few Palaces, with many rooms, many parlors, and soft beds, so that they would be very relaxed and very comfortable.

The King was very happy, he became his good friend and he took some of the left over gold and ordered them to make a statue of Pizarro, sitting on his horse, but it came out green instead of gold. We would have liked it better if the horse had been pink, or blue, and Pizarro a different color, but you couldn't change it and you couldn't, so we had to settle for them both green.

In addition to the Palaces, at the top of the stairs there was a church, which belonged to a saint called San Martín, and in the middle of the Plaza there was a fountain called "*Elpilar*," round and with many fish swimming. The water was green and looked dirty, but those fish didn't care, because I don't think they drank it; it had turned green because that horse put its whole head in to drink, and I think some of his green mixed into the water. The water that came out of the tube was clean, but that horse would mess it up at night, and the fish wouldn't say anything, maybe it was so he wouldn't kick them if he got angry.

In one part of the arcades there were Paula's bar and others of some people that we did not know, and the bank where they kept all the people's money, Pedro Marcos's store, which was a place that our mamás liked very much, because there were many things there and they also knew everyone and could talk for fifty hours straight, and a few other things.

In one part of the Plaza, across from what I have explained to you, there was a very large house that reached all the way across to both sides, called El Mercado.

And there on Thursday mornings they put all kinds of raw foods: fish, rabbits, fruits, vegetables and many stalls with nuts and almonds, dry figs, which on the outside were white because they were covered in flour and then you could open them and stick in a piece of walnut to make them so delicious.

We went to that market one morning with our mamás, but since they were stopping all the time to talk to their friends, we let go of their hands, and we went to a stall where they sold many things made of clay, to see what there was.

There we found several families of piggy banks that were little pigs. There was the pig papá, who was very fat, the pig mamá, who was regular fat, and a few little piggy children. They only had a slit at the top, everything else was covered, I mean totally closed up.

And of course, A-ma-ling wanted to have one, you know she was very capricious and spoiled, so we went back to where Mamá Chong and IsabelM were, to see if they would buy it for her.

IsabelM said she was going to buy one for each of us, so we went back to the clay gizmos.

I didn't care if I had one or not, because those piggy banks were to save money, and when you put in the pesetas, or the fifty-centimo coins, those ones with a hole in the center, you couldn't take them out again, even if you needed the money very urgently to buy something. If you wanted to get it, you had to hit the pig with a hammer, smash open its belly and that's that. Then you had the pesetas and the coins, but the pig was no longer good for anything. And that made me very sad.

But as my friend was very pesky, although I know I explained everything very well, she kept saying that she wanted one of those pigs. And look at me explaining everything to her three or four times! I also asked her how she would like someone to separate her from her parents and her little pig brothers, eh? But nothing, I didn't convince her.

I took a piggy that was very cute, although it was not pink, it was clay-colored, very shiny, and the slit was on one side, and she picked one of the mamá pigs, fat and with the slit on its back, and we went home.

When we were arriving she said:

—I have a great idea! Right now, as soon as we arrive, we are going to see Grandpa Eduar-ding, all my uncles, TrickyJoey, your grandmother, the postmen who live below your house, Dona Ma-rta and all the others, we'll ask them to put money in the pigs, and we'll tell them that we have to save for a secret thing.

It wasn't a bad idea, that's the truth, so we did it.

We were very lucky, they all gave us money, and even Nening and Lupeng.

When we were going to her house, so that she could hide her piggy bank and Titing would not steal it, we met Cheng-Chu, my sister's boyfriend, who was a little hidden behind the lions door, and he also gave us pretty many pesetas, but told us not to tell anyone that he was there. We gave him "Holy Word" and he was very satisfied.

We were going up her stairs, the piggy banks were already heavy, and almost when we were up, A-ma-ling made a mistake on the step and her mamá pig went flying down, buff, it broke totally, the stairs didn't need a hammer, and all the money was left on the floor.

And she started crying like a little girl!

But I said to her, so she would shut up:

—Look at all the money you've saved in just one day! Come on, shut up, I will lend you my little pig a lot of times, and that's that.

So we did that: we took all the coins and pesetas that were lying on the floor, we divided them up, and I left her my pig that whole day, so that she could keep it in her room, and then we had it one day each, but I made her promise that she would have to take great care of it, and take a good look when she was going up or down the stairs.

As we were quite rich (not delicious!) that day, we told our brothers to take us back to the Plaza, but they said no, that they had to ride their bikes in the park before eating, that if we were good and did not make them dizzy, they would take us the next day, so we held on and settled on playing with the dirt, making pictures of faces with a stick, little girls' houses and many other things, until they called us to go upstairs to eat.

The next day we went back to the Plaza.

Until we got there we had to walk many hours, as I have already told you other times, but we did not care, and later in the afternoon we were very tired, but as my grandmother always told us: "To get something, you give something," which was a saying that meant that we had to put up with being tired, trading that for something that we did like.

In the Plaza, under the houses which were not Palaces, were the Arcades. They had put them there so that people wouldn't get wet, if it was raining in the part where you could see the sky, or so they would be a little warmer, if it was very cold.

In one part of the arcades, as I have told you, there were the bars, where all the adulterer people went to have coffee and wine and other things, and in the other part, what there was, was all the treats stands! That was the best part of it all, where we spent a lot of time, first looking, deciding what to buy that day, and then almost when we had to go home, shopping quickly, because Man-o-ling and AngelMaring were with us, hurrying us.

The best stall was that of Miz Manuela.

Because she had everything: roasted chickpeas, chewing gum of many colors, bars of hard licorice and another that was very soft, which we liked less, gold coins that had chocolate inside, sweet stick, square mint candies and strawberry, ordinary candies, café o-lay... everything. It was very difficult to decide what you wanted to buy, because the truth is that we wanted everything, but we could only buy one thing at a time, to make our allowances last longer, so we looked and looked, we thought a lot, and we went to see another stand, in case they had other things. Since there were five or six we could choose, but we always went back to buy where Miz Manuela was, which was where there was more and better.

The day after A-ma-ling's piggy bank busted in smithereens, we had a lot of coins and a few pesetas, so we bought everything, and we still had plenty left over.

Another of the stalls, the ones that were not for sweets, and that had been put in a corner, was full of stories about fairies and princesses, and also had many small books, the kind that you could keep in a pocket, and this was where Man-o-ling bought his books every week. That is why he knew so much, because later, at home, he would read everything that was written in the little book, and sometimes, he would tell us about it. So we got so smart, Ah!

We bought a story each, bought a little book for Man-o-ling, and went to the wafers.

The wafer man had a gadget that was red and gold. It was like a tube, but very big, and the wafers were hidden there, so that no one would steal them and also so that if it started to rain they would not get soaked and all gushy. At the top of the tube there was a wheel, with numbers painted on it, but they weren't numbers in a row, nor were they all the numbers, just a few.

When you went to buy them, the wafer man would ask you:

—Do you want wafers, or do you prefer to spin the roulette wheel?

Which meant that if you gave him a peseta, he would give you four wafers, but if you spun the roulette wheel, you could get different numbers, seven, one, nine or any other number that was painted there, even zero, and then you would be left without the peseta and without the wafers.

As my friend and I almost never had a lot of pesetas, what we did was buy at Miz Manuela's stall and then watch how others spun the roulette wheel, and we knew all the numbers that were painted on it!

But that day, since you already know we had so much money, we decided to spend a peseta with the wafer man, and instead of taking four, two apiece, we decided to spin the wheel.

A-ma-ling was very nervous, in case it stopped on zero, which meant that we would be left with nothing, but I said to her:

—Look, we'll put our hands together, close our eyes and whatever comes out!

And that's what we did.

Before opening our eyes we heard people saying:

—What luck! —Holy cow! —How wonderful!

So we looked and, wow. We won ten wafers!

We couldn't believe it, and I think the wafer man was a little angry, but look, luck is luck, so we grabbed all those wafers, which almost slipped out of our hands and we ran to where our brothers were, in the middle of the Plaza, looking at the posters of the movies that were showing that day.

They couldn't believe it either!

And since we weren't the greedy kinds of kids, we gave Man-o-ling two, my friend kept two, I got two others and AngelMaring as we hadn't bought any of those books for him, because he didn't collect them, we gave four.

They were very happy, they told us we were very good, and since it was almost time to eat, the four of us went home, so friendly and without fights.

SECTION SEVEN: AUTUMN

CEMETERIES AND BONES

Our best outing, once a year, was to go to the cemetery.

And that was when the summer passed, and then it was called Autumn.

Mamá Chong had never ever been to the cemetery, because she liked to talk a lot, and in cemeteries everyone there are dead and do not speak, so, going there was boring for her, because if you asked someone something, even if it was something very simple, like asking what time it was, no one answered you, so she preferred to talk to those who were alive, who were much more polite and always answered, but IsabelM went every year in November, and although she could not speak with the dead people, she cried a little there, and prayed a little.

But Mamá Chong, even though she didn't go, she did let me go.

The first time they were going, Lupeng told us:

—The best and most important thing about the cemetery is the smell of being dead.

We were very intrigued as it must be a stupendous smell.

To go up to the cemetery, which was very far away and you had to walk a lot, we would turn past Doña Ma-rta's house, and from there go up and up, it had to be like a thousand kilometers at least, because it took a long time, and besides, IsabelM had to go very slowly, so that the half needle did not find out that she was walking and did not bug her.

It was called the Saint Andrew's Slope, he must have been a saint who lived there and who had to have a lot of work, because on one side of the Slope, as you went up, many people lived who were a little bad, and surely that Saint Andrew had to pray a lot that they would become good.

IsabelM used to say to us both:

—Girls, don't look to your right, those are houses of low grade women.

So, on top of being bad they got a zero in school! Gee!

But as soon as she stopped to talk to someone, we peeked a little, not much, that's the truth in case she caught us looking, and the women we saw seemed normal to us, they didn't seem bad; it must have been that the nuns at their school had a mania about them and that's why they gave them such low grades, but since we weren't friendly with them, we could never ask them.

Finally, very tired after walking so much, we reached the cemetery.

Our cemetery had three parts: in one were the dead in the ground, in another there were others placed in the wall, in a thing called niches, and the other part was that of the pantheons, which were like little houses, with a door and a roof and all that, and where they put together everyone who was from the same family or close friends, even if they had died eight hundred years ago, and did not even know each other.

As soon as we passed the iron gate, the bash began, because there the dead would not speak, but everyone else did. A lot and very loud.

That day all the townspeople had to go up, except for Mamá Chong; and I thought it was very silly not to want to go, because she would have been able to talk to so many and get rid of that mania; but you know that mamás, even one as good as

Mamá Chong, sometimes do very strange things, and if you got one that was like that, then you had to put up with it.

We started to sniff; and so that it would not show, we put a handkerchief near our nose and mouth, like we were blowing our snot, but we were smelling.

In the part where the dead were in the ground you didn't smell anything, well, you smelled a lot of flowers, because that day everyone who was alive brought flowers to those who were dead, so that they would know that they were still family, even though now they did not eat at the table with them, nor have a bed in the house. Since they didn't have to buy food for them, or clothes or sweets, or anything at all, they kept that money for the flowers, and that's why everything was beautiful: it was like a garden, with roses and carnations and pansies and lilies, and all the kinds of flowers in the world.

I believe that the dead did not care, and that they knew that they were still part of the family, and that even if they had not brought them flowers they would be just as happy, but since that was another mania of the living and they could not speak, well they put up with it.

So in that part no smell.

But it was very nice there, walking among the flowers, and looking at the crosses that were on the ground. In the niches it did smell a little, but very little, and you had to get a lot closer, almost where the name and surnames were, and the age of the corpse, and the "Your family that does not forget you" and all that, which was pretty dangerous, because since we did not know who was stored there, maybe it turned out that he was unfriendly and didn't like that you were bothering and smelling him, especially if he hadn't put on Alvarez Gómez's cologne that day, which was a wonderful cologne that my grandmother always used, so we took turns getting closer, and while one smelled, the other watched, so we wouldn't have a bad surprise. Little smell.

But in the pantheons it did smell!

Good thing Lupeng had warned us!

We went into the family of A-ma-ling first, and while IsabelM was crying a bit and praying a bit, we were getting closer, headstone by headstone, to see how they smelled.

Also, since everyone who was there was their relatives, there was no danger if they realized that we were smelling them.

But don't think it smelled much either, that's the truth.

Maybe it's because they had so many candles lit and it smelled of smoke.

I think that in the pantheons where there should be more smell was in very old ones that had a very large stone instead of a door, and where you had to go down stairs that were full of slippery moss, but we never went to those. We were afraid in case the slab would suddenly close and we would stay there at night and forever; with many flowers and fat candles, yes, but without water or food, and without light as soon as the candles were finished. Really, what a bore, even if we were both there.

Sometimes we were lucky and found smell, but do not think it was very good, that's the truth, although we told Lupeng that it smelled great and a bunch, so she wouldn't think only she could smell, and we were just tiny little girls.

Most of the time, no smell or anything.

But we didn't care, maybe there would be more again, and besides, we had another important goal in the cemetery, which was to find bones.

And that was really difficult!

The first year we went we saw three. Not very big, but three! They must have been from a very short man.

And his family had no idea that this man went around with three bones less!

As we did not know his first or last name, we could not do anything.

What luck for the short man that he was dead, and he didn't have to walk, because imagine the drag it would have been, if you got alive again, to find that you were missing part of your arm or leg, or you were missing your head bone and you couldn't have hair there. Buff.

When a long time passed and it was time to leave the cemetery, we said goodbye to all the tombs, we ran away, and finally we arrived at my friend's house, and we told her sister everything we had smelled, and what we had found. And then I crossed the park and went to eat at my house, and that day, for dessert, we always had two delicious things: Cream Puffs and Saint Bones. The Cream Puffs were a ball that had cream or whipped cream inside, and we all loved them.

But the Saint Bones we liked even better.

I didn't know what they were made of, the taste was a lot like marzipan figurines, but Titing told us that they were made with real saints bones. First the Angels pulled out their bones as soon as they became saints, it was necessary to wait until then, it couldn't be before, when they were still people; then they ground them in a special machine and mixed them with I don't know what he told us, it seems to me that sugar and egg yolks, and the day before going to the cemetery they took that mixture to Basilio's pastry store, and Basilio made the bones tinier, so that more would come out, and we would have them in all the houses, and then he would sell them to our mamás.

Ne-ning told me that this was a fib, that my friend's annoying brother had made it up all over the place, so when I saw him in the afternoon I told him that he was quite a liar, that my sister knew much more than he did and that she had told me that saint's bones weren't made like that, but he blabbed up and down that it was true, and since I didn't care, I turned around and didn't want to talk to him anymore, and that's that.

With so much bash and so much food, we ended up very tired that afternoon, so we played with our dolls and did nothing else, but we were very happy and eager to return to the cemetery to continue smelling the dead, although as we knew we'd have to wait a whole year, we hung on.

CHESTNUTS

The day after going to the cemetery, which was called "All Saints' Day," - but they did not say San Pedro or San Pepe or San Paco or any other saint's name, so that if they forgot one they would not get very mad - the Day of the Departed was coming.

Those were the ones who were already corpses - come on, super dead, even if they had died just an hour before.

That day we had a lot of work, and that even though they let us free from school, thank goodness.

In the morning we had to go to Three Masses! even if we were girls and not nuns. The poor nuns went to twenty masses or more, all in a row, and they couldn't leave the church, not to eat some chocolate bread, or to pee, or for anything at all, all the time in church.

One day we asked Sister Luisina why they had to go to so many Masses and she told us:

—There are some who forget to do their three Masses, and since they have everything written down in heaven, we go to more, so that the accounts come out.

Well what a bore, better not to be nuns.

When they took us the first time to the masses for those dead ones, in church we almost fell asleep; in the first, fine, we were awake; the second a drag, because everyone around, come on, pray, pray, and praying out loud, and crying; and when the third mass came, thank goodness A-ma-ling started crying like crazy, many liters of tears came out, and they had to take us out to the street.

As soon as we were out alone, she winked at me and said:

—We should have both cried in the first one, right?

And really, sometimes she was very smart, you bet!

After mass and lunch, you had to go to something called "Roast the Chestnuts" and it wasn't in Turgalium, it was somewhere else.

The first year that we were best friends, they wouldn't let us go, because our mamás said we were too little and that it was too dangerous, but when we turned six, Mamá Chong asked me:

—Would you like to go roast chestnuts with the older kids? If you do, tell your friend to come over soon and you'll go on a chestnut roasting trip this afternoon.

Oh, well, what a question... We wanted to so much!

So I said yes, and ran to A-ma-ling's house.

As soon as we finished eating, friends of Ne-ning came and a few others who were not close friends but tagged along, and they began to call from the upper park, so we would hurry down.

It seems to me that my sister and some of her friends didn't like having to take us so much either, because they thought that if we got tired they would have to pick us up and carry us, but they didn't say anything.

So a big bunch of us went, at least forty-nine or fifty-four, and Man-o-ling and Angel Maring also with their friends, and others who also stuck to them, as if they were friends.

A-ma-ling's bad brother was punished, and Mamá Chong would not let Feipang go because we had to make a fire and that was dangerous.

We left Turgalium, and after walking through the field for a long time, and pricking our legs with some very bad nettles that were there, we arrived at La Molineta.

La Molineta was a slightly broken tower, that's the truth, that was on top of some very fat boulders, and when you climbed over them you would slip and fall to the ground if you went alone, and you could die right away. But my brother gave me his hand and my friend's brother helped her, and we got to the top very quickly.

The tower was the home of some very good Moors who were always looking through a hole, all the time and even at night, so that no one would enter Turgalium and break our things and take them away. They were like policemen, but they were

Moors and they ate Mooring things, and when they spoke, you could hardly understand them, but it didn't matter because what they had to do was watch.

Nobody was in that tower that day, it seems to me they were at those masses, so we went up, looked at everything, saw the Castle in the distance and went back down.

Meanwhile, the older ones had made the fire, cut the chestnuts and everything was almost ready.

They put the chestnuts in a very large pan, all full of holes that the fire was poking through, and when a long time passed they were already roasted and we could eat them.

Some of the ones that my friend and I got were a bit raw, and others burned, and the ones that were sold in the chestnut stalls in the Plaza were much richer, like delicious, that's the honest truth, but we didn't say anything so the older kids would not be angry with us and not want to take us ever again.

It is because they were talking all the time about their boyfriends, and their heels, and lipsticks and that, that they had not looked at the pan and that is why they were terrible, but hey, we ate them all.

Since a long time had passed we had to go home. Uff! Another hike, and on top of that all our clothes smelled of smoke, our eyes hurt, they were red and we almost had tears coming out, as if we wanted to cry, but it was not that we were sad, it was because of all the smoke from the campfire, and we wanted to arrive soon, but I think it took many hours, so A-ma-ling and I decided that going to roast chestnuts was not as great as they said, and that probably next year we would stay playing in the Park and we'd buy a few of those chestnuts they sold in the Plaza already roasted, which were much richer, that's the truth.

CASTLE AND CORONATION

After that of the Saints and the Dead Departed it was still autumn, we had to go to school all week, we only had Sundays and Thursday afternoons free, until they gave us vacations again a week before Christmas .

Although it was not winter, it was very cold anyway, we did not go to the pool, we could hardly ride our bikes, we did not eat Six-in-One, nor was there a June Fair, and we did not do what we did in the summer, but we also had a good time.

It was the time when we had to set up the Nativity scene and do many things.

We did not have a free minute, neither to rest nor for anything at all, all the time without stopping.

In my house we set up a very nice Nativity scene.

In A-ma-ling's house they put another one that was even more beautiful, because it was huge and took up a whole room: it had a silver river and lights, many women washing in the river and then they put all the clothes to dry in the air and sun, like the real washerwomen, and the three Wise Men were at the top on some very fat camels, we could only see them but not touch them because they were far away, but AngelMaring, who was the good brother, one day helped us to get on a chair, and he and Man-o-ling were watching at the door so that no one would come and we could hold them for a little while.

But before setting up the Nativities first we had to walk to a very far place, at least forty kilometers or so, it seems to me, which was called going to "Outside the Walls," which was behind the castle of the Virgin. Many of us would go to collect the moss: her two brothers, her sister, my brother Man-o-ling, a man who worked with my father and called "Mr. Pérez," very old, very old because I think he was one hundred and three years old or more, another younger man named Cliff, (it must have been because his family lived on a mountain, because we knew from The Book of Our Children that the cliff was like a small mountain), who had a special knife that we could not touch, Aunt Cand-e-itang's maid, well, a lot of people, but we knew everyone, we knew their names, and although we were very tired walking so much, it was a lot of fun.

We had to go very early, which was when the moss was better, green and very soft, if you put a finger on it, it was like a sponge, because first it would scrunch a little, but then it would return to its place almost as if you had not touched it, even if you poked with your nails; we did the test and I know it was true.

When we got to the castle of the Virgin, before going for the moss, we went in to see her.

That Virgin was called like me when she had the full name, but they called me Ma-ring, which was simpler.

The first time we went in together I said to A-ma-ling: — Look, from this very moment, if you don't call me by my full name, I'm not going to answer you, and besides, I'll never ever get together with you.

But she, who as I say was quite silly many times, answered me:

—Yes, María-de-la-Victoria, I understand Ma-ring, I'll always call you that, Ma-ring, come on Ma-ring, let's go now Ma-ring.

Perfectly as silly as you can get. It couldn't be fixed.

And on top of that, Titing, who was always spying on our conversations, said:

—María-de-la-Victoria is not a girl's name, Ma-ring, it is the name of the Virgin and they put it for you to shut you up when you were there crying, while you were baptized, because the Virgin was very sleepy that day, but when she heard the screams that you were making she woke up and went to see what was happening, and said to Mamá Chong "If you put a name like mine, she will for sure shut up," and Mamá Chong then put it for you, but the real name is really Ma-ring, the other doesn't count, I was there and I saw and heard everything.

But since I knew that Titing always told a lot of lies, I didn't believe it, and also I knew that he hadn't been to my baptizing.

The Virgin had a child who was her son and they were both made of stone.

It was very strange because they must be from a very poor family, since they did not wear outfits, everything was made of stone, but the Virgin and the Child had a crown of gold and diamonds and emeralds and sapphires and pearls, and all kinds of precious stones, which were called gems, because it said that in the Book of Our Children, and my brother Man-o-ling had explained it to us, because there was a list of all the kinds of stones that are in the whole world: the green ones that were called emeralds, the blue sapphires, the yellow topaz, and all the others in all other colors, not only the stones that are in the houses of people who have many earrings and necklaces and rings and that, also all the others that are hidden underground, and also those that are kept in the safes.

In summer we could understand that they had no clothes on, for the heat, but in the winter they would be so cold, so when we saw that the first time I told my friend softly, so no one heard us:

—Don't you think that we should bring them a coat at least?

—Yes, and a warm scarf and a woolen hat for the Child, we can put it under the crown, she said.

—Well, as soon as we finish collecting the moss we do it and that's that, I said.

—Okay, today it's very cold and the poor dears are going to freeze there, was her reply.

We took a lot of moss because we needed it for the two Nativities, we put it in some cardboard boxes and we went home.

But that day we were no longer calm, because we had to find a coat, scarf, hat for the Child, and on top of it go back up to the Virgin's castle, which, as I have told you, was very far away and we also did not know how to go alone.

And don't think that getting the clothes was so easy!

First we went into the room of her papá and her brothers, but there was no coat there, because they were wearing them, no hats or scarves.

We only found some gloves in a drawer, and they were useless because the hands of the Virgin and the Child were stuck to the body and they could not be detached to put the gloves on, so we went to look in another room.

Nothing.

Well, nothing that would do us any good.

In my house there was a room called "The Falconry," and it is not because kestrels lived there, because there were none, though many flew around in Turgalium, or at least A-ma-Ling and I did not find them and look, we looked many days; well although it was called that, it did not have kestrels, but it did have a lot of things, because everything was put there that was a bit broken, or that did not work, or that was now too small for us, everything, everything, going there was like entering Ali Baba's cave - we knew about that cave because everything was explained in the Chinese Lupeng book, only in the Falconry room there were no precious stones, no gold in chests, only things, and many.

So we went to the Falconry to look for the coat and the other things that we needed, we were sure to find something.

We looked in a box and right away we saw a coat! It was a bit old and had a few holes, it was also black because it must have been my grandmother's, and although we would have liked it better if it was pink or apple green, we took it because at least with that the Virgin would be warm. In addition, as it was quite large, it could also tuck the little boy in and we would no longer have to put a scarf on him.

But when we were in the middle of this operation, a box fell, making a lot of noise and immediately my sister appeared.

It seems to me that she was quite angry because she began to yell:

—Look, you two are naughty! You cannot be left alone for a minute without getting into some mischief! Let's see, what are you up to now, if you would be so kind as to say!?

Since she had caught us red-handed, or if we speak the truth, coat-handed, we told her everything, the whole truth.

And she, who was almost always bugging us, this time she got very nice, she took each of us by the hand, and out into the hall, and said:

—Don't worry, I have to go out in a little while and I'll take the coat to the Virgin, and I'm also going to find one of An-dong-ni's caps and take it too and put it on the Child.

Buff, what a relief! At last, that night they would not be cold!

So it can happen that older sisters sometimes get nice and help!

The Virgin, who was called like my real name, had been crowned after the summer, in October, because before it was only made of stone and that was that, and she had nothing on her head, but many people began to say that all the virgins of all the towns had a crown, and hey, listen, why didn't ours have any? And what if this and that, and then they decided to buy a crown for her and another for the Child.

I think the Virgin didn't care, because she kept clammed up, she just smiled and let them do it, but maybe she did like the crown, because that way she could show it to her friends, the other virgins, when they went out together for a walk or to take tea snack together, or to buy bread and milk for their children.

Like I already told you, the Virgin was very poor, and as she did not even have money to buy a wrinkle-free skirt, or Gorilla shoes, or socks for the child, all the other people of Turgalium went to the Plaza one day, and The Mayor or the King, I don't remember which of the two, told all of them that they had to give the gold earrings, bracelets and rings, and that if they had precious stones, they could also give them and they would make some very precious crowns, and the Virgin was going to be very beautiful and very happy.

I didn't hear it, but my brother told me everything, he had gone with AngelMaring and they saw the sacks where they put all the gold, and the raw diamonds, and the polished diamonds, and the emeralds and all that.

.Then they took those sacks to Chanquet, who was the one who knew how to make crowns for Kings and the Virgins, so that he could put everything together, and they told him that he had to do them right away, to stop making a ring that he was preparing for Mamá Chong, because the crowns had to be ready for a day when a lot of people were going to come, the priests and the Bishops, and the Pope I think was also going to come, and the fat friars who took care of the Virgin of Guadalupe, who were very friends with priest Don Luis Buenadicha, who was also very fat, because he ate chocolate with croutons every day, and as also all those who wore skirts instead of pants, who are the owners of the churches, and also many princesses and marquesas were going to come, well, they were going to bring the Virgin and her Child down to the Plaza, because there could be more people there than in the castle, so they wouldn't be so squashed.

So that Chanquet, he made two beautiful crowns. And since he had some silver and some gems left over, he also made another two for everyday days, as it happened to us that we had some things for Sundays and others for ordinary days, and when they were ready, he called I don't know who to pick them up, because he had a lot to do and couldn't take them to the Plaza.

When the day of "The Coronation" arrived, Papá Bo-ling went on his own, because he had to be with those who were called "Authorities." It seems to me that he would have preferred to be with us, but since he was very good, he left with the others, even if he would get bored.

My sister Ne-ning also went with her friends and others dressed "Shepherdess," I don't know why they called them that, because what they had on was the skirt, the doublet, the scarf and the espadrilles that they put on us at Easter for the Chíviri, and they were not shepherds like those who are in the field, and they did not even have sheep, but they wanted to be shepherds and they thought they were going to fool us, but as Man-o-ling told me:

—You tell her yes, that she is a shepherdess and that way she'll stay calm, but we all know that she neither is nor has she ever been.

And my brother knew how to act!

Mamá Chong said we couldn't take An-dong-ni to the Coronation because since he was very precious, but a bit dumb, maybe someone would steal him, and Feipang neither, in case he happened to convince the person who was going to put the crown on the Virgin's head, to change it for some decal or something that he had in his pocket, so although Feipang took off his shoes and threw himself on the ground, which was what he did every time he got very angry, this time he couldn't convince Mamá Chong and he had to stand it, even though he kept saying:

—You're going to pay for this, you'll be sorry! You'll find out how you are going to pay me for this!

But he stayed home.

Man-o-ling, Mamá Chong and I went so calm to the Plaza, to see everything from a balcony of the house where we lived before, but which was no longer our house because we had moved to the other one where we lived now; what's going on is that those who lived in that house, I think they knew us, and that is why they let us be there for a while, not to go to bed, or eat, or wash, or that, but to go out onto the balcony.

The Plaza was full, very full of people and the Virgin had been set in a place a little beyond ElPilar fountain; it seems to me that she and the Child were so happy to see all the people there, but since she did not speak, or the Child, well they stayed quiet even when the crowns were put on.

First they said a mass with more than a thousand priests and bishops and all those who know how to say masses, and come on, singing and putting incense, which is something that makes a lot of smoke but smells very good.

That incense seems to me that they had saved it from when the Wise Men gave it to the Child when he was born, they had it hidden so that no one would find it and they'd be able to use it at some important party, and the Pope or I don't know who told those Authorities that they could spend it that day, so the whole Plaza smelled great, and we were all very comfortable, because even if some people might be blasting out poopers, with the incense you couldn't even notice it.

They sang lots of songs, but the one that we all liked the most was one that said:

Hail, hail Judith victorious
Turgalium's Honor and Pride
From the castle's blazon on high
Like the Rainbow of Peace you shine

And many more words.

Mamá Chong and Man-o-ling knew it completely, but I only knew that little chunk, because it was very long and very difficult, and Sister Luisina had only taught us that, but she told us that when they said other things what we had to to do was to open and close our mouths, as if we were singing, that no one would notice because there would be a lot of noise, so that's what I did, but my brother did notice, although he didn't tell anyone, thank goodness that he was a good brother, not like Titing, if not they would have arrested me for deceiving the Virgin.

And then they gave the Virgin and Child the Sunday crowns. They were very happy and all the other people were the same, and many adulterer people cried because they said that everything had been very beautiful and very exciting, it seems to me that they were a bit silly, because instead of laughing they cried, but it was what they did.

When the crowns were on both of them, they all wanted to give them a kiss, but "Authorities" said that the Virgin was very tired, that only villeins could kiss her, that they were her neighbors, and that everybody else go be bugged, so we stood on the balcony so calm.

After the kisses they had to take them again to the castle, which was where they lived all the time. Come on, another procession and more songs, no wonder the Virgin was so tired.

But since everyone wanted to take her back up, they had to do a lottery so that those who won would carry her and her baby, and they gave chits to all of us who were in the Plaza, but Man-o-ling and I gave ours to Ne-ning who had come to see us on the balcony, and had left those shepherdesses that she was with before, but she did not win, and we both were very happy because the Virgin and Child were very heavy and then she would have had a sore shoulder.

Papá Bo-ling did win one of the prizes and later he told us that it weighed a lot, and that they only let him hold it for two minutes, so, if it weighed too much for an adulterer, imagine how it would have weighed for Ne-ning!

The castle where the Virgin lived with her child, the Moors had made it thousands and thousands of years ago, and it was at the top, in a place far away, close to where the Nativity moss, but when the villeins found the Virgin hidden in a closet, one went to see the Boss of the Moors and told him that they had to leave, that they please put all their clothes, their pans and their meals in suitcases, because they needed that place.

It seems to me that the Boss of the Moors did not really want to leave, because there were so many, and he did not know where to find another castle so good for so many people, but A-ma-ling's father, who was the one who commanded all the policemen, called him on the phone one afternoon, a little angry because the Moor Boss said every day that they were going to leave the next day and always the same, and he said: —Look, if you don't leave nicely, I will have no choice but to throw you out, I really need the castle for the Virgin, so let's see if you move! If you can't make the move alone, tell me and I'll send Uncle Valeria with his cart to help you.

Then the Moor Boss was quite happy and told Don AngelB that if they gave them a hand they would leave immediately, and that way they did the whole moving in a jiffy.

Titing told us that, but he told us it was a secret, that nobody but a few who were called "the privileged" knew it and no one else, that he was telling us but that we'd better not even think of telling anyone, not even our own close friends, but we told AngelMaring and Man-o-ling, who were much taller and knew more than him, and they both told us it was a big fat fib, because Titing was a huge liar and spent all day inventing lies, that we should not believe it.

I don't know if it was true or not, but no Moors or anyone lived in the castle anymore.

The Virgin's home was in a room that had a pretty big glass window, and the Virgin was set there, next to the window: in the daytime she looked at everyone in Turgalium so that they would be good and obedient, and at night they turned her around so she could sleep a little, because looking out all the time must have been terribly boring.

But she had no kitchen, no ice box, no bedroom, or anything at all. It was a very naked house.

Only benches so that people could pray, and some very precious vases to put all the flowers that those who went to see her brought her at all hours. On the day of the coronation she had so many flowers that they reached to the ceiling and the Virgin was a little dizzy from the smell, but she held on and continued smiling, pretending that she didn't care because she was so good.

When it was all over, Mamá Chong, Papá Bo-ling and the three of us went home, because it was already lunchtime, and my two little brothers would be very angry that it took us so long, but the truth is that we didn't care if they were mad, because we'd had a yummy time.

Besides, she was my saint, whatever those who believed that it was not my real name said!

SECTION EIGHT: WINTER

SLAUGHTER

When winter came there were many wonderful things, and one of them was the slaughter, which could not be done until Christmas was about to come. Impossible to do it at any other time, because until then the pigs were very small, and they had neither hams, nor sausages, nor loins, nor almost anything inside yet.

When we lived in the Plaza, we couldn't do the slaughter, because Pizarro wouldn't let us. As soon as he found out someone was going to make one, he got off his horse, knocked on the door of the house and said:

—It is forbidden to do that in the Plaza! If I see a pig around here I will put you all in jail and that's that!

And poor Mamá Chong had to put up with it, though she liked to have everything that you got from pig and have slices of homemade chorizo sausage with her cup of chocolate... But if she couldn't do it, she couldn't.

For this reason, as soon as we moved to the house on the upper park, since neither Pizarro nor any of his warriors saw us there, she immediately got a very fat pig, which had a lot of chorizo sausages and blood sausages and loins stored in its belly, so that it would last us a long time. There had to be a lot there, to last us all year, until another pig was killed again, and that's why they hid everything in the pantry, next to the huge tin holding olive oil, the sacks with chickpeas, the cheeses and the other things.

My friend and I were five years old when we saw the first slaughters, at her house and in mine.

In our house the slaughter was much more boring than in A-ma-ling's house, because it was done in the hall, and although there were many people, there was no comparison with all those who were in hers, that always got together a thousand or seven hundred at least.

And look, we could have done it on the large terrace upstairs, I told Mamá Chong a lot of times, but she didn't want to, because she said that it was too cold upstairs, that no one could be busy with us and we could fall to the street, that I should stop teasing. So I had to shut up.

Besides, we only killed a little pig, who cried and screamed for a long time, so long that you almost had time to become his friend, and since we were very, like, couldn't stand it anymore, in the end all of us were crying a lot and the pig looked at us and kept quiet , although he made a very sad face...

But in my friend's family, as they had to make a slaughter to give things to all the houses of the uncles and aunts, the grandfather and many other people, they did it in their garden because they had to kill several pigs, so it was much more fun; also there the pigs, even if they got very angry and screamed a lot like our little pig, it was not so noticeable because they were outdoors, and many of her cousins also screamed, because they were very naughty and a drag, so you didn't know who was screaming, the piggies or the children, and since the garden was on the ground, if we fell, nothing happened, just a few scrapes, but we did not become corpses.

The whole hubbub started a few days before the pigs were killed.

Since it was done in December, they waited in all the houses for us to have the vacations. For both of us the first time we thought it was going to be a total bash, because we could be in the middle all the time, asking questions and finding out about everything.

So the first time we went we looked at the ones who were preparing the troughs, which were like the coffins that my papá told us, only they didn't have a lid, then they would throw the pigs in there when they were corpses; while other lady adulterers were all the time cooking potatoes to make potato sausages, which were really black pudding but they called them that so that people would know they weren't blood pudding, or rice or whatever; a few of her older cousins, her aunts, Lupeng and Ne-ning were preparing the guts to put them in the pigs' belly and then turn them into sausages or loins, or some other things.

Others prepared the fire, to burn the hair of the pigs, because under the skin was the bacon, which was put in the cocido stew, but on top they had some very ugly hairs, and I think that they were never washed or combed, so they were horrible.

But as soon as we got closer to the bonfire everybody started to yell:

—Get out of here, you're going to get burned, or if cinders pop out you can go blind!

Neither A-ma-ling nor I knew who those Cinders ladies were, but it seemed to us that they were not like Cinder-ela, but must be like tigers or leopards, who make huge leaps, so we saw Titing there and asked him:

—Hey, do you know who are those called Cinders?

He told us:

—Well, they are some witches who get into the fire, they get very tiny and disguise themselves as ashes, but they have fire inside and as soon as they see a girl nearby they jump super fast, and they burn their eyes, but only girls, boys never because they know witches are hiding there. As soon as they get in your eyes they become witches again, and they laugh with a very evil laugh. I have told you but you cannot tell anyone, it is a top secret secret.

We were a little scared and nervous, because although we wanted to see those bad witches, we did not want to go blind either, so we were trying to think of a girl that we did not like, to put her close and see if what he had told us was true, but we didn't remember any.

When we were doing that, my friend's goody-goody cousin Eng-a-ning appeared and wanted to play with us for a while. We almost never let her, because she was dopey and she was always very goody, but that day we told her that, well, she could be with us if she obeyed us in everything we ordered, and right away she said yes, she would do everything and that's that. We approached where they had the bonfires and A-ma-ling said:

—Look, get a little closer, so that you can see everything very well, there are some very beautiful embers there!

(That was to do an experiment so that we could see the Cinders Witches)

The silly was going to do it when her mamá came and took her hand and said to us:

—But how can you think of putting your cousin so close to the fire? Look, you are naughty and never come up with anything good!

And she took her away, so we carried on, we didn't see those evil witches and we went to look at other things, because we had to keep an eye on everything.

But they were all just working and working, and they told us to get out of the way and stop getting in the way.

What sillies! on top of we were not doing anything!

On the day of the slaughter at her house, I got up very early, had breakfast fast, and as soon as they helped me put on my clothes, I crossed the park and went into her house.

Everything was already prepared.

The pigs were terribly loud and one of them even looked at us with a very mad face since he did not know how to speak thank goodness Turgaliuman, and we did not understand pig language either, we did not find out what he wanted to say, but for sure it was something very ugly.

The vet, who is the animal's doctor, came to cut a piece of meat from them to see if they were poisoned. I do not remember if they did that before or after killing them, it seems to me that before, because if they were already corpses it was a huge nonsense, but since there was so much hubbub we did not find out.

None of the pigs had poison, so even though they screamed a lot and they spat it didn't help them at all: They threw them into the troughs, they slit their bellies and everyone started to get the sausages and hams and bacon and everything that goes into the cocido and that's that .

As many hours had passed, A-ma-ling and I were very tired, so we went to my house to play with the dolls, change the shepherds in the Nativity and hide their sheep behind a boulder, so that they would sleep very warm, because today they hadn't killed our little pig yet and there was no hubbub there, and we could have been so calm, but as soon as we got to my house, my brother Feipang wanted to go see the slaughter, and we had to go back with him.

When we arrived, what they were all doing was eating and drinking, what a drag...

And look, we told him a thousand times that he was going to get bored, with so many grownups, but no, he started telling jokes and saying silly things and they all burst out laughing.

On top of that they gave him a whole ham and eight sausages for himself!

And to us, who had been working there all day nothing... Well thanks so much!

So we decided that we didn't like that about the slaughters so much and that maybe it was better to see the piggies alive, playing in the mud, doing their pig stuff, and that's that.

A few days later came the slaughter at my house.

The pig we had was very cute and since he had been living in the rooms upstairs (where the terrace was), he had become quite polite and did not squeal so much, also my brother Man-o-ling had even bathed him a little and he was quite clean.

He also gave him a name: Dan-Sing, because he told us that that way he would feel much more in family, that since we all had a name, if we called him only a pig, he might think it was an insult.

We told him that it was a very stupendous name, because the truth is that if that piggy heard some music he started lifting his feet and going around in a circle, dancing and singing oink oink oink, so happy, and he told us that he had been searching many of his books and that Dan was the name that fit our pig the most, although he had to fight for a while with Feipang, who wanted him to continue calling him Pig, or if he wanted to put another name, it would be one calling him Hog, but in the end he convinced him that his name was Dan-Sing Pig, so, name and surname, like us.

They prepared all that about the troughs and the guts, they lowered Dan-Sing tied with a string around his neck, the Veterinarian came, tore a piece of meat from him and said:

—Mamá Chong, this pig seems to be poisoned, it has "tricky notions."

Luckily we both knew what those were, ha, because we had heard my grandmother a thousand times, that when one of the nanny maids did something she shouldn't do and then changed the story to fool her, she always said:

—This nanny maid has many tricks! We will have to be careful with her!

But the nannies did not have poison, only those tricks, and as they did not have to be killed because they did not have sausages or anything like that, it did not matter.

But with pigs I guess it was different.

The truth is that all of us were happy that they did not have to kill him, although he had a fairly large wound where they had removed that piece of meat, but since my sister knew how to sew everything, even pigs, she did a few stitches, put on some Band-Aids and the poor guy was so happy.

Mamá Chong was a little sad and almost crying, because she wanted to have her slaughter, and since Dan-Sing had those trick things, she couldn't, but immediately Mr. Pérez came from my papá's office and said:

—Don't worry, Mamá Chong! In a jiffy I will bring you a very healthy pig!

He ran to a nearby orchard and in less than half an hour he returned with a very fat pig, very mad because he had woken him up from his siesta, which only said oink, oink, oink, he looked at us with a very ugly face and on top of that he started to blast poopers, that dirty pig, there in front of everyone. It seems to me that what he wanted was to stink us up so that we would go to another room and they would not kill him, but we covered our noses and we did not pay any attention to him, come on, because he thought he was going to scare us, doggone it, and although he was kicking and spitting at us, three or four men grabbed hold of him and put him in the trough to get his loins out and all that.

Poor Dan-Sing was looking all the time, but it seems to me that he did not know much, because one eye looked towards the kitchen and the other towards the living room, and since the stinky pig was in the middle of the hall, he did not see well what happened, almost better this way, so that he did not suffer so much.

Then Papá Bo-ling said,

—Okay, we issue a pardon for Dan-Sing. You can keep him to play with! The only condition is that you will be the ones who are going to take care of him.

My brother Man-o-ling immediately picked up a paper and a pen to make out turns.

It happened that that day it was A-ma-ling's and my turn, so we put the string around his neck again and took him upstairs. We gave him a few acorns and a bowl of crumb milk, covered him with an An-dong-ni blanket, told him a very precious tale of a pig fairy, and he fell asleep in no time. A super great pig, that's what he was.

When we went down to the hall, there they were all eating pork loin and drinking wine!

It seems to me that this slaughter thing was said to fool some dummies, because what they really did was eat all the time....

So, taking advantage of the fact that no one was watching us, we went to the park to jump rope. We decided that we didn't like the slaughters at all and that we weren't going to go to any never ever again, not even when we were nineteen and were already adulterers, and period!

COCIDO

In winter on ordinary days, from Monday to Friday, afternoons we always ate something called "El cocido," and almost all the people, if they had food, would eat the same, because as many things were stuck into the pantries, I think it was very easy to go there and take them, and that was that.

At night no, at night we ate other things.

The cocido had many courses: the soup, which was made of fine noodles or letters; I liked the letters a lot more, because if none of the grownups were looking at you, you could find many words and many things, if you were lucky you almost could write a story, well, or a piece of story, or at least the beginning, or look for names of gods and goddesses, or put what your brothers and sister or cousins were called, but you had to be very careful because if they saw you you could no longer continue, and the word got broken and very ugly.

We all ate soup with a spoon, except for my brother Feipang, who ate it with a fork because he had that mania. He said that he did not like the broth and although Mamá Chong tried to convince him, he, come on! kept on with the fork, and always the same.

Every day, Mamá Chong would say to him:

—Look, Feipang sweetie, try once, you'll see how delicious the broth is.

But he was very stubborn and said no and no, and poor Mamá Chong finally got very tired of telling him all the time, so she let him do whatever he wanted.

One day when A-ma-ling's bad brother was eating with us, he saw what was happening and said,

—Don't worry, Mamá Chong, you're going to see how he'll take the broth too.

And he took a straw out of his pants pocket and began to sip his soup.

As soon as Feipang saw him, he put down the fork with the noodles and said:

—Get me a straw right away!

Like that, and not even please, and we always had to ask for things "please" and then say thank you, but he was not very polite, and when he got angry he got terrible and screamed a lot and threw himself to the ground, and none of us wanted him to get angry, because then our heads hurt from listening to him.

When the straw was brought to him, he put all the noodles to the edge of the plate and in a moment he sucked up all the broth!

We were all delighted and Mamá Chong almost cried with joy; after she tried so many times he had finally taken everything, and from that moment my Mamá became quite friends with that brother of my friend, and gave him pesetas and sweets when he came by my house.

And it's just like A-ma-ling told me:

— Bad brothers know many tricks!

And in that I had to agree with her.

After the soup came the chickpeas.

The chickpeas, when they were in the sack and had not been put in the pot, were very hard, like a small stone, but at night they were put to sit in a bowl with a lot of water and they also added salt, and that way they believed that they were in the sea and they were getting soft. But you could not forget the salt, because otherwise it was like they were in the river and they were hard. We were very smart from that Book of Our Children, and we knew totally well about fresh water, which was that of the rivers and lakes and the arroyo freshet of the Vineyards, and about salt water, which was the kind in the sea and in the ocean. I don't remember who had to put the salt in the sea every day, but I think it was Conrado, who had a store with many bags and he carried it in the afternoon, and he did it even on Sundays and even when he had tonsillitis, because if he missed one day the sea became a river or a lake and that could not be.

You couldn't drink the sea water, you could drink the water from the freshet and that's why we sometimes drank it.

At my friend's house they ate the chickpeas with cabbage, but my mother didn't like the smell of the cabbage while it was cooking, so they didn't put it with ours. What our chickpeas had were squares of potatoes and a salad of roasted peppers in strips.

And look, that salad was very dangerous!

Because you could die while you were eating it if you weren't careful.

We all liked it very much, but my mother liked it more than anyone else and she always said:

—I just love the salad of roasted peppers with oil and vinegar!

And she liked them so much that she would have eaten a whole platter but, since she was very good, she would put a little for the rest of us and she would put on a lot, fill the plate, and she wanted to eat them all so quickly so that we wouldn't take any from her, that many times they went to the other side of the neck and got into the tube that is inside to breathe, and one day she almost became a corpse.

When she saw us all crying and super sad for being left without a mamá, she promised us that she would never ever again eat them so quickly, but it seems to me that she crossed her fingers behind her back, because she kept doing it secretly as soon as we were not looking.

When they took away the chickpea dish, "Main body" came, which was the meat and the chicken and the chorizo and the bacon and the blood sausages and all that; what a weird name that part had because it didn't look like any body, but it was called like that.

As we were very curious and we liked to find out about everything, we dedicated ourselves to asking questions about some corpse, but they all laughed and didn't tell us anything, it must have been a secret and they didn't want us to find out, so after thinking about it a lot, I told my friend:

—It seems to me that that "main body" must be very fat and very strange, because what they put in my house looks like chicken and meat and bacon and all that, and it is not like any of our neighbors, like the daughters of Don Eli-ang, nor like Lo-li-tang... they are not missing...

—Well, the one at my house is the same, she answered. — Maybe they were some very bad neighbors and they killed them at night, they kept them in the pantry and it's a secret.

—Well, we can tell your dad, who is in charge of all the policemen, let him find out and tell us later.

So one day in the afternoon after school, when we were at her house painting our nails with a small bottle of paint that we had swiped from my sister Ne-ning without her knowing, while she was writing those long letters to Cheng-Chu, as soon as we saw her father arrive we immediately asked him:

—Do you know why the third dish of the cocido is called "main body"? Where did they get so many? Is it that they were very bad and that is why they have been killed and we are eating them? Can you ask your policemen?

Her papá, who was always so serious started laughing like crazy!

We didn't know what to do. Were we super dummies or what? Everyone just laughing and laughing at us...

At last Don AngelB stopped, and he sat down with us and said:

—It's not called body like a corpse, or even a live human body. Body can also just mean the main part of something, like the most filling or delicious food.

And since he was very serious and spoke very little, he said nothing more and was so calm. Well gosh.

I mean, they hadn't killed anyone, it was just critters meat and we both thought that we were, well, a bit silly, and that's why they laughed at us, that's the truth.

And after those three dishes came something called "The First," which was also a silly name because we ate it at the end of the other dishes and it no longer seemed like the cocido, because it was a potato omelette, or steaks with tomato, or croquettes, or many other things, but things that were not thrown into the pot, they had to be done separately so that they would not mix and get confused, I think that was why.

By the time we got to that "start" we were pretty full and we didn't want to eat more because then we wouldn't have room for dessert, and we liked dessert a lot, whatever it was.

Well, all that cooking stuff during the week would stop when the time of Christmas Eve and Christmas and New Years and the Three Kings arrived.

Then we ate one thing a day.

JOSEFA

A few days before Christmas Eve, my father's students began to send him many live animals: turkeys, chickens, bunnies, lambs, everything, it seems to me that it was to give them good marks, because the dumber they were, the more things they sent him, but maybe it was not for that and what they wanted was for him to get very fat and very happy, and since next to the large terrace above we had a few rooms to store the coal and the charcoal and other things, when the critters arrived, they would put them there so that they would be very warm and become friends, because since they were no longer with their families, at night they did nothing but, come on, cry and scream and bother us, and we could not have them inside our house, not even one of them, because even when they were alone they behaved awful.

One afternoon when IsabelM and Mamá Chong were having coffee and perrunillas pastries from the nuns, not from our nuns who did not know how to make them, but from others who lived in another convent, my friend's mother told her:

—Mamá Chong, today they have given me a very good and very easy recipe to make the pepitoria. Right now you are going to write it down and you will see how delicious it is. But for it to come out well it needs to be made with a hen, which although they are tougher, have much more flavor.

Mamá Chong, as she saw that we were there doing nothing, said:

—Very good, stupendous. Girls, do you want to write it down in my recipe book?

Because she had a notebook, with black covers, where she had written down how to do all the things we ate, and when they made them they had to put exactly what the recipe book said because if they made a mistake and put two tablespoons instead of one, something else would come out and that was a mess, and instead of the French omelette, there would be macaroni and tomato or salad or whatever, and if we had asked what we were going to have for lunch or dinner, and then something different came out for not having followed the recipe, that was a lie and they had to confess, so they always read it.

We took the notebook and while IsabelM was saying it very slowly, we wrote down, but it was a lot of work and we only wrote one row and on top it came out a little crooked because that notebook was not like ours and it had no lines not to go out of, so Mamá Chong took it to write and we watched.

And this is the recipe that my friend's mother gave us:

—You take a hen that is very fat (that's what we wrote, and that was that), and after killing it and removing all the blood it has in its body and on the head and on the legs, the feathers are pulled out, although it yells a lot and becomes very scandalous, and you break it into many pieces. Then those chunks are put in a frying pan with oil and fried until they are not raw so that you do not want to puke. Meanwhile, with another hand, you take bread and soak it in vinegar, like you had a cupcake, but you have to do it with vinegar, if you do it with milk or chocolate it cannot be, it does not work, just vinegar, and then it is fried in another frying pan and when it is fried it is squashed a lot, and also there you put garlic and onions and parsley and red peppers and then, when all that is very fried, you put water, or water broth, I no longer remember that, and then with another hand you put all of that in the Chinese thing with the crank and blades, and put it on top of the fried chicken and keep it in the pan for many hours, until the meat becomes very soft and that's it, eat the pepitoria.

It was a very simple recipe, but you had to have at least four or five hands, even we could make it if they let us into the kitchen, because if we were missing a hand we could tell Ne-ning to lend us one of hers for a while, but they wouldn't let us because they said we were going to get burned, that we were too little and all that — Pwahf! what silly nonsense, I mean it!

Among all those gifts they gave my papá during the Christmas Eve holidays, although we had a lot of raw critters upstairs, they were all turkeys and chickens and roosters and bunnies and that, none of them was a fat hen. In Las Viñas, yes, there we had many hens and roosters, and sometimes, yellow chicks, which were very cute and very soft, so Mamá Chong told Josefa the guardian to send us a fat one, the one who was the fattest of them all.

Josefa took good care of all the hens and especially one, which was like her daughter; well, her daughter was really Petri, she was a girl, but she also loved that hen very much, she made her some very good meals, and she made her very fat.

The day the hen arrived at my house, the poor thing was a little dizzy because since she had never left her hen house, nor had she even ridden on a donkey, she was very tired and I think it was a bit sad to be so far away, but we put her with all the others to make her happy.

Since we didn't know her real name, A-ma-ling and I decided that we were going to call her Josefa too, like the guard, and she immediately became our friend.

While we still had school, whenever we were free, we would go up to see her in the afternoon, to play with her and teach her things because she was very smart, and when she saw us she came running to our side and all the time what she wanted was to sing with us.

As soon as we got the holidays we started to be with her in the morning, and in the afternoon if we had a free time; we dressed her with a cloth to be warm, we gave her milk and cookie crumbs, well, as if we were her mamá or her family, and she was never sad and I think she loved us a lot.

The day before Christmas Eve we had a lot of work because we had to go to all the neighbors' houses to sing Christmas carols and ask for the Christmas gift, and we could only see Josefa for a moment early in the morning.

When I got home it was late, but I went up to see her and she was nowhere to be found, well, I thought, "she must have gone to sleep because it is already a little nighttime and hens like to go to bed very early," and I went downstairs.

The next day, as soon as A-ma-ling came, we went to see Josefa and again we didn't find her. That's weird! She liked to be and play with us!

We looked everywhere, and nothing; the few animals that were left did not know how to speak Turgaliuman, they could not tell us anything, so we went to search my flat in case the poor thing had gotten into some trouble.

Come on, look and hunt around, even under the bed and even in the girls' room and the "falconry" room. She did not appear and did not appear.

We asked everyone we met in the rooms and they all told us that they were very busy, that we go play, or look at Nativities and that we leave them in peace, so, since we had been looking for Josefa for many hours and we did not see her anyplace, we went to the park to play with some other girls who were also friends of ours, but a little less friends, not close ones.

Dinner time came and we said goodbye for a while because she had to be with IsabelM, her father, her brothers and sister, her grandfather and all her aunts and uncles and all those people at a very long table of more than two hundred meters, and I with Mamá Chong, my papá and Ne-ning and Man-o-ling and Feipang and my grandmother; the baby was not allowed to be with us because he did not know how to sit in a chair and they had hidden him somewhere so that he would not cry if he saw us.

Feipang promised that he was going to be very good, that he was not going to get up from the grownups' table, and that he was not even going to take off his napkin, or anything like that and that's why they let him.

The Christmas Eve dinner was made up of many dishes, and it lasted many hours because we had to eat a little of each one, and we all sat at the dining room table, which was very large and very beautiful, and on top it had a white tablecloth that we only used that night and New Year's Eve. The dishes weren't the ones we used every day either, they were special for Christmas Eve and Christmas, and as that night we could drink a little cider, we all had a drink, not just the grownups.

First we ate the appetizers, chorizo sliced, cheese, tenderloin, ham, salad, dwarf croquettes, and so on. Everything was delicious, and since it was the first thing, my older brother Man-o-ling and I, we ate a mountain.

Then came the consommé, which although it was called that was like the soup broth, but it seems to me that on Christmas Eve we had to call it that way, and it had no noodles or letters: it had pieces of ham and chopped hard-boiled egg.

When they took away that broth, they brought us a glass dish with eggs stuffed with béchamel, and that was the best thing about the whole dinner, because it was a secret to know what they were stuffed with, nobody knew, not even Mamá Chong; on top they were all the same and as they were half eggs and on top was the béchamel and tomato sauce and the yolks that had been taken out of the eggs without them knowing, and they had been squashed so that they were no longer hard yolks but very tiny balls, everything was very nice, but they all looked the same. The same.

Then Papá Bo-ling would ask us:

—Let's see, what filling do you want the egg with?

And he lifted the dish with both hands so that we could see underneath and choose.

Because the half eggs were filled with many things, and you had to think a lot not to be wrong, and if you chose one with the inside of tuna you couldn't say later that you didn't like it, you had to eat it and that was that, because otherwise you were very capricious.

Ne-ning chose quickly and Man-o-Ling also quite quickly, but when it was my turn, although I had looked while they were asking so I could see where the ones I wanted were, it took a long time and Feipang, who was after me, started to get a little angry, so I had to take some that I didn't like so much, but hey, I ate them.

Then came a fish called sea bream, which was on a platter surrounded by slices of potato and lemon. It was awake, well at least it had its eyes open and looked at us a little serious, I thought he was alive, but my brother told me no, to stop talking nonsense all the time, well, what a silly, if people and other critters, even if they are fish, have their eyes open, they have woken up, right? But I had to shut up.... Then the prawns, the crayfish and the shrimps and those critters that live in the sea, but could no longer swim, or even dive, came immediately, because they were cooked and put on a platter for us to eat, but we didn't even look at them, because we were no longer hungry.

So they took the seafood, and then Mamá Chong told us:

—This year, in addition to the roast chicken and the turkey with spun egg, we have a surprise: Hen in pepitoria. You are going to like it very much!

Because the last dish of Christmas Eve dinner was that hen with fried potatoes and turkey cold cuts, which although it was called turkey, did not look like a turkey, because first they put some strips of white breast, and ham and hard boiled eggs. And then all that, when it was already inside the turkey's belly, they would squeeze it a lot in something called "The Press" and when it left there it no longer looked like a turkey or any critter, but we knew it was a turkey because our mamá had told us, and then they cut it into slices and around the platter they put the spun egg, which wasn't like an egg either, but it was really called that, it was sweet and delicious.

Then, my brother Feipang took out of his pocket something that he had made with some very precious feathers, like a crown of a king, and put it on his head and we all laughed a lot because it was very funny, and he looked like a Comanche Indian who came in the stories.

I don't know where he got the feathers from, but they were very pretty and I thought I had seen them somewhere before, but I didn't say anything and we ate in peace.

The pepitoria was delicious, so as I knew I had made it a little, because I was there when we wrote the recipe, not like Ne-ning who was elsewhere that day, we ate almost the entire plate.

Buff, we couldn't get any more full! And the nougat turrón, the marzipan figures, the chocolates and the cider were still missing!

And we couldn't fall asleep because they were going to take us to the midnight mass, the Mass of the Rooster!

The turrón we only had two days a year to eat, Christmas Eve and Christmas and that's it, and that was a drag, because in those days there were many other different foods and we had to try them all, but it was like that, in my house, in my friend's and in all the other houses in Turgalium. It was forbidden to eat them on other days, it seems to me that if you ate them on other days you would become a corpse because they had poison or something, and if there were any turrón or some marzipan figurines left after Christmas they had to throw them away, they were no longer useful even to give them to a dog in the street, because then the poor thing would also die.

Mamá Chong ordered all the turrones and that at Basilio's pastry shop, and they were rich, rich, delicious; that night we had hard turrón (which had to be broken with a hammer and it was full of almonds hidden in the middle so that we wouldn't find them), soft turrón , which was delicious and the one I liked the most; and guirlache turrón , which was also very hard and very bitter, but that Mamá Chong liked very much; "Cádiz bread," which Ne-ning liked the most, and was not really bread but a fat turrón of many layers; marzipan figures, coconut balls, polvoron pastries.... Well, lots of nougats turrones and things like that, and some chocolates that had liquor inside and you could only eat one or two, because if you ate more you got drunk and fell to the floor as if you were sleeping, but everything was fallen asleep inside, the heart, the guts, the liver, the lung and everything, and that was a drag, so my older brother and I only ate one just in case.

With the nougat turrones and figurines that night we had a sip of cider, which tickled your nose and made you laugh a lot. Feipang drank I think the whole glass, because he started telling jokes and he didn't stop and he didn't stop, and we were all hurting from so much laughing and so much of a bash, and even the baby woke up and crawled into the dining room, and even though he didn't understood anything at all, he was also laughing a lot.

When we were all so amused sitting around the fireplace they brought A-ma-ling, because she had already finished dinner at her house and in a short time we had to go to church for that rooster mass.

As they had not been able to make that pepitoria at home, she tried ours and also liked it very much.

As soon as she finished trying it, the first thing she asked me was:

—Have you found Josefa?

—No, I told her, I've looked everywhere and she wasn't anywhere. If you want, let's look in the cupboards, because she has to be very hungry and a little bored from being alone for so long.

So we went to look and dig around through all the rooms that had closets, but nothing, we didn't see her.

We were already starting to get a little sad, but suddenly we realized that that night was Christmas Eve, and that everyone, even the animals, had to be having dinner with their families, so surely Josefa had also gone to Las Viñas, and she would be very happy there with her relatives and with the guard woman, and then we were happy again.

It was also time to leave for the midnight mass of the Rooster!

It was the first time we were going to go, and look, it was late, but that day our mamás let us and we did not have to go to bed, even if it was late at night, because it was the day the Child Jesus was born and we wanted to be there.

Baby Jesus was born in Bethlehem, not in Turgalium, that's the truth, and not because the Virgin remained there until the child came with the Wise Men, because it was a village very itsy-bitsy and much uglier than ours because one day they took us there to roast the chestnuts, we saw it, and we didn't like it at all, nothing, but hey, the poor kid was born there, and in the church of San Martín the one there was not the real one, the flesh and blood one, they had one they had made with I don't know what to make him look like the real one, and they had done him very well because he was so cute, chubby, laughing all the time and it seemed like he was real.

They put our coats, gloves and scarves on us and we both ran off with my sister Ne-ning, because it all started at twelve, which was called midnight, and even though we had never gone to bed so late we were still awake.

As it was the first time we were going to see the rooster crow, my friend was very nervous and came to ask and ask:

—Ne-ning, how is the rooster? Where does the rooster live? What songs can the rooster sing? Does the rooster have brothers and sisters and grandparents? What color is the rooster?

And many more questions, the truth is that she tired us out, but we didn't say anything to her because she was my friend and that night my sister was very kind.

We got a great place, almost in the front row, to see everything very well, but A-ma-ling was still very pesky, nothing more than asking all the time, and I also started saying things, so Ne-ning was getting tired of hearing us and to make us shut up at once, she told us:

—If you are good and you are still and quiet, then I'll tell you where Josefa is.

Look, after looking for her for two whole days, we were finally going to see her again!

So we shut up and waited for the rooster.

But the rooster did not come out!

And look, we looked front and back, and up and down, nothing, no rooster crowing, come on, there wasn't even a rooster, well, after spending so long in church, with so many people there praying and singing and all that and pushing us, and come on, say "Merry Christmas," "Merry Christmas," "The God Child is born" and many more things, when we finally went out to the Plaza what we wanted was for Ne-ning to say things about our friend the hen.

When we were going down the shopping street, my sister stopped next to La Giralda, which was that place where they sold many stockings and dresses and belts and everything we used to not be naked, she crouched in front of us to be just as tall and she said:

—Do you remember IsabelM's recipe for making hen in pepitoria? Well, yesterday Mamá Chong went up to see Josefa, told her about it and told her that they had brought her to make that dish with her, and not to worry, that she would be with us all the time and many other things; Josefa was very happy and the two of them went to the kitchen and there it was prepared and we ate it tonight.

At first we really wanted to cry, but as we were already quite sleepy, we told her that, well, that since it had already happened and there was no remedy, okay, and we continued walking home, and that's that.

The next day it was Christmas and we were still free, without having to go to school.

CHRISTMAS

The day after the night when Jesusito was born it was Christmas.

We were still on vacation.

That day in all the houses of Turgalium no food was made. We ate something called "Leftovers," look how silly to call them that, because they were all the platters that continued from the night before, and many of the things had gone to the kitchen just as they had come, because we were already full and nothing else entered us, but they had been given that name.

I did not care what food there was for those who stayed home, because Ne-ning and I had been invited by her godmother, and since she was from another place she did not have to do that "Leftovers" thing like all the rest.

Man-o-ling also went to eat at his godparents' house and there surely Ga-bing would fill his pockets with those chocolates that she made so delicious, so Mamá Chong, my papá, my grandmother and my two little brothers were left alone.

But they were enough.

That godmother's house, you know I didn't like it very much, but that day they had less furniture there and it was a little better.

When we arrived, we met Cheng-Chu, my sister's boyfriend, but it was a secret and no one could find out. Ne-Ning made me use up one of my Holy Words and another of those of Honor and also a Formal Promise that I was never going to tell Mamá Chong, well, like I was a stool pigeon, and for her to leave me alone I said yes to everything and that's that.

Cheng-Chu was a very handsome and very nice boyfriend and my sister said that he was exactly like an actor from the movies called Kirk I don't know who, who lived in America with the Indians, but he looked like himself to me and of course since I did not know that other man, I couldn't compare either, what happens is that since I had promised my mother that I would be very good and very well-behaved, I also told her that, well, he was exactly like that, and she was very happy.

They gave us a pretty rich meal, almond soup (which I had never tasted, although I had eaten soup many times and also almonds, but not mixed together), and then orange duck, which was a duck without feathers, as if it were a chicken but a little fatter, and with an orange in the mouth. He was very funny and we laughed a lot when we saw him.

The godmother said that at coffee time my friend could come to play with me, so she sent one of her maids (who was not the terrible pincher), to get her.

That house was where the strange little sofa was, with the seats facing each one to one side, so A-ma-ling and I started to play on it, as if we were some fine ladies who did not know each other.

I said to her:

—Good afternoon, ma'am, it's very good here today, right?"

And she:

—Excuse me, I don't know you. Are you from Turgalium or La Cumbre, if I may know?

—Well, from neither place. I'm from Zorita and my name is Sinforosa García, I replied.

—Ah! Nice to meet you Mrs. Sinforosa, what a stupendous name you have, my name is Marcelina Pérez, but my girl friends call me Marce and my boy friends Lina, and so I know quickly if they are boys or girls, A-ma-ling told me.

And a lot more silly stuff that we were coming up with.

As we were so entertained as Doña Marce and Doña Sinforosa, we had not even realized that everyone at the coffee table had shut up and were dying of laughter listening to what we were saying, and as each of us was looking to one side we didn't notice them either, until suddenly they applauded us and we were very embarrassed, but the godmother said we were stupendous artists and gave each of us a bag full of candies.

What luck! And on top of that, inside each bag, Cheng-Chu had put a five pesetas bill! Can you imagine? All his allowance he got on Sunday, and notice that we were only talking and telling each other things about how terrible our children were, and that Doña Lina's husband was a bricklayer and had fallen off a roof, his brain was broken but still he was not a corpse, ordinary things like that of life....

So that day we had a great time and when it got dark we ran to our house and as we were going downhill we arrived in a moment.

INNOCENTS

Between Christmas and Old Year we had a few days off from so many huge meals and so many jobs.

Thank goodness we didn't have to go to school, because I don't know where we would have found time....

The afternoon before the twenty-eighth Lupeng warned us:

—Tomorrow you have to be very careful. It is the day of the Holy Innocents and this is when the hooligans play a lot of pranks.

We didn't know who those hooligan gentlemen were, but so as not to look like sillies and tiny girls, we pretended we did and went to my house.

We wanted to ask Mamá Chong, but she had gone "on a visit," which was what she did every second day, like the other mamás in Turgalium: one day she went to a friend's or a cousin's house, the next day another friend or another cousin came to my house, the other my mother went to see another friend or another cousin, and so on. Not on Sundays, that day she stayed without having to go anywhere or having one of those come to see her, uff, what a rest. But it was what she liked to do.

And look, I said to her one day:

—Hey, Mamá Chong, why don't you see four or five at the same time so that you don't have to go out every other day?

But she told me no, that it was much better how she did it, besides that some of her friends didn't hang out with others and it couldn't be, and in that she was right, because A-ma-Ling and I also had some of those we didn't hang out with because they were silly, and we couldn't mix them with the good ones.

Since my mother was not there, we went to the middle floor, and thank goodness Fel-i-crung was there and we could ask her about what Lupeng had told us.

She said that we did not have to worry, that she was going to cut out some paper dolls, and that what we had to do was put them on the backs of those we met on the street, but without them noticing and that way we became hooligans.

Look how easy and what a thrill! Surely my friend's sister did not know about the paper dolls, and that if we had them we would become hooligan ladies in no time, instead of being girls.

She made a lot for us and her mother even painted eyes and mouths looking up, which meant that they were laughing, that lady was very good to us, but she told us not to tell anyone that we had them because then there'd be much more laughter, and she put the little men in a large envelope.

When we were leaving her house we met Feipang who asked us in a very scary voice:

—Quickly show me what you have in the envelope, or you'll find out!

We told him it was a letter that we had to post, but as he saw that it had no stamp, he did not believe it, and we had to show him everything.

He was very happy when he saw the paper dolls and told us:

—Since you are a pair of sillies, you'd better give them to me to do a business, and then maybe I'll give you a peseta each so you can buy balls of bubble gum.

The truth is that we did not want to give them to him, but he got so pesky and started in with his threats thing of throwing himself to the ground, that we had no other choice.

And we could not go back to get more made.

We went to A-ma-ling's house again, to see if Don AngelB could draw us at least some of those doll figures, but he wasn't there either. He had gone off with his police to chase some guys who had escaped from jail.

We crossed the park again and entered Telegraphs, in case my papá could draw us a few, but we were not lucky there either: he was teaching and we couldn't interrupt him.

So we held on and stayed girls since we could not be hooligan ladies.

On Innocents Day I said to Amaling:

—Look, so that nothing happens to us, we'll stay alone, playing in one place and that way they won't attack us. Since it is very cold in your garden, we'll go to my house, sit at the brazier, play house, change the dolls' dresses and that's that.

She thought it was a very good idea and that's what we did.

So we would not have to separate and get caught by those hooligans, she stayed to eat with us.

The bad brother of my friend came when we were sitting down and mamá Chong told him to also remain, that where three ate, four could eat (and do not think that was true, but I did not tell her, because another at the table squeezed us together and they had to put plates and cutlery and a napkin, but since my mamá had become friends with Titing I shut up).

And there we were so calm sitting at the table eating the first course, when suddenly a horrible plague.

Papá Bo-ling asked:

—Who has let loose a pooper? You already know that this cannot be done at the table. It is prohibited. If anyone needs to do it, go to the bathroom.

It seems to me that he was a little angry.

We all looked at each other, to see who had turned red, because when you did something you shouldn't do, your face would get very hot and red, so everyone knew it was you, that you had told a lie or whatever. That was called "Being the culprit" that Sister Luisina had explained to us one day in class, and see what a good method, because even if you didn't speak, or if you spoke and said it wasn't you, that didn't count: it was the face that told the truth.

But no face was red and the plague was still there. Much mystery.

A little more time passed and my dad said again:

—We're getting stunk up. The balconies will have to be opened because this smell is unbearable. If you don't want to confess, at least stop throwing poopers!

We looked at each other again and nothing, no red.

What could it be?

Because sometimes the braziers had something called "stinkers" and when those got into the braziers you had to run them out of the room fast so as not to die in a minute. One day when one got into the brazier in the living room, and we were so calm, when they took it out I ran after the girl to see what it was like, and don't think it was a small devil or something like that. It was a fatter piece of charcoal, but instead of having fire inside it, what it had was very bad smoke. I don't remember who put that smoke there, Man-o-ling told me about it but I was thinking about something else and I didn't know.

As soon as they discovered who "the stinker" was, they had to catch him with a pair of tongs and although he got very angry and wanted to stay in the brazier, they took him to the kitchen faucet, they covered him with lots of water and, yippee, to the garbage.

And they could put the brazier back under the table.

But that plague was different.

Very stinky.

Of poopers.

We were all half dizzy by now when suddenly it sounded like a small explosion near one of the balconies. First it went piufff, piufff, and then Bamm! and fell silent.

And the plague suddenly disappeared. Thank Goodness.

Then Titing confessed:

He told us that it was an Innocents joke, that he had brought something called the Stink Bomb, that it was the stinkiest thing you could find in the world because it was made with the poopers of some very filthy swine demons, and pardon for doing it at lunchtime.

And Mamá Chong and my papá burst out laughing!

I did not laugh at all, well what an idiot, it seems to me that he was one of those hooligans, even if he looked like a boy.

OLD YEAR

On the thirty-first day of December my grandmother's calendar pages ran out and then we knew that the year had also finished.

Because my grandmother bought a package every year that was like a little book, but it was not a book because the sheets were only together on one side and as soon as you pulled a little they came off. And that was the calendar.

On each sheet it put the day it was, five or nine or whatever, then the day of the week and the month and the year.

Also many other things, like prayers and that, but the important thing was the days and months.

Because look how stupendous, just by looking there you knew a lot and you didn't need to ask anyone what day it was, if Tuesday or Friday or anything else.

The calendar, at first, was very fat, but when the days and months went by, it got skinnier and skinnier, and I tell you, when it was December thirty-first, it only had one page, but it did not matter because they brought a new one and so we all knew what month we were in.

A-ma-ling and I went to my grandmother's room every day to look.

But once we were very scared because every time we looked at the day it was the same as before, although it seemed to us that it must already be another because we had gone to bed at night and then we had woken up when it was in the morning , and that meant that it was a different day, but on the calendar it was still the same.

When they didn't change, I said to A-ma-ling,

—Look, maybe we're in a dream and we think we're awake. I'm going to give you a pinch and if it doesn't hurt, we are dreaming. If it hurts, tell me, but don't make a big fuss.

She said all right and then I gave her a pinch, a very small one, just in case we weren't asleep but awake: she jumped into the air and said:

—Ow! It hurt a lot!

So we went to ask my sister why this day did not change.

Ne-ning explained to us that my grandmother had a bad cold and that she had forgotten to tear off the leaves. Thank goodness! Well, I did not want my grandmother to be ill, but always being on the same day was a real problem, look, if it was Sunday or your Saint's Day, stupendous, but imagine if you stayed on a rainy day, or that your throat hurt or things like that....

That time what we did was to tear off all the sheets that were stuck and that their days had passed and that's that, we were so happy and knowing that we did not have to worry ourselves sick.

The last day of the year was called "Old Year" and it was also very special.

That night we would go back to dinner in the large dining room, again with many different foods but without turrones, because now it was forbidden to eat them.

That's why they made a huge cake for dessert, it seems to me that it was a meter or more, which was called a drunk cake, which we pretty much liked to eat, but the best thing was to see how they made it.

Because although the cake was not a person they had to get it very drunk, and that was quite complicated.

First they put a lot of sponge cake all together, like it was a mountain, and when it was all squashed together they began to pour in liters and liters of a liquid to get it drunk, I don't remember if it was sherry, or wine, or Liqueur 43, or something that was in the bottles in one of the dining room furnitures and they waited until they saw that it couldn't be more drunk.

When the cake started to act silly, it was already ready and then, so that it would be good and quiet, they put a paste on it (which they had made with egg whites, that's the truth, but they were no longer like drool, but pretty meringue), and then they put sugar on top of that pasta and they burned everything with a very hot iron paddle. Imagine how hot, it was no longer a bad color like the braziers, it was red, super red and as soon as it touched the sugar it went Fiuu, Fiuu, Fiuu.

The sugar was turning a little black and that meant that the cake was done and we could eat it right away.

In Old Year there was also another mass of the rooster, but A-ma-ling and I decided that we were not going to go, come on, so that later that rooster would not show up? — let dummies go — and we both stayed at my house, nice and warm by the fireplace waiting for twelve o'clock to arrive.

Because at exactly twelve o'clock was when the year changed and we had to be awake and eat the grapes, one for each month; if you did not eat a month, that was a disaster: either you would turn into a corpse, or you would get a fever, or they would scold you a lot, or, well, a lot of misfortunes, so we each had our grapes on a plate and although we wanted to start a little earlier just in case we didn't have time, Man-o-ling said no way, that we had to wait and that you couldn't cheat because the grape wise man was seeing everything and writing down in his notebook anyone who started too early.

My silly friend was very sleepy, but I yelled very loudly and said:

—If you don't wake up and stay wide awake, you'll see what will happen to you! Come on, let's sing until the time comes.

And we sang a lot and that way she didn't fall asleep.

At last twelve o'clock arrived, what a thrill: the chimes began and we were almost choking, with the whole mouth full of grapes that did not want to be swallowed, but with the last one they all slipped inside us. That was almost a miracle! Now nothing was going to happen to us any month that came... They came to pick her up right away and I got into bed to sleep.

NEW YEAR

When I got up, even though I knew from my grandmother's calendar and the grapes that it was a different year, it seemed like one more day.

But I knew that no, that it was a new year, good as a little baby, because the other old one had gone very far and was never coming back.

But we were still on vacation. And that was the most important thing.

And Doña Ma-rta that day even went down to the park with us!

We were really worried about whether those bones of hers would start to bug her, but they were good, they stayed still and we were even able to teach her to play potato ring, which was a game where with three it was much better than with two.

She had a yummy time, she told us we were great girls and she wanted to be a close friend, so well, we let her.

And she gave us a whole box of chocolates! The chocolates were delicious rich and I'm not telling you about the box: Tin and even with a princess and a prince painted on the lid.

The princess was wearing an orange dress with many emeralds just like her earrings, and some green shoes; the prince was dressed so-so, I didn't like what he was wearing, but A-ma-ling said to me the thing was that princes at the end of the year, after the grapes and that, go around all night to drink and sing with their friends the other princes, and that he had not had time to change when they put him on the tin box, which is why his pants were gray and with many wrinkles. He had fallen into a puddle while he was walking around to the bars and that is why he was a bit messed up.

The princess must be very good, because despite how dirty he was, she was smiling; maybe inside she was a little mad, but since it was the first day we saw her we didn't want to ask anything.

From all those chocolates that were inside, we gave a few to our brothers and when they were all used up we were left with the empty box, and there we put our silk worms.

Although they weren't from the same family, as we both had five each we put them together.

Man-o-ling and AngelMaring gave us plenty of mulberry leaves, which was their favorite food, to make them good and fat and shiny.

It was the first time we had silk worms. Mr. Pérez, who worked with my papá and had a whole farm of them, had given them to us.

He explained everything to us like this:

—You put the worms in a box. If it is very pretty, much better, because that way they are happier. The leaves have to be changed every day and they have to be mulberry, they cannot be ordinary leaves from other trees. Do not forget because if you put banana leaves or other kinds of leaves they get a lot of stomach pain, they go and get themselves poisoned and they turn into super corpses. That is very important.

I asked him:

—Mr. Pérez, do we have to give them water or milk? What do they like to drink?

But he told us that there was no need, that in the mulberry leaves there were already some "mercoscopic" things, like dwarf glasses of water, and that they drank from there.

We had never heard of those mercoscopicas, so we went to have Man-o-ling explain it to us.

He was very busy inflating his bike and he told us to wait a while, that as soon as he finished he would consult one of his books, but that it seemed to him that we had misunderstood the word, that maybe they were microscopic; well, my friend and I did not care, what we wanted was to make sure that our worms had water and that they did not stay dry.

My brother searched and hunted through all his books and then said to us:

—Indeed, you have heard wrong, or Mr. Pérez, as he is so old, has already become confused. The word mercoscopic does not exist. It is microscopic and means that it is so small that you cannot see it, not even with glasses.

With that we were at peace.

The only problem we had was who kept the box at night, because Titing was in her house, he could take it from us and steal the worms, and in mine Feipang, if he saw them he would take a shine to them because he would want them for one of his businesses, and if we did not give them to him, he would throw himself on the ground, take off his shoes and all that he did and Mamá Chong would have a tremendous upset, and that could not be, it was forbidden, so we asked my neighbor girls to keep them for us at night.

As they were terrific, they told us yes, not to worry, but so that our worms wouldn't catch those microbes critters from their papá's cough, we told them to keep the box tightly closed and in the pantry.

Those worms must have really liked the leaves we put in, because very soon they started poking holes in them and then they ate whole leaves.

And every day they got fatter, they got really fat for us.

Well, one of them was a little bit weakling for some time, I think he had tonsillitis, but we didn't know if he liked the syrup they gave us so we left him alone, and if he had a little fever, then let him put up with it and that's that.

After a few days, one morning when we opened the box, they had disappeared! Where had they gone? What a problem and what a worry....

We ran to ask Mamá Chong who told us:

—It's okay, don't worry, they're there, but now they don't need you to give them more food, they're making their silk cocoons and as soon as they finish them they will turn into butterflies and they will leave you the gift of their cocoons.

Wow! That's for having been so good and having treated them as if they were our little children....

So we stayed very calm and let them continue doing the silk thing, we only looked at them once in the morning and once at night, to see if they were warm and happy.

But the box remained at my neighbors' house, just in case.

We couldn't risk it being stolen from us now, after so much work...

And a few days later, the butterflies came out, looked at us, went to the lower park and we never saw them again.

But they left us ten precious balls of yellow silk, well nine, because one was a little squashed, it must have been because of the tonsillitis.

THREE KINGS

Almost the day we liked the most, of all of all, was the day the Three Wise Men came, and that was when we were in a brand new year.

The night before day six, Mamá Chong took my friend and me to the Plaza, because the Three Kings were going to arrive from the East (which was very far, even further than Cáceres), with all their pages and with many gifts for all the children who had been good.

They also brought three chests, they called them chests, but which were like very precious boxes filled with gold, incense and myrrh for the little Jesus who was in San Martín.

It was very cold, but we did not care, and also we had almost been super good so we would have gifts.

Because to all those who misbehaved, what those wise guys left them was a lump of coal, and that was that.

Next to my house was the coal store.

Well, before it was a very beautiful Church, but some bad guys had stolen the Saints and the Virgins and all those and as it was already empty and the Three Wise Men had no place to keep the coal, they took it over and then it was called the coal store.

But since those three Kings were very good and not greedy, they told Uncle Man-o-long:

—Look Man-o-long: we only need coal for the fifth of January at night, for the bad children; if you want, every other day you can take care of giving people coal and charcoal so they can cook their meals and get their braziers going.

And Uncle Man-o-long did that: he had a lot of coal and charcoal there and all the people of Turgalium would go in the morning and at night to take a bag so they could be warm and cook their stews so that they were not raw.

When we got to the Plaza, A-ma-ling was already a little calmer, because when we had picked her up at her house she was terrible, all full of tears, very sad and I think she was a bit angry too.

I asked her what was wrong and she told me she would tell me later.

I was very intrigued and while we were going up I did nothing more than ask her:

—Come on, tell me, come tell me now!

But she was all the time with her mouth closed and without saying a peep.

In the Plaza there was no place you could fit, with all the people who were there, but some friends of Mamá Chong had found a great place and we got together with them and their children.

When a long time passed and it was already very dark, with the sky full of stars around a very fat moon, by the arch of Sillerías Street the Kings appeared!

They were riding on three camels, with many pages who threw candy at us as they passed.

A-ma-ling let out a huge sigh and said,

—Uff, thank goodness! What peace!

I had no idea what she was talking about, but then she told me everything.

It turns out that her bad brother, Titing, had told her that the Three Wise Men did not exist, that it was a made-up story, that those who left the gifts were the mamás and papás, that is why they knew if the children had been good or if they had told lies or done evil things, that only tiny girls like her believed that about the Kings and many other things, fifty or eighteen at least.

A-ma-ling told him that she didn't believe him, that she was going to ask IsabelM or Lupeng, but neither of them was at home and we immediately came for her and she almost didn't even have time to cry.

Then I said to her:

—But are you dumb or what? Don't you know that brother of yours is always telling a lot of lies? If he had told me I would have kicked him in the shins and that's that. Well, what a demon for a brother...

My friend was very happy and then we were able to enjoy watching the entire Parade.

As the camels were very thirsty, they stopped for a while at the ElPilar fountain to fill their humps with water. The poor guys had not been able to drink since they left the East and they were quite dry, and meanwhile the Three Kings began to talk to all of us.

A-ma-ling and I went over to see them and yes, they were flesh and bone like us.

As the day before Ne-ning had helped us to write the letters putting all the things we wanted, we had them with us and that way we would not forget anything.

Some children would send their letters from the post office, but as the East was very far away, Lupeng told us that it was better to hand them to the Kings, because sometimes they did not arrive on time, buff, what bad luck.

She spoke with Don Melchior, who had a very large white beard: it almost reached to his waist! And a white suit with a fur-lined cape to stay cozy. And some beautiful boots, red and with the borders also made of leather. We really liked those!

And we whispered to ourselves that next year we were going to ask for the same ones.

She told him again everything she put in the letter and to not forget to leave her a doll called Tatiana, who was almost as tall as us, very beautiful, and who talked a lot.

We had seen that Tatiana one day in upper park. A girl who was a bit of a friend of ours had it and she let us play with her. It could walk and say many words, but always the same and I told A-ma-ling that it was better to have a parrot for that, but she insisted that she wanted the same one and all the time she was making me dizzy telling me all the words that she was going to teach her Tatiana, and was going to make this and that for her, very tiresome... Well, maybe I didn't want that to become her close friend, because since they were going to live in the same house and not in two different houses like us... But she told me no, that Tatiana was still a bit slow and didn't learn much, that I shouldn't worry because we were flesh and bone and much greater friends, that we were close friends, so I got calmed down.

Since Don Gaspar was with another girl, I went to talk to Don Balthasar, who was black but not from Africa, no, this was not a kaffir, he was super good.

Although I had my letter in my hand, I knew everything by heart, so I told him real fast. He asked me if I had been very good and I told him the truth, that I had been so-so, because sometimes people (especially my little brothers), bugged me a lot and that is why I could not be as good as I wanted, but that Yes, I was going to become completely good.

—Then no more talk! was what he answered, —You will have your gifts!

Oh, how good!

When they had already talked to all of us who were there, they went to San Martín and gave the Niño Jesusito all the gifts that they had brought him, that of gold and other things, but since the Child did not know how to speak, he couldn't even thank them.

On top of that, a nun who was there took everything very quickly and hid it under her clothes, we saw it, do not doubt that. How greedy.

Meanwhile, as there was very beautiful music, the camels were dancing and having a wonderful time, until the pages told them to be still, put a stop to such carryings on, and they stopped.

It was ten o'clock, it was very late, and we still had to go home and go to bed in case the Wise Men arrived early....

The next day, when I woke up, I only saw a very small package and a letter! What a scare! And I who had told him the truth...

I first opened the package and inside there was a chunk of something that looked like coal, but it wasn't black: it was gray and not as ugly as coal, but I didn't know what it was, so I opened the letter and this is what it said:

"As you have told me the truth, that you have been so-so, I leave you a piece of coal, but a sweet kind that is very rich; I have put all your gifts in the hall so as not to make noise and so Ne-ning does not wake up. I hope this year you are very good. Signed Balthasar."

Goodness!

So that telling the truth worked.

I ran to the hall and there were all my things: a little kitchen with many pots and pans and plates and everything that is in real kitchens but tiny. Even a slop bucket for Mrs. Swill! All very beautiful and I really liked it.

Also colored pencils, a notebook with many pictures to fill in with the colors and a doll.

The doll was not a Tatiana. She was smaller, uglier and it seems to me dumber, because she did not know how to speak, not like the one I already had, yes, the one who believed that I was her mamá and was calling me that all the time, but hey, she was a doll and right away I gave her a name, Carmina, so that she wouldn't be unfaithful, in case she suddenly broke and the poor thing had to go to doll limbo.

When I was finishing breakfast, A-ma-ling came with her things, and don't think she was very happy.... She also had another letter, but not from Balthasar like mine. Hers was Don Melchior's and we gave it to Man-o-ling so that he could read it to us more quickly.

The letter said:

"A-ma-ling: I have no Tatiana left, I have searched all the stores, even at the North Pole and the only one I have seen was very ugly and she did not even speak, I am very sorry, but I leave you a few other things. Do not be angry and be good. Signed: Melchior"

And yes they had left her a lot of things, so as we saw that poor Don Melchior, on top of how old he was, had looked and searched so much and not found a single Tatiana, her sadness passed, I gave her some of my sweet coal candy and we immediately started playing, until it was time to go to the Plaza with our nannies and new dolls, to see what the Kings had left other girls.

Two of them had Tatianas, but with very ugly suits and they also seemed very disobedient.

We told them how lucky they had been, but quietly we said to ourselves that it was much better not to have those, because we would need to scold them all the time, like my sister did with us, and on top of that those Tatianas weren't even sisters, what a job....

That afternoon was the day that we had a very stupendous Kings' Ring Cake snack for tea time: Roscón de Reyes.

We could only eat that once a year, the other days it was forbidden.

The ring cakes were very beautiful and very rich, with little chunks of dried sweet fruit on top. They were like a big ring, with a hole in the middle and then the frosted cake all around. And it came on a paper tray but it wasn't right on top of the tray, because in between there was a paper with many little holes cut like lace that we really liked and Ne-ning told us that one day when we didn't have school she would teach us to make some just like that.

What happens is that those roscones had a very bad trick: inside, which was what you ate, there were two things, one good and one bad, a ring (I think it was made of pure gold), and a dry bean.

If you got the ring, it was stupendous, because it meant you were the princess, or the fairy, or I don't quite remember who, but someone phenomenal; but if you got the bean, that was a drag: everyone who was having a snack with you could give you a pinch or a kick or something, so when Mamá Chong started to cut the roscón we were very scared, but we were lucky and in the first chunk we only got roscón and that was that.

My friend wanted to get the ring, and she asked for another piece, but I said,

—Look, don't be greedy. It is better to have only roscón than to get the bean, which has not yet come out either.

But she ignored me.

And I was saying to her under my breath:

—Wait for the bean to come out... When it comes out you ask for another piece. You are going to blow it!

But nothing, she even stood up and held her plate high so that Mamá Chong could put another piece on it...

And of course, what I was saying all the time happened; the ring did not come out, but the bean.

And she started crying like a little girl!

Luckily, since my mamá was very good, she told her that there was a mistake, that that chunk was for her and that's that, so she stopped crying and stayed still.

In the end, neither of us got the ring, but after the disgust about the bean we didn't care.

And we had to play a lot with our new things, because that was on the sixth and on the eighth the holidays were over and we had to go back to school.

That night they let us stay up much later, it was at least eleven when they came to pick up my friend, and it seems to me that neither of us slept much because we had to meet early the next day.

I let Carmina, my new doll, lie in bed with me, because it was the first time she was in my house, in case she started crying or something, but I told her very clearly that only that day, not to think that she was going to be so comfortable the other ordinary days and she didn't say anything. Since the poor thing couldn't speak...!

The day after Kings we were playing all the time, changing our dolls' outfits, painting and doing many things, but since we had to go to school the next morning they put me to bed at nine.

The holidays were over.

What a shame!

But we had a yummy time. And soon we would have others.

And maybe this year we were getting so old we could wear needle heels!

The end

EPILOGUE

A-ma-ling, as I have already pointed out, existed and was my first friend. But she left us when she was not yet forty, due to cirrhosis of the liver, so her dreams of doing things when she was older did not come true, although I am sure that wherever she is she will be waiting for me so that we can continue getting into mischief and standing up to face the world.

IN MEMORIAM

NOTES ON SOME OF THE CHAPTERS

Titing: JoeyStreet - for a man named Pepe La Calle, called Pepelacalle by the narrator. Pepe is a hypocoristic nickname for José, as Joe or Joey may be for Joseph. La Calle, a real surname, means literally "the street."

An-dong-ni: *de villela* - made of villela, a soft cloth of cotton and wool. TrickyJoey, for Pepeltuno, conflation of Pepe el tuno (Joe the tricky one).

Feipang: *churrería* - a place where *churros*, a kind of Spanish cruller, are made and sold.

Lupeng: *santos*, usually "holy" or "saints" or "saints' days," is also used colloquially for printed illustrations, such as Mamá Chong looked at.

Relatives - Neighbors: national teachers (Em-i-long was one) were certified to teach anywhere in Spain. Talavera of the Queen is Talavera de la Reina, a Spanish city famous for its manufacture of tiles and ceramics.

One Hundred Pesetas: *duro* means five pesetas, a term often used in reckoning value or price.

Sponge Cake: here and elsewhere in this book translates *bizcocho*, a special cake made by the Turgalium nuns, very high, fluffy, delicious. The Cakies ladies were named Bizcochitas, little Cakies, a hypocoristic nickname invented when they were children by their father. Whimsical cognomens were very common in the town.

San Lázaro Pond: *migas* are a specialty of Extremadura, made principally of diced hard bread, chorizo, paprika, olive oil, garlic...

Paquito: the name is a hypocoristic diminutive of Paco, itself a nickname for Francisco, in this case for Spanish dictator General Francisco Franco in a child's fantasy.

Cinema: Jose Maria Gabriel y Galán was a famous Extremanian writer, one person!

Good Friday: Jews - This chapter and the preceding one (Holy Thursday) narrate a small child's view of the Passion in early 1950s' Spain, before Pope John XXIII in 1959 removed the phrase "perfidious Jews" from the Good Friday Mass; stereotypical views, though perhaps not virulent, were not rare at the time.

Paper Bull - Ma-ring must be thinking of the papal bull, granted Spain, that eased certain fasting rules.

Slaughter: Poor Dan-Sing... did not see well... - originally the name Casimiro, a real name that can be interpreted as "I almost see." This is one of many puns the translation has had to maneuver around with creativity!

Cocido: Main body - in the original, *cecina*, which is misheard as *vecina*, female neighbor, and the narrator does speculate, as here, on some skullduggery. After the multicourse *cocido*, comes el *principio*, "the start" - a curious designation indeed.

Josefa: Coal - see below.

Turrón: Christmas time treats usually of some sugar and almonds variation.

Polvoron - pastry basically of flour, sugar, lard.

Bethlehem - in Spanish, Belén, which besides being the designation for a nativity scene, is also an outlying village administratively part of Turgalium.

Three Kings: Coal, charcoal - All coal referred to in this book is wood coal, that is, charcoal. What is here called coal (*carbón*) burned strong and fast, used for cooking; charcoal here is *picón*, slower burning, processed from branches and used for heating rooms in braziers, often placed under round tables, and diffusing heat for many hours.

ACKNOWLEDGMENTS

Putting the adventures of these babies in writing would not have been possible without the constant support of my sister, who has encouraged me since I started thinking about this project, and my faithful companion the wonderful Roberto who has put up with all the stories that I was telling him while he ate, walked, took a shower and even when he slept.

Thank you all!

ABOUT THE AUTHOR

Victoria F. Leffingwell is a young writer with almost three quarters of a century on her back. She is defined as "a storyteller", understanding that as someone who likes to tell and write stories. She has written crime stories, children's stories, haiku poems, and essays.

She distributes her life between Spain and North America and try to enjoy every day. As she is a nomad, she does not live more than four months in the same place, although she has fulfilled her dream and when she is in Turgalium she lives where the *villeins*. But you can always find her at: shuinero@icloud.com, where she will be happy to communicate with you.

Bibliography

"**Childhood with A-Ma-Ling**" It takes us to the Spain of the 50s from the perspective of two small girls. Their adventures, problems and joys are shared by many people of that generation and also by the subsequent ones.

Her series of stories "**Memories of America**" is a fun collection that spans several decades in that country, with a slightly acidic vision at times, but always friendly.

Her stories **"Escritos y Tontunas"** are also a series of childhood experiences and memories.

The **"Tales for Ariel"** are stories with magical animals, and it is a series that periodically continues to grow, as Ari's interests change, aimed at children's audiences.

"A Serpent in the House" is a novel based on real events: a murder attributed to the Maquis, but which was simply a crime of passion.

"Cousins" is a historical novel about the experiences of five cousins, spanning four generations and developed in several countries.

Printed in Great Britain
by Amazon